PENGUIN BOOKS

IN THE MIDDAY SUN

Guy Bellamy was born in ⋯ of his life in Surrey. After National Service in Germany with the Royal Air Force, he went into journalism and has worked on newspapers in Cornwall, Bournemouth, Brighton and Fleet Street. He has written several short stories for *Punch*, and his previous novels include *Drinker*, *I Have a Complaint to Make*, *The Sinner's Congregation*, *The Nudists* (Penguin 1987) and *The Secret Lemonade Drinker* (Penguin 1988). He is married and has a young daughter.

Rave reviews for *The Nudists*:

'It is rare for a book to be comic, happy and readable all at once, but Guy Bellamy's *The Nudists* is just that' – *Daily Telegraph*

'Whip-crack wit and street-smart prose ... funny, caustic and gloriously readable' – *London Standard*

'Cruel hilarity' – *Mail on Sunday*

and *The Secret Lemonade Drinker*:

'An expertly engineered sexual comedy' – *Observer*

'Sparkling ... It cracks open a thousand jokes, some old, some new and some blue. As hideously addictive as drink' – *Sunday Times*

GUY BELLAMY

IN THE MIDDAY SUN

PENGUIN BOOKS

PENGUIN BOOKS

Published by the Penguin Group
27 Wrights Lane, London w8 5TZ, England
Viking Penguin Inc., 40 West 23rd Street, New York, New York 10010, USA
Penguin Books Australia Ltd, Ringwood, Victoria, Australia
Penguin Books Canada Ltd, 2801 John Street, Markham, Ontario, Canada L3R 1B4
Penguin Books (NZ) Ltd, 182–190 Wairau Road, Auckland 10, New Zealand

Penguin Books Ltd, Registered Offices: Harmondsworth, Middlesex, England

First published by Viking 1988
Published in Penguin Books 1989
1 3 5 7 9 10 8 6 4 2

Extracts from 'Mad Dogs and Englishmen' by Noël Coward
are reproduced by permission of the Noël Coward Estate
and Chappell Music Ltd

The extract from Cannery Row by John Steinbeck is
reprinted by permission of William Heinemann Ltd

Extracts from 'The Hungry Years', words and music by
Neil Sedaka/Howard Greenfield, © Don Kirshner Music, are reprinted
by kind permission of Kirshner-Warner Music Ltd

Printed and bound in Great Britain by
Richard Clay Ltd, Bungay, Suffolk
Filmset in Plantin Monophoto

For KATE
aged two
who helped

ACKNOWLEDGEMENTS

I am indebted to several people for their assistance with this book, and I should mention first Roy St John of St Louis, Missouri, who has written all my favourite songs. I was also helped by Bryan Jackson, Ian Pert, Diana Sewell, Michael and Carol Weeks and Ron Ronchetti. In Gibraltar I was assisted by Dan Twiddle, and in Puerto Banus by Lloyd Hulme, the piano star of the port. Mark Cowling, who has played there and in many countries, was also a great help. On the Costa del Sol I talked to people who would not like me to mention their names but I must, above all, acknowledge the invaluable cooperation I received from J. After all, he really did stitch £200,000 into a pillow.

SPRING

What to do in case of emergency:
1. Pick up your hat
2. Grab your coat
3. Leave your worries on the doorstep
4. Direct your feet to the sunny side of the street

– Graffito

ONE

WHEN Matthew Ward stuffed £200,000 into a pillow, and carefully re-stitched the seam, he knew that a comfortable past was about to be followed by an uncertain future. The false passport on the table in front of him lay there as a bleak reminder that his life had already taken an irrevocable lurch towards the unknown, but what he did know was this: if he didn't move very quickly his newly discovered talent for needlecraft would soon be devoted to sewing mailbags, not pillows.

He finished the sewing and picked up his new one-year passport. The face was his own but the name was Bradley. He checked the ferry tickets that were clipped to the passport, and then he counted the money in his wallet. He had just over a thousand pounds. He stood up and toured his hotel room, opening drawers and cupboards to see that he was leaving nothing behind.

Matthew Ward was a tall, thin, restless man, with long hair brushed back over his ears, and a face that had changed perceptibly over the past few weeks from a certain plump joviality to a slightly haggard expression of permanent concern. His tour of the room ended in front of a mirror where both it and he reflected that the transition from a millionaire aged thirty to a man on the run with much less than a million pounds stitched into a pillow had not done a lot for his looks.

The pillow, he hoped, was an inspired idea. Nobody, in the history of the internal-combustion engine, had ever stolen a pillow from a car, and the police, who these days could tear a machine apart in search of exotic substances, wouldn't look twice at a grubby pillow on the back seat.

He looked out of the window of his room and saw Kim's yellow Scirocco in the car park. She was a short, dark-haired girl with bright eyes and a pretty mouth, and he could see her some distance away exercising his dog, Lady, a cross between an alsatian and a collie, who today represented one more complication in his complicated life. The British laws on quarantine meant that leaving the country with a dog looked rather final, and could attract attention; he wanted to look like a tourist.

He collected his luggage and his pillow and went downstairs. The receptionist took his key and his money and said, 'Thank you, Mr Hurst.'

In the car park Kim gave him a hug and Lady jumped up, trying to lick his face.

'Let's go,' said Kim. 'I never could stand the English climate.'

Matthew put his luggage in the boot and the pillow on the back seat with Lady. He kissed Kim's cheek and wished that he had met her before he had met his wife. She was a very bright girl who had never found her niche in life: she had been a model, a receptionist and even a journalist and she was still only twenty-five.

She drove north briefly to join the motorway and then they headed south towards the M25 and the kennels at Heathrow.

'Aren't we cutting this a bit fine?' Kim asked. 'The ferry is at six.'

Matthew lit a slim cigar and stared out at the English countryside, wondering when or if he would ever see it again.

'We're cutting it fine because once the dog is checked in she becomes cargo and won't be fed,' he told her. He threw some biscuits on to the back seat of the car but Lady, who did not know that this was her last food for some time, ignored them.

It was almost four o'clock when they reached the kennels and it took an hour to have Lady weighed, measured and checked by a vet. Matthew paid £430 to have her booked on an Iberian flight to Malaga on Monday.

'Three days without food,' he said, shaking his head.

'Get in the car,' said Kim. 'There is no alternative.'

'I'll drive,' Matthew told her. 'We have sixty-five minutes to reach Portsmouth.'

His worries about Lady, his false passport, the momentous move that he was making today were now all submerged in a nightmare drive of skids and screeching tyres on the wet March roads as they tore down the A3 – Guildford, Liphook, Petersfield – in fear of being waved down by the police.

But the luck that had been conspicuously lacking in his life in the recent past had begun to return, and they reached the boat with five minutes to spare.

Half an hour later they sat in the bar as the ferry crept out of Portsmouth Harbour, and Matthew wanted to jump on his seat and shout: 'I've escaped!'

Instead he sat quietly and held Kim's hand.

'I could never have guessed three months ago that this would happen to me,' he said. 'And if I had, I would never have guessed that you would be with me.'

She smiled and said nothing. She had wanted him for years and now she had got him. She had no intention of losing him – particularly as she had every reason to believe that she was pregnant.

John Ward heard about his son's disappearance while drinking gin at his golf club. The man he was drinking with, who had just accompanied him on eighteen competitive holes, was a police inspector at county headquarters. It was a cold March day for which a pale sun had produced light but not heat, and the policeman, whose name was Gillespie, had snapped up two birdies on the inward nine, so John Ward's morning had already been ruined.

'I would have told you earlier but I didn't want to spoil your game,' Gillespie said.

'What do you mean – disappeared?' John Ward asked.

'He left his home ten days ago and his wife doesn't know where he is. There's a tax problem, John.'

'What tax problem?'

'His wife told the revenue he had been lying for years. They reckon they are owed about £600,000 and there was a warrant out for his arrest for criminal fraud. I'm sorry, John.'

'Criminal fraud?'

'Tax evasion. He didn't turn up for the hearing and now there are other warrants for contempt of court. They've frozen all his assets. They've got the skin but not the animal.'

'Where is he?'

'I thought you might know, John. We traced him to the Aubrey Park Hotel in Redbourn, but he had booked out before we got there.'

John Ward slumped in his seat. 'Is this an official inquiry, Gillespie?' He wondered why he always called the policeman Gillespie, but the policeman always called him John.

'Of course not, John.'

'I know nothing about Matthew's affairs. I knew his firm was doing very well, but that's all. I see him once a month. He rings occasionally.'

'But not in the last ten days?'

'As it happens, no.'

John Ward picked up his drink and took a large sip. He had always regarded Gillespie as an amiable golfing partner with not a lot happening above the eyebrows, but now he was seeing the professional in action, eliciting and withholding information, a hound with the scent in his nostrils.

'You're not thinking of going abroad, are you, John?' he asked now.

'Abroad? No. Why?'

'I go abroad whenever I can. I find that television encourages me to travel.'

'Really? I thought it had made it unnecessary. But I see what you are driving at.'

'We thought Matthew might join Danny in Spain. We've been watching the ports.'

'Good God.'

'Can I get you a drink, John?'

John Ward pushed an empty glass at the policeman. 'A large gin and tonic, seeing as it's obviously on expenses.' He waited while Gillespie was served. 'Matthew and Daniel aren't very close. There was a lot of tension there.'

'But they've got something in common now, haven't they? Do you ever hear from Danny?'

'Not often. I disapprove of him and he knows it. I don't put Matthew in the same bracket.'

'Danny made a million pounds out of thin air in a week. It was the cleverest crime I've encountered in thirty years.'

John Ward drank his gin. 'Forgive me if I don't share your enthusiasm, Gillespie. He's a disgrace to the family. But not everybody regards tax avoidance as a criminal act. You make it sound like rape.'

'You can get longer prison sentences for it than rape, John.'

'That's because the English law has always put property above people. It's a hangover from the past when rich landowners wanted to protect their possessions.'

'That is as may be, John. But Matthew was facing a sentence of five to seven years.'

'That's bloody scandalous, Gillespie,' John Ward said angrily. 'I hope the boy escapes. There was a nineteen-year-old in the paper this morning who got twenty-seven months for battering his two-month-old daughter to death because he wanted a son.'

'Property not people, John. I don't make the laws, I just try to enforce them.'

When the policeman had gone, John Ward ordered himself another gin and contemplated the fresh calamity that had afflicted his family. He considered himself a fortunate man in many ways. The small petrol station he had started after the war had grown into a car showroom with the franchise for many of the best cars. But the disasters had dropped into his life like bombs at irregular intervals.

The first one had prevented him from creating a family of gospel writers. His first son, now thirty-five, had arrived in 1952 and been christened Mark after a television serial at the time. The choice was his wife's but John Ward, a deeply religious man, a practising Catholic, liked the name for its biblical association. When his second son arrived five years later he had already decided on the name of Matthew and hoped that one day he would have a third he could call Luke.

It didn't happen. His wife was told that another birth would be dangerous, and she was advised by a specialist to settle for the two sons she already had. John Ward went to the family priest to seek special dispensation for some form of birth control, but the response was uncompromising and unsympathetic. The medical advice was waved to one side: contraception was a sin. Five difficult years later Mrs Ward gave birth to their third son and died that day.

John Ward reneged on his silent promise to create a quartet of Matthew, Mark, Luke and John, and he never went to church again. He called his third son Daniel, a name which still remembered his Christian upbringing and pleased him greatly. It sounded softer than Luke. His father always used it in full, but to his brothers and friends he became Danny. John Ward was not to know that a quarter of a century later the name, which he felt had a quiet dignity, even a certain gravitas, would be a gift for the sub-editors of Fleet Street who would christen him anew in the more lurid tabloid papers with huge headlines that would shout: DAN, DAN, THE BANK SCAM MAN!

John Ward never really recovered from the death of his wife, but he did the best that he could. He threw himself into his work, masterminded a long programme of expansion, and became rich. The money arrived in time to give Daniel advantages that his brothers had missed.

Mark's education had been a rudimentary affair, with two young, inexperienced and busy parents having little time to supervise the progress of his learning. His academic headway remained stunted, and he sought solace on a small piano which had been left to the family by a grandfather. Matthew was brighter, with an inventive and independent streak. With more encouragement from his father he collected certificates and prizes.

But Daniel was sent to public school – to Westminster, one of the nine original public schools in 1864 – and John Ward, determined that he should not be at a disadvantage, now had the time, money and experience to give more care to his youngest son than to either of the others. His schooldays, according to the only humorous schoolteacher that his sons ever met, had been spent 'in a daze of whines and ruses'. Dismissing the judgement as a poor pun, John Ward overlooked the perceptive warning contained in the word ruses.

John Ward, a tall, smart man with a lot of grey hair brushed neatly back, sat at the bar drinking gin, thinking about the past. He liked the past: you knew where you were with the past. The present was becoming too terrible to contemplate, and the future frightened him. Every Sunday he visited the cemetery: the flowers on a grave are to comfort the survivor. The boys had grown up and left home, and there was no sign of the grandchild he craved. Now that the Pill had severed the connection between fornication and propagation there seemed to be a new generation that never even imagined becoming a parent. Procreation was the enemy of recreation.

At fifty-nine John Ward was in semi-retirement, dropping into the showroom two or three times a week to confer with the manager he had appointed. It had been clear from an early stage that none of his sons would take over the business: Mark was only interested in music, Matthew was too independent to join a family firm and Daniel's mental agility was too large for a car showroom.

John Ward had his golf and his roses. Money might not buy you happiness, but you could rent a lot. Ladies found him exceptionally attractive, but he discouraged their invitations. To the toothless come many nuts, he said. The only unwelcome problem in being alone (mysteriously overlooked, he thought, by the concerned crews who trawled these sociological waters for facts that would shock) was that one trip to the lavatory in a bar or a restaurant and your drink or meal had been borne away by an efficient waiter before you got back. There was no one left behind to tell him that you still existed.

He decided to have one more gin before going home to see whether the deer had been eating his roses. Life was full of choices but his own seemed to diminish annually. Soon it would come down to old age or death. And what sort of old age? A terminal stay in a home for the bewildered?

He shook himself as if the thoughts would fall away, and began to think instead of what Gillespie had told him. He had trained himself not to think about Daniel, the second disaster to hit his family. Already he could feel himself resisting thoughts about Matthew, who was now the third.

To have one son wanted by the police could be counted a misfortune; to have two looked very much like carelessness.

Appropriately enough in a car called a Scirocco, Matthew Ward drove like the wind. Down the 137 to Rennes and on to Nantes and the Loire, he thought only of Lady now, hungry, thirsty and cold and classified officially as 'cargo' in the hold of a friendless jet.

He did not feel that he was fleeing justice; he was in flight from injustice. He stopped at Nantes to change some money into francs and to fill the petrol tank, and then drove on under a low, leaden sky. Kim, beside him, studied the map on her lap.

'Where will we get to by tonight?' she asked.

'The border,' Matthew said. 'France today, Spain tomorrow. I want to be in Malaga by tomorrow evening, ready to meet Lady.'

They drove past a Bentley driven by a man who seemed to be wearing a Union Jack tea cosy on his head. He waved at their number plates.

'Are we officially on the run now?' Kim asked. 'It's exciting, isn't it?'

'We're not on the run. We're tax exiles.'

He gave her a collusive smile.

They stopped in Bordeaux for a snack and, defeated by the signposting, took two hours to get out. Eventually they were cruising through the pine forests of Les Landes on a long, boring journey to Biarritz. The tedious scenery seemed to stultify conversation but they both had a lot to think about. 'One small step for a man but a giant leap for a girl,' Kim had said as they boarded the ferry.

When they could finally relax over dinner in a café in Biarritz – where they could watch their parked car through the window – they became quite playful with relief at their getaway.

'How would you sum up your marriage, Mr Ward?' Kim asked, offering him a pepper pot as a microphone.

'Stormy and volatile,' Matthew said. 'Emma had a tongue that could rasp flesh from a carcass.'

'You don't regard marriage as a cure for loneliness?'

'Yes, and the guillotine is a cure for headaches.'

'Could you describe your ideal woman?'

'A deaf mute who has won the pools.'

'You won't be getting married again then?'

'The day after the Pope.'

He poured Kim some wine and felt apologetic.

'You're a lovely lady, Kim. Who knows what will happen? It was very brave of you to come with me.'

'I thought so.'

'If there is something you would like to tell me about women, you have the microphone. I was a supporter of feminism before women took it up.'

'They are half the world's people, they do nearly two-thirds of the world's work, but earn only a tenth of the world's income and own only one per cent of the world's property.'

'Very good. And they spend ninety per cent of the world's money.'

'Yes, on men.'

They slept in the car that night in a car park at St Jean-de-Luz, beneath the shadow of the Pyrenees. Kim, hugging the pillow that contained the money, was asleep at once, but Matthew, although he was exhausted, twisted uncomfortably in his seat, his mind too full to relax.

The collapse of a life that he had carefully created had been so sudden that even now he could hardly pull all the threads together. But his downfall, he knew, had been due to his love of new gadgets – in this case, the car phone.

Driving home from work one night he had decided that

a short visit to his new girlfriend would provide a pleasant prelude to what promised to be a dull evening. Kim Bradley, the estranged wife of a man with strange sexual tastes, was an unusually bright model who had done some work for the public relations and publicity giant that he had created, and they had now met half a dozen times without their friends knowing. To make the time for an assignation, he rang his wife on the car phone and told her that he was still in London and would be home in two hours.

But Emma had a car phone, too, and calls to the house transferred to it. Her reply was a shock.

'That's funny, darling,' she said. 'You're just in front of me at these traffic lights.' It was the last time she called him darling. Within a day she had noted the numbers on his car phone's memory, rung those she didn't know and spoken to Kim.

Emma had always been a hard lady. She was three years older than Matthew which had sometimes – for reasons that he could never quite pinpoint – given her an edge over him. But the ruthlessness which she now showed was quite outside anything he had experienced in a business in which deception, equivocation and the knife in the back were all tools of the trade.

Matthew had set up the business eight years ago when he was twenty-two. It began as a public relations outfit but expanded rapidly. Soon there was a separate firm dealing with publicity and then there was a small advertising agency. The latest addition to the empire was an office that dealt solely with the organizing and presentation of exhibitions. If a firm wanted to gather all its European representatives for discussion and instruction in London, Paris or Geneva, Matthew's men would be there in advance, setting the scene. The expansion was so fast that early on he had to give two brilliant colleagues equity in the business. At the same time he gave his wife twenty-six per cent and was left with forty-two per cent himself.

The first thing that Emma did after the car phone incident was to get him voted out of the firm. It wasn't difficult: the two partners, seeing their stake in a thriving business almost double in an hour, agreed at once. After a brief and extraordinary career, Matthew found himself unemployed at thirty. For a week he didn't worry: he thought he could see advantages and the job had become a huge strain. And he had an awful lot of money.

But what Emma did now made the loss of his business seem a trivial setback. For five or six years the money had come in so quickly that he hardly knew what to do with it. He bought property, developed it and sold it, forming new companies at the rate of one a month to handle the deals. He opened accounts offshore – in Jersey, Switzerland and the Isle of Man – thinking more of the interest rate than the claims of the tax man. His last tax bill had been £210,000 and he had paid it promptly.

But now Emma told the Inland Revenue that her husband had been lying for years. Tax officials moved in and went back through his books for six years. The summons to the High Court in the Strand arrived just after a new tax bill for £340,000.

Matthew's accountant took him to see a QC. The QC, a large, fat, balding man with an astonishingly red nose, was gloomy from the beginning.

'They will charge you with criminal fraud, Mr Ward,' he said. 'You won't walk freely from the court.'

'You mean prison for sure?' Matthew had asked.

'Unquestionably. You could rape and mug two old ladies and possibly commit one murder and get the same sentence.'

'What do you mean, possibly?'

'It depends what form of murder you chose.' He leaned forward and pointed at the small cigar that Matthew had nervously been smoking. 'I'll tell you something else.

Smoking may damage your health, but prison will crucify you.'

The unspoken message, surprising from a Q C and the more alarming for that, was clear, and in the street outside his accountant endorsed it.

'Disappear,' he said.

The court hearing took place in Matthew's absence. The Inland Revenue were given power of attorney to freeze his assets, his bank account and put a claim on his houses, offices and cars. They also issued a warrant for his arrest for criminal fraud and, following his non-appearance, contempt of court.

Matthew and Lady had moved in with Kim. She rented a small flat, but he had only been there for two days when a policeman called to see if he was there. Kim persuaded him that he wasn't, and within the hour he had moved into the Aubrey Park Hotel at Redbourn under a false name while Kim looked after the dog.

He sat on the bed in room 167 and drew up plans that would keep him out of prison. His planning had always been brilliant: it was the reason for his success. He realized that he needed three things: money, a false passport and a booking on a cross-channel ferry.

He phoned his accountant and then he rang Kim.

'How's Lady?' he asked.

'I'm fine.'

'I meant the dog.'

'I know.'

'Listen, it's only a matter of time before I'm caught. I'm leaving the country this week.'

'I'm coming with you.'

The thought had never occurred to him.

'Are you sure?' he asked.

'I'm certain.'

'Well,' he said, 'company would be nice. Stay by your phone.'

He tried to get a place on the ferry to Santander in northern Spain, but they were booked up for a fortnight and he couldn't risk the wait. Instead he found room on the Friday evening crossing from Portsmouth to St Malo. Then he went to London. At St Catherine's House in the Strand he provided all the necessary details, supplied by Kim, about her husband, Robert Bradley, and paid £4.50. Two days later he returned to collect a copy of Robert Bradley's birth certificate. He had three pictures taken of himself in a booth, and returned to the sanctuary of his hotel with a false one-year passport. He and Kim could now travel as man and wife.

He rang his accountant again and received the first good news for weeks.

'The Revenue haven't found out about the Jersey account and an open draft for the whole amount is on its way to the Nat West,' he said.

'I had £200,000 in there,' said Matthew.

'That's right. I've arranged with a solicitor to collect a draft from the bank in his own name. He doesn't know what's going on. He just thinks he's receiving funds on behalf of a client.'

'And he'll pay me in cash?'

'On Friday morning.'

'I've got £35,000 in a current account at Luton.'

'Well, you won't see that again,' said the accountant. 'Take care, Matthew.'

He woke up in the Scirocco with his head twisted awkwardly against the door.

'Is it still today or has tomorrow arrived?' he asked, but Kim was still asleep, with her arms around the pillow. He got out to have some air. St Jean-de-Luz was a beautiful town and he would have liked to stroll through it, but there was too much money in the car to wander far, so he walked round it a few times to take the ache from his legs.

When he opened the door again Kim had woken up.

24

'A wash would be nice,' she said.

'Some luxuries aren't available to fugitives,' he told her. 'Are you hungry?'

'Not yet.'

But when they had crossed the border and turned their money into pesetas they stopped in San Sebastian and sat at pavement tables for coffee and rolls. An hour later they had crossed the Ebro and were in Burgos, and then they headed south towards Madrid. The roads were not so good now and they could see that it would be late evening before they reached the south.

'Tell me about your brothers,' Kim said, 'as we're obviously going to see them.'

'I haven't seen them myself for two years,' said Matthew. He couldn't remember whether he had discussed Danny's crime with her. 'One of them is a real villain, not a poor, hounded tax-payer.'

'Daniel. I know about it. What did he do?'

'He worked out a method of relieving several banks of a million pounds without actually using a gun and the next thing I knew he was in Spain. I've never had the time to visit him, but my elder brother Mark, who can best be described as an itinerant musician, flew out immediately to bring him home and liked the place so much that he wound up working in a piano bar. He's been here ever since.'

Kim found some sweets in the car's glove compartment and pushed one into Matthew's mouth. 'What are they both like?'

'Danny is five years younger than me. He's an intellectual who used to work in computers. After Danny has explained something to you, a subject which you half understood becomes incomprehensible. He was the pampered youngest son, the only one to go to public school. He rewarded his father by stealing a million pounds with an extraordinary scam.'

'What's a scam?'

'Trick, ruse, swindle. American, I believe. Here, would you like to drive?'

He pulled into the side of the road. There was surprisingly little traffic. The countryside, green in the north, was becoming browner as they progressed south. Kim drove off quickly.

'We'll need petrol soon,' she said. 'Where do we head after Madrid?'

'Granada.'

'And what about Mark?'

'Mark is five years older than me – we arrived very regularly until mother died giving birth to the criminal. He's thirty-five and is what you might call an under-achiever. He marches to a different drum, although his chosen instrument is the piano. He's so laid back he's practically unconscious. At least he was in England and I don't imagine that the land of *mañana* has livened him up. He treats life like a rehearsal, and doesn't seem to have realized that this is the real thing.'

'What does he do apart from play the piano?'

'Sings, writes songs that nobody else ever sings except Mark. In England he was with a remarkably unsuccessful group who didn't even get on to television when television was screening musical illiterates every night.'

'Have you noticed that it's getting hotter and the sky is completely blue?'

'Drive on, Mrs Bradley. I think we're going in the right direction.'

TWO

DANIEL WARD sat on the patio of his villa in the foothills of the Sierra de Mijas doing the crossword in yesterday's *Daily Telegraph*. Daring action in one who believes all is lost. Nine letters. Feat, he thought. Defeatist. His record for this crossword was just over five minutes, and he liked to keep in training. His life now was devoid of the mental challenges that he loved and it was important to him that he kept his mind occupied. When he ran out of crosswords he played chess with himself, determined always to make the best move he could see for both black and white.

Daniel was smaller than his brothers and, unlike them, was losing his hair. It began receding dramatically at the front when his salary reached £20,000 a year, and then a bald spot appeared and expanded on top. Today no one would readily name him as the youngest among his brothers and with his accent, polished during six years at school, there would be plenty who would refuse to believe that he was a brother at all. Short, suntanned and with a sad, heavy look about the eyes after two years in exile, he found it increasingly difficult to get satisfaction from his life: there was too much time, and not enough to do with it.

In the early days, naïvely, he had sought the company of people in the same situation, men whose absence from Britain was an enduring source of frustration at Scotland Yard: runaway jewellers, bullion robbers, insurance fraudsters, middle-men in all sorts of transactions who never quite passed the money on to the next in line. All had arrived before Spain joined the European Economic Community in 1986 and were safe from the threat of

27

extradition unless Spain decided for other reasons that their presence was undesirable. At that time they all drank in a bar at Los Boliches called The Office. It evidently gave them a homely feeling to tell their wives that they were going to The Office, but fashions change and they moved to Wyn's Bar in the hills behind Benalmadena. Daniel had driven up there a couple of times in a blue Ford Escort that he had bought within days of arriving. He found himself sitting in a single-storey shack with tiled floors, a few tables and a dartboard. Was this where you drank when you had a million?

When he did make a friend it was, ironically, a retired bank manager called Nash, who was led to believe that Daniel had started his own computer firm, built it up to an enviable state of profitability and sold out to the Americans before voting for a life in the sun. They played a game of tennis twice a week, followed by a dip in the pool and a drink on the terrace. The routine had remained unbroken now for more than a year and was itself producing the *cafard* it was intended to dispel.

For Daniel, a lifestyle which had once seemed idyllic was now as confining as the prison sentence he had plotted so diligently to avoid: he could travel anywhere in the world so long as he didn't leave Spain, and he was becoming tired of Spain. He was tired of sudden and gigantic holes in pavements; he was tired of the contours of the lavatories that retained what they were supposed to dispatch; he was tired of *platos combinados* and Union Jacks on menus; he was tired of donkeys covered in earthenware jugs and old ladies selling what evidently was the same tablecloth; he was tired of reading day-old newspapers; he was tired of seeing large signs outside cafés saying FILETE – CHULETA – BROCHETA – SAL-CHICHA – PINCHITO, when neither he nor his lacuna-riddled dictionary knew what it meant. Even the remorseless sun was beginning to unnerve him.

He cheered himself up by devouring the English newspapers, even if they were a day late, and listening gratefully to the BBC World Service. He even listened to the football commentaries on Saturday afternoons. When he was in England he had not the slightest interest in football, but now the noisy Saturday ritual helped to alleviate his homesickness by removing him for a couple of hours to the land he had left. Another solace was the local video club that rented out films in English. Daniel was nearly top of the waiting list for *Crocodile Dundee*, although no one seemed to know when it would reach the Iberian peninsula.

It wasn't quite what Daniel had expected when he first arrived in these parts, optimistic and suddenly rich. He had taken to the hills within an hour of landing in Spain. His inclination was to avoid the clamorous coastline and its occasionally observant visitors, and buy himself something in the country from which, re-styled and possibly bearded, he could make forays to the fleshpots on the coast. And so, getting an airport taxi south, he turned off the main road quite quickly and, heading inland, found himself at Mijas. It was a tiny town of cobbled squares and whitewashed buildings which offered a marvellous vantage point over both the coast and the Mediterranean. Sipping beer on the balcony of the Hotel Mijas less than two hours after his arrival in Spain, he felt like a man in a castle who could see his enemies approaching long before they saw him.

He rang Leanda as soon as he had unpacked.

'Where the hell are you, for God's sake?' she asked. 'Dinner's been ready for at least an hour.'

'I'm in Spain,' he said.

'Spain?'

'It's just below France in your atlas.'

'What the hell are you doing there?'

Daniel had to concede that his wife's bewilderment was

understandable. He told her: 'I have a lot of money and I'm not coming back. I want you to get a plane.' He did not tell her that on the two-hour flight out he had wondered whether to ring her at all; he had not been in Mijas for half an hour before he knew that he was going to be very lonely without her.

But when she arrived at the hotel two days later, she had company herself. She had brought Daniel's brother Mark. He was a big, shambling man, ten years older than Daniel, with lots of black curly hair and a fat, contented face.

'I've brought Mark,' said Leanda, kissing her husband on the cheek.

'So you have. How are you Mark?'

'Fine.' He seemed embarrassed to be there.

They sat at a table on the magnificent balcony and stared down at the Mediterranean five miles away. A waiter brought them drinks.

'Dad asked me to come,' Mark said. 'What's going on, Danny?'

Daniel looked at his wife. 'You phoned my father?'

'I had to. I didn't know what to do.'

'All you had to do was what I asked you. I'd have rung Dad myself, eventually.'

'He's pretty worried,' said Mark. 'What are you doing, Danny?'

Daniel drank his beer and wondered how much to tell them.

'I'm looking for a house,' he said. 'I think I've found one. I'll show you it in the morning.'

Mark looked at him. 'And what was this about lots of money?'

'I'll tell you what I did yesterday. I deposited a quarter of a million pounds in the Banco Atlantico, the same again in the Banco de Jerez, and in the Banco de Bilbao. I then put a quarter of a million in the Banco de Granada here in

Mijas. I can afford to buy you another drink, should you want one.'

Leanda stared at her husband, but couldn't bring herself to ask the question. Mark had no such compunction.

'Where did it come from?'

'It came from where all money comes from, Mark. The bank.'

'You robbed a bank?'

'Well, I didn't rush in with a gun in my hand, if that's what you're thinking. I just discovered a flaw in their system. I made several million in a couple of weeks but let them off lightly. I only withdrew a million.'

'But why, Danny? Why?'

Daniel turned his beer round in his hand, studying its colour. 'That is the question, Mark, I agree. I could say, "because it was there", but there's obviously more to it than that. Matthew has money coming out of his ears, in case you haven't noticed. I am told that he is a millionaire several times over. You have your music, which gives your life a purpose. What did I have? No money, no purpose. I had nothing.'

'You had the best education that money could buy,' Mark said with more force than he had so far shown. 'Something that neither Matthew nor I were given.'

'Education alone isn't enough, is it?' Daniel said, putting down his glass. 'It gave me aspirations and no means of fulfilling them. It gave me dreams, but no talent. It showed me how the rich live, and there were some very rich people at my school, but it didn't give me the money to live like they do. I was educated to a high state of dissatisfaction.'

'You'll regret it.'

'Probably. In the meantime, don't you think this is a lovely place?'

Leanda looked at Mark. 'I don't believe any of this,' she said.

'I can hardly believe it myself,' Mark said. 'However, I

know it's all true. I'd better get to reception and book myself a room.'

The money was never mentioned again; it was as if everybody was too embarrassed to bring the subject up and had already consigned it to the cupboard that is kept for family skeletons. There was a quite different atmosphere the following morning when Daniel took his wife and brother for a walk round Mijas. The landscape was so steep that even when you were close to a building you could still see the trees growing on the hills above it.

The town had been built in layers on this sloping land, with the square at the bottom where the children played in the evenings. Steep steps led up to another part of the town, narrow, car-free pathways in green-and-white tiles where the shops displayed most of their goods outside. They sold leather bags, sunglasses, postcards, straw hats, fans, tablecloths, bracelets, belts, bottle-openers, china cats, chess sets, crinoline dolls, key-rings and – a local product – rugs and carpets.

They walked past an 'English tea-room', which made Leanda feel at home, and a museum which offered 'the most curious collection of tiny things in the world'. This included Churchill sculpted in school chalk, a naval battle with thirty-seven aircraft and twelve ships painted on the head of a pin, a Leonardo da Vinci painting on a grain of rice and some clothed, stuffed fleas.

At the top of the town, on a third layer, was a square bullring, a parish church that was originally a mosque and built in 836, and an open-air auditorium that seated more than a thousand people. There were also three fountains.

'I could live here.' said Leanda, enjoying the spectacular view. 'How much money do you say we have?'

'You don't want a butler, do you?' Mark asked. This morning, in the sunshine, he felt quite differently about mysterious departures to Spain. His life had been cruelly short of foreign travel.

'Let me show you the house I've been looking at,' said Daniel. 'Then we'll have lunch.'

The house that he showed them that morning was now, two years later, considerably improved. The eight-foot white brick wall that surrounded the entire grounds – the elephant-grass lawn, the swimming pool, the tennis court – was a refinement that Daniel had paid for, as was the tennis court itself. New, too, were the hidden cameras in two palm trees that revealed on a screen in the house the identity of the caller at the gate. The gates themselves were remote-controlled and could only be opened from inside the house, which had wrought-iron grilles over every window.

The house now seemed to him to be the last word in luxury, with its cedar sauna, oversized jacuzzi and butler's pantry that he had turned into a bar. It was an open-plan design so that you could see through the drawing room and dining room to the garden and the pool. Out there, among the eucalyptus trees and aromatic shrubs, the only sound to disturb the peace was the hiss of the lawn sprinkler, toiling to keep the grass green. Inside, the floors were white marble throughout, with a plentiful scattering of rugs. The drawing room had two sofas, four armchairs with footstools, all in a floral-pattern material that matched the full-length curtains. There was an enormous open marble fireplace which they used, just for atmosphere, at Christmas. Beside the drawing room, but on a higher level, was the dining room with table and chairs for eight and a sideboard covered in silver. Upstairs – a wide staircase with a white carpet – were six bedrooms and four bathrooms. The smallest bedroom was Daniel's office, although he seldom used it. A new Amstrad computer sat there, waiting to be asked something. The bathrooms were in dark-blue ceramic tiles, with matching bath, basin, shower, lavatory and bidet; and their own bedroom, the largest, had a four-poster bed and one wall

33

made entirely of glass which, when the green silk curtains were opened, offered a view of the coast. There were delicate white radiators everywhere, which were rarely used, and the house itself was surrounded by a terrace with many white pillars, several cushioned chairs and sun-beds and a conservatory where guests could drink if the unthinkable happened and it rained.

While millions of families lived in high-rise two-bed-room flats in dusty cities, Daniel relaxed now among this conspicuous opulence and felt thoroughly miserable.

Stalled by an anagram, he took ten minutes to finish the *Daily Telegraph* crossword, threw the paper down and went to find a beer. The advantage of drinking as a pastime was that you enjoyed yourself even when you weren't enjoying yourself.

At a loss for something to do, he turned on the tele-vision. He had the greatest difficulty in understanding Spanish television, but some scenes on the news bulletins were self-explanatory. Today a bunch of hard-eyed young men with funny moustaches were waving the cameras away, but they panned nevertheless to a dozen black sacks containing the newly dead. Today's terrorist outrage. He couldn't even remember yesterday's.

He heard Leanda arrive, and turned the television off. In many ways she had adjusted to the life here better than he had. She had made friends in the English tea-room whom he had never met, and three times a week she at-tended the Centro de Artes in Mijas, learning Spanish on Wednesdays and Fridays and, today, joining other ladies in holding back the years with a keep-fit class.

She was a tall, blonde girl, taller than Daniel, with a rangy, athletic build and a lot of energy. The tennis court and the swimming pool provided compensation for her exile which she referred to less these days, although Daniel knew that she would prefer to live in Britain, where she would find more scope for her social ambitions. She looked as if life wasn't at all what she had expected and was a continual source of dismay. Her eyebrows, plucked inwards from the side of her face, registered permanent surprise. Leanda was a conventional girl who had been given a comfortable and protected upbringing. She believed in chastity before marriage and fidelity after it. At twenty-five she was still waiting for her first orgasm.

She came in now, wearing a silk shirt, white linen trousers and flat white sandals.

'Miss Joan Hunter Dunn,' said Daniel. 'Furnished and burnished by Mijas's sun.'

She flopped down on a sofa and kicked off her sandals. 'Very good, Danny.' she said. 'Not that I've ever seen you read poetry.'

'Not since school, thank God.'

He had met her drinking champagne framboise in the terrace bar at Harrods: it was love among the roof tops. He rushed her to the Verbanella in Beauchamp Place for a meal. Now the conservatory in Mijas was a replica of Harrods' terrace bar, complete with tiled floor, ersatz bamboo chairs and green Harrods ashtrays.

Daniel was about to suggest dinner at El Capricho, his favourite Mijas restaurant, when the buzzer told him that he had visitors at the gate. Leanda, for whom almost any visitor was a welcome distraction, jumped up and switched on the screen. They saw a dog, a girl, a man and, behind them, a car.

Daniel jumped up, too. 'That's Matthew, isn't it?' he said. It was more than two years since they had met. Excitedly, he pushed the remote-control button that opened the gates and they both went out to greet their guests. The dog jumped up and down incessantly, as if freed recently from a long incarceration.

'Hallo, people,' said Matthew. He looked pale and tired,

and much older than when Daniel had last seen him. 'The dog is Lady and the lady is Kim. I think I've got that right. Hallo, Leanda.'

He kissed her cheek and hugged his brother.

'Hallo, villain,' he said. 'We need a bed.'

'Come in. Come in,' said Daniel. Nothing as nice as this had happened to him for a long time. He had hero-worshipped Matthew as a boy, the brother just five years older than him who had taught him all the things a boy wants to know. Mark had always been too old to be interested, but Matthew had shown him how to play games, ride a bike, fire a catapult, climb trees, catch fish, skate, smoke, swim, hit people. The saddest part of his boyhood had been when Matthew grew to prefer boys of his own age and told Daniel he was too young to join them.

Later, when Daniel was doing well at school and felt that he might now be regarded as an equal again, he could see that Matthew resented the expensive education that his younger brother was receiving, the advantages that were denied to him. In his more perspicacious moments, Daniel imagined that his own sudden emergence as a privileged public schoolboy had been the goad which drove Matthew – the independent bastard, who wouldn't even work with his father – towards his extraordinary commercial success. And so they had spent their lives growing apart but now, suddenly, they were together again and Matthew needed him.

He led them through the house and out to the patio where they could sit in the shade and admire his pool. He produced champagne. An hour later, when he had been thoroughly briefed on his brother's situation, he felt that they had never been closer.

'We're in exactly the same situation,' he said. 'Cheers!'

'Well, not *exactly*,' Matthew said. 'I ran away with my money and you ran away with somebody else's.'

'It wasn't your money. It was the government's.' Daniel

didn't care for this distinction. 'If we went back we'd face more or less the same prison sentence.'

'That's all part of the injustice of British justice, Danny. The Revenue have confiscated far more money than I owe them. This bit here is definitely mine.' He held up his pillow. 'Can I put it in your safe?'

Daniel took the pillow into the dining room, removed a painting of the Alhambra in Granada from the wall, and fiddled with the combination on his safe. It was big enough to take several pillows.

'How are you both liking it here, anyway?' Kim asked. 'This is the sort of house I always wanted.'

'When I was a girl I wanted a Georgian home, a grandfather clock and a Persian carpet,' said Leanda. 'Then I met Daniel.'

'Women never enjoy themselves anyway,' said her husband. 'But they think they are enjoying themselves if they are surrounded by luxury.'

'You patronizing little pillock,' said Leanda cheerfully.

'She wanted a millionaire who had been educated at public school,' Daniel told the others. 'And that's what she's got.'

'Presumably it isn't quite as she envisaged it,' Kim suggested.

'Well, we all have to make adjustments,' said Daniel. 'Let me show you round. There's a wonderful bedroom here for you somewhere.'

What Matthew saw during a conducted tour persuaded him that there was life after England, although he had to remind himself that his brother had arrived here with five times as much money as he had in his pillow. He took Lady for a romp on the lawn: the dog's delight at their reunion that afternoon had still not worn off, and she seemed none the worse for her ordeal. Daniel joined him.

'Our ladies are grilling steaks for us,' he said. 'I take it that you and Emma are –' He made a throat-cutting gesture.

Matthew nodded. 'She's after a divorce and she's welcome to it. The whole thing is her fault.'

Daniel patted his shoulder and led him back towards the food. 'You know what they say, brother. Hell hath no fury like a woman's corns. I think that's what they say.'

Matthew looked at his brother and thought he detected a nervous hilarity that was created by alcohol.

'What do you do with yourself,' he asked, 'in the evenings?'

Daniel shrugged as if the problem of evenings was one that he had never managed to solve. 'What would you like to do? You're the guest.'

'See Mark,' said Matthew.

The piano bar was like a bear pit, and there was something heroic about Mark at the centre of it, singing his heart out with song after song while 200 customers crowded round, not all of them listening. They sat, with their drinks on his grand piano, in the middle of the room, and they sat at tables for four or six round the edges; but most of them stood in the space round the bar, listening, shouting and clapping, and demanding that Mark sing their own obscure favourite.

Jay's Piano Bar was red: red carpets, red leather-covered bar stools, red flock-paper on the walls and red drapes over the windows which looked out over the marina at Puerto Banus. It was designed like an old-fashioned English pub, with ornate woodwork over the bar that ran the length of one wall, and gas lamps that dimmed when the pianist was working, to be replaced by candles on the tables.

Mark knew more than 3,000 songs, 300 of them perfectly. If he was asked twice for a song he didn't know, he learned it. He had a prompt book for words and chord sequences, but seemed magically spontaneous to the customers at Jay's, hurling himself into songs that had enjoyed a brief success ten or twenty years ago. He worked for three hours a night – six half-hour sessions alternating with a bespectacled genius from Knoxville called Alvin who, nearing forty and unable to settle, was working his way round Europe for the umpteenth time. It was understandable that the owner, a shrewd, silent Spanish tycoon, wanted an American in the cast list. That was where most of the popular songs came from. The top six in Jay's were 'New York, New York'; 'Summertime'; 'Yesterday'; 'St Louis Blues'; 'San Francisco' and 'Don't Cry for Me, Argentina'.

Tonight the first shift was Alvin's and he ended, as usual, by introducing Mark as the man who knew 3,000 songs. Mark put his glass of beer on the piano, alongside another glass that was supposed to fill with tips before the evening was out, and adjusted the synthesizer at his side, which he had only recently and reluctantly mastered. They knew him here and the welcoming applause was enthusiastic. He still became nervous before he played; pianists who didn't, he thought, had a clock inside instead of a heart. He only knew roughly what he was going to play, because the requests could not be ignored. On the other hand, there were some songs with funny chord sequences that had to be played regularly, requested or not.

'I'm going to play a Hoagy Carmichael selection to start with,' he told the bar, and went straight into 'Up the Crazy River', 'Sweet Georgia Brown' and 'Sunny Side of the Street'. He wasn't even sure whether they all were Hoagy Carmichael, but nobody disputed it.

'"Rock Around the Clock",' somebody shouted.

'One of the few songs to reach number one three times,' said Mark. 'Do you mind if I play it after this?'

He was finishing 'Sunny Side of the Street' when he saw his brothers come in. Daniel was with Leanda, but Matthew was with a girl he had never seen before.

'Here's an old Cat Stevens hit,' he said, and started in on 'Matthew and Son'.

Matthew waved.

The arrival of his brothers distracted him. Daniel visited the bar only rarely, and he hadn't seen Matthew in two years. He could hardly see him now through the crowd and the gloom. He pushed the visitors from his mind and sang his favourite Presley number, 'Love Me Tender'.

But when his first shift was over he grabbed his drink and hurried to the bar, where the four of them were standing.

'Let's go outside,' he said, when Matthew had introduced him to Kim.

They sat at banquettes under a marquee roof where they watched the boats bobbing in the harbour. Alvin's round-up of some of the better known New Orleans numbers was being relayed to the passers-by through loudspeakers, an invitation to come in and see the face behind the voice.

'I am the unsuccessful brother,' Mark told Kim. 'I expect you've heard of me?'

'I think you do a wonderful job,' she said. 'I loved it.'

'It's the hardest job in the world. A singer should sing in a club, and a pianist should back somebody. You try to combine the two and you need a bullet-proof vest.'

'Well,' said Kim, 'at least you are the only brother who is not on the run.'

Mark's big, smiling face suddenly went serious. 'Is there something I don't know?' he asked. Watching him, Kim found it hard to believe that the three men were brothers.

'I had a difference of opinion with the tax man,' Matthew told him.

'What was his opinion?'

'That I should go to prison, having first been made bankrupt. It wasn't something I could agree with entirely. You didn't think I was on holiday did you? I don't have holidays.'

'Jesus,' said Mark. 'Two of you. Dad will be delighted.'

The reference to their father plunged them all into silence. Alvin's deep voice bounced round them from the speakers.

Puerto Banus was a magnetic spot on this coast. Its tall, white buildings were so narrow and odd they looked like something from a Disney cartoon. They looked down on a harbour that was filled with yachts, the biggest of them worth millions of pounds. Along the front, behind the palm trees and bougainvillaea, were boutiques with the very best labels in haute couture, bars and restaurants and the occasional property and investment consultant with extravagant plans for you to buy your own place in the sun.

Mark loved to sit out here between his sessions at the piano and watch the world walk by. It sometimes seemed as if the crowds who wandered along the water's edge had been licensed by a very selective casting agency which had scrutinized them for looks, clothes and style before awarding a coveted permit to stroll in public. What was strange was that so many of them were nocturnal creatures, emerging after dark and staying up until dawn, when the days here were so beautiful. If all they wanted was night-life, Mark thought, they could have gone anywhere.

He looked out at the water where black fish a foot long searched for scraps from the rich men's tables. Judging by their numbers, it was a search that was usually successful.

'How is he anyway?' he asked.

'Who?' asked Daniel.

'Dad.'

'He was fine when I last saw him,' said Matthew. 'Playing golf, enjoying himself.'

'He's sixty in September.'

'Is he?'

'Didn't either of you know that? I want to get him out here for his birthday. Now Matthew is here he's got to

41

come, unless he's washed his hands of us. Does he know you're here?'

'Not yet. I'm going to ring him.'

'Be sure you do.'

It was as if they were boys again, with Mark, the eldest and most powerful, pushing them in directions they hadn't chosen. It had always been Mark who had urged them to be helpful to their father, struggling to bring up three boys without the help of a wife. His efforts had never received appreciation, even from his father, but the habit had stuck.

Daniel called the waiter and ordered them all drinks.

'They're expensive,' said Leanda, 'compared to other places.'

'That's how they pay me, Mrs Ward,' Mark said. 'How are you, anyway?'

'Daniel gets bored, but I'm all right,' she said.

Mark turned to his younger brother. 'Why don't you do something, Danny? To stop the boredom.'

'Like what?'

'Buy a boat. Play golf. Get a job. Before you decline into permanent melancholia.'

But Daniel had drunk enough to feel cheerful now. 'The climate has affected me, brother. I've become a great believer in doing nothing. Positive moves produce negative results.'

'Not necessarily.'

'God's done nothing for 2,000 years and look at the loyalty he inspires. Harold Wilson was the same. Not for so long, of course. How's the song writing?'

'Well,' said Mark, 'I'm still doing it.'

'But it doesn't produce pesetas?'

'Headaches, yes. Pesetas, no. That's why I sing for my supper.' He looked at his watch and stood up. 'I'm on again. I'll see you later.'

He hurried into the bar, leaving them outside under the marquee roof.

'The man who works the most has got the least,' said Daniel, reaching for his glass.

Unlike his brothers, who had, before their respective set-backs, taken the conventional route from school classroom to professional success and considerable affluence, Mark Ward had left school with no qualifications and the following day joined a pop group which, unusually for the time, needed a pianist. He mixed, almost immediately, in a world of deeply insecure men, carnal gymnasts, suicidal poets, barroom bullshitters, pear-shaped women, upside-down beer-drinking champions and musicians consumed by ambitions beyond their grasp or reach. These frequently drunk and constantly complaining malcontents never ran out of plausible explanations for their blameless failures, their crippling poverty or their glum futures. If they had invested half their creativity in a career, they would have had three bank accounts by now, one of them quietly fructifying in a sunny tax haven. But Mark empathized with this noisy team of losers: he was a failure, too.

He had in his time made music of a sort from the Orkneys to the Scillies and from Anglesey to Ipswich, and he was now sustained by a quixotic determination to stay with music until music rewarded him for his loyalty. The closer he looked at the alternative life the more it depressed him. Trade union leaders were fond of talking about 'the dignity of work', but Mark could see nothing dignified about shuffling into a factory at half past seven in the morning with your sandwiches in a box. The thriving industrial society, so popular with today's chatty pundits, was a concept so alien to him that his mind instinctively leapt right over it to other, happier images. Only that week he had read that in Japan, that busy little offshore island in the north Pacific, there was a suicide every twenty minutes

43

His life had changed for the better at the time that Daniel had vanished with his mysteriously acquired million. Discovering quite quickly that his impetuous flight to Malaga would not bring his brother home, he abandoned the doomed mission and looked for the fun. He found Puerto Banus a couple of days after arriving, and he found the piano bar a couple of minutes after finding Puerto Banus. It was a timely arrival at Jay's: one of the two resident pianists, a pioneer until the end, had just died of Aids. An audition the following morning when the customers had gone home was followed by the offer of a job.

Mark lived frugally in a tiny one-bedroom apartment at the back of the port which belonged to the bar's owner and was let to him at a considerable discount. He had a small kitchen, a shower and a living room where the main feature was a Casio keyboard that could sound like a grand piano if he wanted it to, or a guitar or violin. The piano was dead, long live the keyboard. It was a birthday present from Daniel who, being ten years younger than Mark, was ten years ahead of him in the new technology and the latest electronic toys. Next to the keyboard was a table on which stood a gooseneck lamp and piles of songs, the product of ten years of lonely brain-ache. The songs had been sent to, and returned by, some of the biggest names in show business, apart from assorted music publishers and record companies. The latest, called 'Peacock in the Morning', was even now, he imagined, being played excitedly in some London impresario's sumptuous office.

On the day after his brothers had made their unexpected visit to Jay's, Mark rose at noon. He took a shower, slipped on a T-shirt, jeans and a pair of espadrilles, and made himself a coffee. This was the time of day when he would write a song if he had a song to write. They were timeless and, usually, romantic; he always had an eye on the largest possible audience. But today he wondered whether there

44

wasn't a novelty number to be written about his brothers or, possibly, the tax man.

He picked up one of the pop-music papers that he had sent from England so that he could keep up with developments in a wildly unpredictable business, but they seldom told him what he wanted to know.

> He should be made a saint, sobbed 50-year-old Valerie Constable, who named her Clapham council house Gracelands after Elvis's mansion.

Was it really ten years since Presley died? That told you how fast the time was passing. Every year seemed shorter then the last, and although he was in his twenties only the other day, he was now looking towards his fortieth birthday. As his father had once said, he had aged but never grown up. But he was thirty-five and quite old enough to be alarmed by the young, by their furious energy, their raucous music so unlike his own sweet songs, their penchant for illegal substances and their icy contempt for anybody who had reached that advanced stage of senility and degeneration that is marked by a thirty-fifth birthday.

He felt like a twenty-year-old himself – the trouble was he couldn't find one! But perhaps that was the answer to the fleeing years that failed to bring success: a fresh-faced young thing with breasts like tennis balls and buttocks like footballs. Or was it the other way round? Life, he was beginning to think, was a game in which you were only given the correct information when it was too late.

It was a strange thing, he reflected, that at a time when marriage was moving out of fashion it should be he who had stayed single while his younger, with-it brothers had promised to love, honour and dismay. Daniel had been only twenty-one when he put his head in the noose.

Perhaps it was part of the lessons in correct living that you were taught at public school: clean your shoes, wear a tie, get a job, find a wife, rob a bank. Mark had always imagined that public schoolboys were a bunch of pillow-biting shirt-lifters who joined the secret service, and was relieved at the time by his brother's orthodoxy. It was about the only time that he had been pleased with his father's youngest son, the pampered favourite who caused his mother's death. These days, when he thought about Daniel at all, he thought about the million pounds and wondered how he had got it. He would never talk about it now, but he had let out once that the bank had never made the theft public because they feared imitators.

He played a chord on the piano.

> My brothers are both villains
> They're running from the police
> They're homesick in the sunshine
> They search in vain for peace.

Like many of his songs, it was derivative. The debt here, he realized, was to 'My Old Man's a Dustman', and he started again with a song about the tax man. This had not progressed very far when the post arrived.

He could see immediately what it was. 'Peacock in the Morning' had flown straight back to him, with a letter.

Dear Mark Ward, *he read.*

You wrote a song once that we rather liked here at TPA, although we were unable to do anything with it. (That's show business!) However, this latest, 'Peacock in the Morning', is so far removed from today's sound that you could honestly save yourself some postage. This is not what the kids want to hear today and it's kids who buy the discs and kids who fill the discos. Yours faithfully,

Conrad Gambardella

TPA Music

Mark imagined Conrad Gambardella, some swarthy, tin-eared philistine with two Rolls Royces and a mansion in Buckinghamshire, and thought of the hours he had sweated over that song. Then he thought of his brothers with their ill gotten gains.

Then he hurled the cassette across the room.

THREE

AFTER a week Matthew and Kim abandoned the olive groves, almond orchards and vineyards, and went down to the sea. Seven days in his brother's villa had persuaded Matthew that this was the place to be. All he needed was a home.

They drove down to the coast, with Lady on the back seat, and came immediately to Fuengirola, a mid-way point, geographically and qualitatively, between the neon-lit clamour of Torremolinos and the expensive elegance of Marbella. It was an old fishing village that had gradually, under the pressure of tourism, become a town. It lay between the mountains and the sea, and the mountains protected it from the north wind and gave it a wonderful climate. Cars were banned from many of its narrow streets, so you could walk around unharassed, admiring the buildings, all with little balconies bearing terracotta pots and geraniums, and many decorated with handmade tiles. At the centre of the town was the church square with white tables alongside a huge fountain and trees that filled with birds at dusk.

On the seafront was a four-mile esplanade stretching out of the town in both directions and clearly ideal, Matthew thought, for exercising the dog.

They booked into the Hotel Florida, a clean little hotel that was separated from the sea only by its own tree-filled gardens, and went out to look for an apartment. They were directed at first, by one of the many offices that eagerly dealt with such matters, to the Palm Beach apartments, a somewhat grandiloquent name for an edifice that overlooked only a few ailing palm trees and a narrow, grubby stretch of sand.

Discouraged by this, they seemed to lose their impetus, and the search was never pursued with the vigour that was necessary. They slipped into the aimless existence of the expatriate rather too easily, and the freedom was exquisite. Matthew, once an immaculate dresser in his double-breasted box-cut suits, now settled for white short-sleeved shirts, scruffy jeans and sandals.

In the mornings they went first to the churros bar for coffee and doughnuts dipped in chocolate, and then they looked around the shops before establishing themselves in a bar where they could drink for ever. But they usually left before two and headed for the beach, where they rented sunbeds and gently changed colour. The town was full of good restaurants and in the evenings the restaurants and the bars carried them along quite happily until it was time to go to bed.

One afternoon as they were lying on the beach Kim had an idea. She had taken to this leisurely existence as readily as Matthew, but she could see its hazards. She was sitting topless on her sunbed reading a very old paperback that she had bought secondhand in Julian's Book Market (three used paperbacks for fifty pesetas). It was Muriel Spark's *The Mandelbaum Gate*.

Matthew lay on his back contemplating the great changes that his life had recently undergone. It was nice, he decided, to lie here and forget the grey skies, the wet roads and the steamy windows of England, where for many months the sun, if it was visible at all, rested complacently on the horizon at midday.

He lifted himself on to an elbow to watch a topless but lymphatic blonde with a small boy on a nearby sunbed. 'Don't get sand on your banana,' she told him. The male obsession with the female breast had been killed stone dead by the topless revolution, he decided. This, however, did not apply to Kim. He was very fond of her breasts and liked the way that they were tanning

49

with the rest of her body. They always gave him ideas.

'This is the sort of afternoon that should be devoted to fornication and curry,' he told her.

Kim put her book down. 'I'm not sure those activities go together.'

'It depends what order you take them in.'

He leaned over to find a packet of Capote mini-club cigars in the pocket of his jeans. They seemed to have replaced quite adequately the slim cigars to which he had been addicted in England. The addiction had begun with a Clint Eastwood film. He fancied himself as Clint Eastwood. Or Tex Ritter. Or Rex Titter.

'Most people can't afford a decent holiday in the first half of their lives and haven't got the time for it in the second,' he said. 'Not a proper, six-week job. Aren't we lucky?'

'How do you know which half of your life you're in?' Kim asked.

A black man with a strange variety of goods came up to them. He was selling wooden elephants, drums, whips, beads, ivory and bracelets. On the beach now you were offered everything from carpets to watches. To the man's great joy, Matthew bought an elephant.

'I never worry about dying,' he said. 'Dying is what other people do.'

'I'm glad,' Kim said. 'In my experience when a man can't find anything else to worry about, he worries about his health.'

'You're thinking about Robert Bradley,' he told her. 'He's probably worrying about Aids by now.'

The reminder of her brief, calamitous marriage was unwelcome. Robert Bradley was the best-looking man she had ever seen and when he proposed marriage a week after they met she had thought herself lucky. She was only twenty and was not to know that Robert Bradley's tastes excluded women. He had married against his own perverse bias in the naive hope of overcoming it, but the marriage was not a month old when Kim discovered him in the back of a camper with a bisexual hairdresser from a unisex hair salon. Camper was appropriate, she thought at the time, and 'camp' was a word that she carried around for months afterwards. Like For Unlawful Carnal Knowledge, it was an old police acronym, she discovered: Known As Male Prostitute.

She looked at Matthew's gangling frame on the sunbed and thought how lucky she was. There was nothing ambiguous about his sexual tastes.

The beach was noisy now. Waiters had arrived with their cassette players to look for girls. Children were screaming with excitement at the pedalos. Overhead a small plane flew past trailing an advertisement for a disco up the coast.

The smell from the suntan oil was of citrus and coconut. It wafted across to them on the breeze. To the women, sunbathing was a serious cosmetic business, like choosing clothes or having their hair done, although none were quite so methodical as Leanda who a few days earlier had laid beside their pool at Mijas with a kitchen timer. For half an hour she tanned her front, and then spent half an hour doing her back. The third half hour was spent in the shade of an orange parasol, and then the rota started again.

'I've had an idea,' Kim said.

He rolled over on his sunbed and looked at her. 'You don't have to have ideas, Kim. Your role is to look beautiful and wait on me foot and mouth.'

Kim didn't much like the assumptions contained in this remark, but she didn't respond: when two people each have a broken marriage behind them, tolerance becomes the greatest of the virtues.

'Listen to it, anyway. If we are going to spend so much time and money in bars, why don't we buy one of our own?'

Matthew sat up on the sunbed. 'Why don't we buy a bar?' he repeated. 'When I was a proper person I used to have good ideas like that. It would be a better investment than leaving the money in a pillow.'

'It might even make a profit.'

Matthew shook his head. In the old days when he had made more money than he could handle he had a flawless instinct for what would produce it. 'There are a thousand bars round here within a mile or two. I wouldn't expect it to make much profit, but an investment in bricks and mortar on this coast couldn't go wrong. I think I'll buy you a drink.'

While thousands of people in cloudy Britain' were poring over glossy brochures designed to lure them to Spain, Daniel Ward lay on a luxurious sun-lounger on his marble patio studying Spanish brochures which urged travellers to head for Britain.

The one he was reading now, called Gran Bretana, had a strange picture on the cover that placed Nelson's Column immediately in front of the Mansion House with St Paul's Cathedral peeping over the top. At the bottom of the picture the streets were so full of large red buses that it was hard to see how traffic could move.

Daniel studied the picture for some time and then wrestled with the Spanish below: '*En un abrir y cerrar de ojos estara en Heathrow, el aeropuerto mas cercano a Londres.*' Even after two years his Spanish was poor but he tried to read the brochure in English, to savour in full this glimpse of home. 'Now the great experience begins with the quality and beauty of statues, legendary palaces and museums. The city of excellence enjoys many and varied clubs and theatres, all with peculiar character, which are situated in colourful streets, where buses and activity are prime. London is extra special because of music centres, the

Houses of Parliament and Big Ben and the changing of the guard at Buckingham Palace, the British Museum and Westminster which is the area to visit as it is busy with famous faces.'

Like all his translations it sounded odd, although not as peculiar as his very first attempt to read the instructions on a packet of soup to his wife. 'Duck the contents of the purse to the west wind moreover,' he had told her, before she collapsed in hysterical laughter.

He put the brochure down and closed his eyes against the sun. He had stopped thinking about how he had made his money a long time ago – it was almost as if he was trying to convince himself that the cash arrived honourably. But today, with Leanda away at her Spanish classes, the curious montage of London – London, the scene of his crime – brought it all back to him. It had begun as a cerebral challenge, developed into a puzzle and ended up as straight theft, but even now he had to admire the breathless ingenuity of it.

The challenge was to make a million pounds out of thin air and it nibbled at his mind for months. He had spent his life wrestling with chess puzzles, crossword puzzles and computer puzzles, but here at last was a puzzle worthy of his protean talents.

The idea had come to him in his bath, the one place where he could lie without distraction, and a few minutes later he was in the room that he used as an office at home, playing with a pocket calculator. Soon sheets of paper were covered with figures, each bearing a one-pound sterling sign in front of them. He couldn't believe what the figures told him. He discarded the pocket calculator and switched on his Amstrad home computer. The computer agreed with the pocket calculator: in four working days he would make £1,132,275.

He went downstairs feeling light-headed, and opened a bottle of champagne.

'What's that for?' Leanda asked.

'We're going to be rich,' he told her.

'When?'

'Soon.'

The following day he arranged a fortnight's holiday from work. It was a month before the firm could fit it in, but Daniel didn't mind; there was some preliminary work to be done before the great plan could be put into action.

The first thing he had to do was find an area where there were ten banks within reasonable distance of each other, ten banks that he could cover on foot in an hour or so. When he had found them he opened an account in each under a false name with a deposit of £100. Had there ever been a better way to invest £1,000, he wondered.

He had been working his way up in the world of computers, having turned his face against further education in favour of joining the future now. And the future was computers, or so everybody was saying at the time. From the classroom he applied for a job as a trainee operator in the data-processing department of a city-based financial institution. Within six months, his trainee status behind him, he was assigned to the graveyard shift as a fully-fledged junior operator, and set about learning everything he could about what made a large financial institution tick. And between 11 p.m. and 8 a.m. what made it tick, he discovered, was a large black-and-grey box labelled I B M and called a C P U, some tapes and tape drives, some disks and disk drives, card readers, a console like a fancy typewriter and some printers. A few friendly chats with the night-security guard, some confidences exchanged, encouraged by his endless supply of cigarettes, and he was able to wander uninterrupted around the five floors occupied by his company during the day, including the inner sanctums of the top floor where the general manager and his executive colleagues drank fresh percolated coffee provided by beautiful secretaries. This was where Daniel wanted to be. Over the next year he learned that what he had discovered was completely useless unless he could in some way direct the work being done by the large black box. And so, while his contemporaries were directing their energies towards wine, women and probably song, he enrolled in an assembler language programming course at a polytechnic during the day, while doing the graveyard shift at night. By the end of this course he was deputy shift supervisor, which meant that he would be in charge of the shift for at least three weeks every year while the supervisor was in Provence. But by the time he had reached this first plateau – the chance to test his own ability to manipulate the bits and bytes of the company's computer systems run by the big black box – another discovery was beginning to dawn on him: nobody ever made any real money working for somebody else.

On the first day of his holidays Daniel was so nervous that he was physically sick. He felt that he had already painted himself into a corner and there was no escape. He told Leanda that he had a bug which, in a way, was true. They were living then in a small house in Holland Park. He had married young but was a high earner and could just manage the mortgage repayment of £700 a month.

He told Leanda he was meeting a colleague for lunch and caught the Central Line train east towards the country's money.

The banks were now numbered one to ten in his mind; he planned to visit them every Monday, Wednesday and Friday for two weeks.

It took three days to clear a cheque!

At the first bank he paid in a cheque for £75, drawn on Bank 10. He now had £175 in the first bank and he hurried to the second to present a cheque for £150 drawn on Bank 1. The third bank was less than a hundred yards away and there he paid in a cheque for £225 drawn on Bank 2.

The nervous attack that he had suffered that morning

soon evaporated in a mood of euphoria. Whenever the banks saw him he was paying in money!

It took him just under two hours to complete the round. At the tenth bank he had paid in a cheque for £750 from the £775 which by this time was deposited in Bank 9, and the ten accounts, which had sheltered a miserable thousand pounds when he left home, now showed a credit balance of £5125.

He took his mind off the great plan on the Tuesday by going to the cinema with Leanda, but he was in action again when the banks opened on Wednesday morning. He began by paying £825 into the first bank from Bank 10, and moved quickly to the second where he paid in £975. He didn't want to be overdrawn.

With the discovery of some short cuts, the second circuit of the banks was quicker than the first, and by eleven o'clock he was sitting down with a coffee and reflecting on the fact that his credit balance now stood at £29,125.

It wasn't until the Friday of the first week, Day Three of the plan, that he began to feel nervous again. His credit balance at the end of the circuit was more than £173,000. He went through the figures, still partially mystified by the arithmetic which confronted him. Five days earlier he had £1,000 in the bank and now he had £173,000. And all he had done was write a few cheques! At this rate he would soon become the banks' most important customer and start receiving luncheon invitations from the managers.

Day Four, the Monday of the second week, was the day he became a millionaire. Although he began the day by paying only £41,000 into Bank 1, his last call, at Bank 10, was to deposit a cheque for £221,100. The total, as his calculations had told him, was £1,132,275. He stared at the figures in utter stupefaction. From the first cheque, he had never written one that would put him in the red and yet in eight days his £1,000 had become a million.

He did the rounds on the Wednesday, but this time he didn't even bother to work out what the grand total had become. As soon as he got home he rang each bank and told them he would want to withdraw a certain sum in cash the following day. The sum varied from bank to bank, but was nowhere near the total credited to him. From the first bank he only wanted £40,000, and there were only four banks from which he wanted more than £100,000. The highest figure, from Bank 10, was £190,000.

It came to exactly one million pounds.

When he left his home on Thursday, Daniel took a taxi and a hold-all. The banks were wonderfully cooperative, almost deferential. He tucked the money into his bag, jumped back into the taxi and hurried on.

'Where to now, guv?' asked the cabbie when he had run out of banks.

'Heathrow,' said Daniel, groping through the money for his passport and air ticket.

Leanda, who was cooking a chicken for them for dinner, was surprised to receive a telephone call from him at seven o'clock – from Spain.

The prospect of owning a bar gave Matthew something to think about. It gave his life a direction again. He had once had the idea of buying a public house and running it in a way that nobody else seemed to have thought of – making customers feel welcome was one of the revolutionary ideas he planned to introduce – but his growing commercial responsibilities had made the scheme impracticable.

The day after Kim had floated the idea he left her in the bath and took Lady out for a walk round the town to see what premises were available. There were plenty of bars and shops on the market but what was on offer was the *traspaso*, a Spanish equivalent of the lease, which meant that you never owned the building and could be evicted very suddenly if you defaulted on payments.

When he found the bar that he wanted it was closed 'due to illness'. It had been closed ever since he arrived. It was a small bar, right on the front, and peering through the window he saw white walls and ceiling with black oak beams, a fireplace and a pool table. There were about six small tables in the bar with the chairs piled on top of them. As he looked through the window a man appeared at the back of the bar.

Matthew tapped on the window and the man came over and unlocked the door. He was a big man with white hair and, it turned out, German.

'We are closed,' he said, pointing to the notice.

'I want to buy the bar,' Matthew told him.

'To buy it? The bar?' the German said. He waved Matthew in and sat down. He did not look well. '*El ataque cardiaco*,' he said, reverting to Spanish. He tapped his heart. 'How much you pay?'

'The bar,' Matthew said. 'No *traspaso*.'

'How much?'

Matthew had only a vague idea of the property values round here, gleaned in a few days from the pictures and advertisements in the windows of the property dealers. He looked round the room: it was exactly what he wanted.

'Fifty thousand pounds,' he tried.

'No, no,' the German said, standing up with an effort. 'Look, I show you. Upstairs.'

A door behind the bar opened on to the stairs. He followed the German up and found himself in a small one-bedroom flat, with the living room at the front overlooking the sea.

'Down below is cellar,' said the German. 'I show you.' Matthew followed him down both flights of stairs, fearful that the effort would produce another heart attack. Finally they sat down in the bar again.

'How much?' the German repeated.

'Seventy-five thousand,' Matthew suggested.

'Is not enough,' the German said breathlessly. He didn't seem to be much older than forty, but Matthew had visions of the man expiring before they could complete a deal. It was good to be doing deals again. He had already decided that he would pay £100,000 to get this place: the game was to see how much he could save.

The German was counting items on his fingers. 'Bar, *el piso, paseo maritimo.*' He had gone into Spanish again. Did this German ever speak German?

The bar, the flat, the seafront position. If it was an investment that he was looking for, the seafront position made it gilt-edged.

'How much do you want?' he asked.

The German didn't hesitate. 'Eighteen million pesetas.'

Matthew worked it out at 200 pesetas to the pound, which was where the exchange rate seemed to hover this summer: £90,000. He looked round the bar again, not wanting to seem too eager. There was a notice over the counter that said: 'Credit will only be given to customers aged over eighty if accompanied by both parents.' That would have to come down.

'It's a deal,' he said, offering his hand.

The German smiled for the first time. 'You have the money here in Spain?'

Matthew nodded. 'When can I have the bar?'

'We waste no time. We go to see my *abogado* and he will act for us both.'

Matthew thought that he had seen quite enough of solicitors to last for some time, but he said: 'Fine.'

It was lunchtime before he got back to the hotel. Kim was sitting on the bed looking thoughtful.

'I've got one,' he told her. 'I've bought a bar.'

'That's wonderful, Matthew,' she said. Her enthusiasm fell some way short of what he had expected.

'Aren't you pleased?' he asked. 'It was your idea.'

'I'm very pleased. Aren't I, Lady?'

She was stroking the dog.

'What's up, kid? You're not getting homesick, are you?'

She looked up at him. 'Homesick is the last thing I am. I have some news of my own, Mr Ward.'

He sat on the bed beside her. 'Sock it to me.'

'I went to see the doctor while you were out.'

'The doctor? We don't have a doctor.'

'Leanda gave me the address of hers. An English bloke with a surgery near the bus station.'

'And?'

'I told him that I thought I might be pregnant. I expected tests, samples, come back next week, but he just put a stethoscope to my stomach and said, 'You're certainly pregnant. I can hear the heart beating.'

Matthew's own heart seemed to miss a beat at this news.

'When is it due?'

'He thought September.'

'A Christmas-party baby,' he said, remembering. 'That's terrific, Kim.'

'You're not annoyed then? I thought you would be.'

'Why did you think that ? I love children. It's adults I can't stand. Actually after five childless years of marriage I was beginning to wonder if I'd ever be a dad.'

She kissed him then and held on to him. 'As long as you're pleased,' she said.

'This bar has got a small flat above. It'll be perfect for three.' She stretched across for the cigarettes that she occasionally smoked, but he pushed them out of her reach.

'They are versatile little things, cigarettes. They cause premature death in men, and premature births in women.'

'I've given them up already, but I think you could buy me one small celebratory drink.'

'An excellent idea, Mrs Bradley. I trust this new condition of yours won't prevent you from helping me in my new business enterprise?'

'Certainly not. Pregnancy isn't an illness.'

'Then come and have a look at the premises. We fathers-to-be need to earn money.'

Punctiliousness with paperwork is not among those many characteristics for which the Spanish are renowned, and so it was thought afterwards that the speed at which Matthew became the owner of a bar on the coast probably owed much to the disparate nationalities of the principals: the vendor was German, the buyer was British, and the lawyer for both of them was a tireless and eagle-eyed emigrant from the Rann of Kutch.

The only problem in the transaction was extracting the right amount of money from the pillow and passing it swiftly through the bank's innards so that it emerged at the other end as a bank draft made out in pesetas, rather than a hoard of creased plastic envelopes, with the name of a British bank printed on the side. This process filled Matthew with alarm: he imagined some legal instrument, originating from London, reaching across Europe to intercept the loot while it was in the hands of the bank – nobody had ever served a court order on a pillow.

When the German had been paid £90,000, there was still another £7,000 to pay for licences and legal fees, and then Matthew returned what was left to the pillow.

From the German, whose vulnerable heart seemed already strengthened by this inrush of cash, Matthew bought the stock of drinks, the coffee machine, the ice machine, the chip-fryer, a microwave oven, a fridge, a fan and the pool table. Elsewhere he bought a cash register and a music centre. And then, while Kim cleaned the bar, he drove up to the *hipermercado* and bought spirits, cigarettes, cigars, food, tea towels, brushes, dustbins and disinfectant.

Two days after first visiting the bar, he held an opening party. A sign saying MATT'S PLACE had yet to be fitted.

'You hate to be called Matt,' protested Daniel when he heard the intended name. 'You would never let any of us use it.'

'They were charging me by the letter,' Matthew told him. 'Actually, Kim wanted to call it The Tax Haven.'

Daniel and Leanda had cruised down from the hills for this special social event; Mark had jumped in a taxi but had to be back at his piano by half past ten. All three seemed to be more interested in the birth of the baby than the birth of a bar, but Matthew kept pouring champagne and allowed them to choose their own toasts.

'Father will be pleased,' Mark said. 'He must have given up all hope of a grandchild.'

'Will his pleasure be spoiled by the fact that it will be illegitimate?' Kim asked. 'Is that the sort of thing that will worry him?'

'He won't even notice,' Mark told her. 'With sons like this pair he's got too much else to worry about. A grandchild is what he always wanted. In the old days he used to say, "Be fruitful and multiply."'

'But you didn't?'

'It's easier said than done in my experience.'

More difficult now than ever, he thought. The girls who came into Jay's and fancied piano players and the glamorous life they imagined they led were invariably accompanied by younger men who became jealous and then abusive, and by the time Mark had finished work they had gone.

'You're a very attractive man, Mark,' said Leanda, pouring herself more champagne.

'That's a bit sexist, isn't it?' said Daniel. 'Don't worry, Mark. I was reading in the *Telegraph* today that marriages have gone up by a third in twenty years, but divorces have quadrupled. If this trend continues we'll all be single and you'll be right in fashion.'

But it wasn't a fashion that Mark particularly welcomed. Unlike many of his contemporaries, he thought that children might be fun. His sexual dreams as a young man had mostly involved his frequent marriages to Princess Anne, a romantic sequence which was abated not a whit by the lady's sudden attachment to a man the newspapers called Fog. He found the royal wedding quite extraordinarily depressing, but he still compared the girls he met with the new bride and found them wanting.

'I always thought I would be the only one to marry,' he said. 'I thought my frantic little brothers would be too busy for that old-fashioned sort of thing.'

'We went ahead and tested it for you,' said Daniel.

'Like canaries in a coal mine,' Matthew added. 'Do you want to know what you missed? I was married once.'

'You still are,' said Kim.

'You eat when you would prefer to drink. You stay in when you would prefer to go out. You watch television when you would prefer to read. You talk when you would prefer to think. You stay awake when you would prefer to go to sleep. And if you go out, when you would prefer to stay in, you dress up when you would prefer to dress down, and sit down in bars when you would prefer to stand up. You meet this couple when you would prefer to meet that couple, and see this film when you would prefer to see that film ...'

'That was marriage to Emma,' said Kim, looking strained.

'It's the only marriage I know, Kim, and it led me to this conclusion: nothing puts a woman into a bad mood faster than the sight of a man enjoying himself.'

'If you go on like that, Matt's Place could be the haunt of homosexuals,' said Leanda.

'They've already got a place up the coast,' Mark told her. 'It's called The Halfway Inn.'

A sunburnt old lady came in with a rush and threw her handbag on the bar. The first customer.

'A gin, dear,' she said with a Scottish accent.

'You wouldn't prefer a free champagne, would you?' Matthew asked her. 'This is our opening night.'

'I know it is, dear, but I'll have a gin all the same. What did Adolf Hitler rush you for this place?'

The champagne drinkers filled their glasses and watched Matthew at work.

'It's just right for him,' said Kim. 'He was always in bars anyway.'

'It's better than being behind them,' said Daniel.

SUMMER

Mad dogs and Englishmen
Go out in the midday sun.

– Noël Coward

FOUR

QUITE OFTEN at six o'clock Matthew would go down to the port at Fuengirola with Lady to watch the fish come in. He liked to enjoy the fresh air before long hours in the bar. The walk took him along the white, yellow and brown tiled promenade that was separated from the one-way *paseo* by a line of dusty palm trees. Most of the sunbeds on the beach to his left were empty now, but the beach bars were doing good business. On the other side of the road three cranes towered over half-built apartment blocks that were replacing a row of old Spanish houses. After a lifetime of poverty, whole familes were rich but homeless. It was a good promenade to walk along, apart from the dogs' mess and the skateboarders who came at you silently out of nowhere, and he kept promising himself to walk five miles a day on it.

He went past the big blue water chute that never seemed to be operational, and the sand sculptor who used to be a miner in Scotland. The man, in flight from some domestic horror story, had arrived without a pillow full of money, but still managed to spend his days on the beach. He made three life-size horses' heads in the sand and sprinkled them, for effect, with white powder. Sometimes he added a Snoopy or a mermaid to the ensemble, if yesterday's work was still intact and there was nothing else for him to do. But occasionally rain or malevolent children had wrecked his masterpiece overnight. He lived on the coins that people threw down to him, but he didn't need a work permit because Spanish bureaucracy decided that his wages were voluntary donations.

Matthew turned into the port tonight feeling especially

cheerful. He was glad he had bought a bar – endless leisure didn't suit his restless nature.

Battered old white boats, laden with ropes and nets, were tethered to the jetty. The skipper's accommodation up front had less space than a telephone kiosk. When the boats were tied up, the fish was produced, already covered in ice in large flat boxes, and passed from hand to hand before it was laid on the jetty for the tourists to admire. Some of the fish were still alive and Matthew watched an octopus who thought it still had a chance. The trays were piled four at a time on the back of a motorbike which took them, not too quickly, to refrigerators on the other side of the port, but on other days Matthew had watched them auctioned off immediately in the hall on the jetty.

He turned away from the trays of fish and saw that he was being watched by a young man in a green suit. The man had thick, horn-rimmed spectacles and a lot of greasy, curly hair, but he stood out because of the green suit. Nobody around here wore a jacket or a tie, let alone a green suit.

Matthew left the port and walked back along the promenade towards his bar.

A thousand voracious appetites prowled the seafront: the most common sound on this coast was of cutlery meeting crockery. He checked the board on the beach side of the road which was supposed to direct aimless holidaymakers towards Matt's Place, and then crossed over to the bar. He could see the man in the green suit heading in his direction.

The bar was already attracting its own customers, and to Matthew's great pleasure they were not mostly here-today-gone-tomorrow tourists, but people who actually lived on the coast and could be putting money in his till indefinitely.

There was a German blonde with the bulging eyes of the unslept, called Sylvia, the daughter of a wealthy local property owner, who often arrived at the bar on horseback. Her boyfriend, caught in possession of marijuana, was spending the summer in Malaga jail, and every Wednesday Sylvia would take him an orange, injected to its maximum capacity with vodka. There was a small, nervy Italian called Pepe, who survived by playing pool for money and could conduct three conversations simultaneously in three languages. An old couple, who looked for all the world like pensioners on a cheap package holiday, were actually enjoying a comfortable retirement in the sun after selling a chain of fish-and-chip shops in the north of England. There was a silent Spaniard called Manolo, who was thought to be some kind of government spy, assigned to infiltrate the British community so that some faceless bureaucrat in an office knew who was doing what where. There was also an aggressive Welshman who had opened a bar in a backstreet with his redundancy money. But his bar stayed stubbornly empty so he drank, fuming, in Matt's Place.

Kim was sitting behind the bar compiling a shopping list for the supermarket. Matthew kissed her cheek and pulled himself a small glass of Cruzcampo. The man in the green suit had followed him into the bar and now sat on a stool in front of him.

'I'll have one of those,' he said.

'On holiday?' Matthew asked when he had pulled the drink.

'Sort of,' he replied evasively. 'You're Matthew Ward, aren't you?'

Matthew looked at him, surprised. 'Why do you ask?'

The man sipped his beer before answering, as if he needed time to think.

'I'm a friend of Danny's,' he said.

'Where do you know Danny from?'

'I was at school with him.'

'What school was that?'

'Westminster.'

'Really?'

'Well, I wasn't there long.'

Matthew doubted he was there at all.

'This is a great place to stay,' the man said, to change the subject. 'I went to Majorca last year. I couldn't find anybody who could talk English properly, and that was just among the English.'

'You didn't enjoy it?'

'Dreadful place. I was the only British male who hadn't been tattooed.'

'You have something against tattoos?'

'It's a certain sign that the conversation isn't going to be about Schopenhauer.'

'We don't get to chat about him much in here. Did Spurs sign him from Inter Milan?'

'He was a German philosopher who said that the will was greater than knowledge.'

'Well, I could have told you that.'

The man in the green suit was studying the pool table. 'Do you fancy a game?' he asked. 'My name is Russell, by the way.'

Playing customers at pool was part of the job. It encouraged them to stay and have another drink. They also had to put 100 pesetas into the table. Matthew usually played what he called a 'customer game'. This meant that the customer won and remained happy, although Matthew was playing so often now that he could usually win if it was necessary to retain the customer's interest.

Russell put a coin in the table and racked the balls. He removed his jacket, but not his tie, and insisted on buying them both drinks. While Kim went to the supermarket, they played two games. Matthew, suspicious of this visitor, beat him in both while trying, tactfully, to find out what he did for a living. It was like trying to nail jelly to a wall. Questions seemed to slide round their target and disappear and when answers came back across the green baize they were answers to questions that had never been asked. Russell was here on a 'working holiday', he was on 'exes', he 'earned a few bob'.

When Kim returned with three bags of goods from the supermarket, Russell put on his jacket and finished his beer.

'I must go and find a steak,' he said. 'I'll see you again. Where did you say Danny lives?'

'I didn't,' said Matthew. This didn't seem the sort of person his brother would enjoy finding at his front gate. Keep it vague, he thought.

'Mijas.'

Russell nodded. 'Cheers,' he said.

The tourists had arrived in Mijas now. They came in on coaches and took photographs of the donkey taxis with their bells and their colourful headgear. They combed the shops and filled the streets with a dozen different languages, and the locals made what they could and looked forward to the peace and cool of autumn. Every day the temperature topped eighty and you could tell at a glance who lived here and who was visiting: the tourists were the ones with tans. They were also the ones with money, at any rate to start with.

Daniel strolled up the hill into the town, as he did every morning, looking forward to his appointment with yesterday's newspaper. There was talk of an election and he wanted to read as much as he could about it. That he would not be in the country when it happened was just another source of regret.

He walked past the new Barclay's Bank – one of the few banks around here that he steered clear of – and made his way to the newspaper shop. He bought a *Daily Telegraph* and Iberia *Sun*, the English-language paper that sometimes carried later news.

At the Casa Pepe bar he ordered a large Victoria beer, bought himself twenty Fortuna for 115 pesetas from the cigarette machine on the wall and sat at a table outside from which he could see all the new arrivals.

He liked watching the Spanish with their children. They treated children like gods, but were careless with their animals. This was the opposite of the British and, as usual, he thought bitterly, the British had got it all wrong. There were few teenage hooligans in Spain.

The waiter brought his beer and when he had drunk a quarter of it he opened his *Telegraph* at the financial pages. The tourists read the sports pages, the expatriates read the financial pages. He was glad that he no longer held shares. Even with a Tory victory looming, he could see that something very nasty was going to happen soon. The boom had gone on too long. He turned back to the news pages and learned that a Euro MP who was trying to save his life by giving up smoking had choked to death on his nicotine chewing gum. He lit a Fortuna and read that there were talks planned to peg the yen–dollar rate. He didn't want to read about financial affairs, but when he turned to the *Sun* he found that people were making money there, too.

It won't be a vintage year for Bekaa Valley hashish, but growers say connoisseurs will still get good value from each puff of Lebanese Red.

'There hasn't been enough rain this year, so it won't be as good as last year,' said Abu Abbas as he inspected his 11-acre field of shoulder-high cannabis, the plant from which hashish is made.

'But it's still OK – our hashish is never bad,' he said as he crushed

the head of a cannabis plant, the
most prized part.

'I don't know about wine, but
smell this – definitely the Johnny
Walker Black Label of hashish.'

The paper seemed to specialize in off-beat stories:

Frederick, a bull elephant that fell
while being chased by seven amorous
she-elephants, has died of an appar-
ent heart attack at Givskud nature
park in Denmark.

A taxi pulled up right in front of his table and a man in
a green suit climbed out. He appeared to have difficulty in
finding the right money for the driver, but eventually the
taxi drove off and the man turned and gazed about him.
Initially he made for the bar, but as he approached it his
eye caught Daniel and he stopped at his table.

'Are you Danny Ward?' he asked.

Daniel didn't answer questions like that. Once, when
approached by a stranger who thought he had found a
fellow Englishman, he had managed to convince the in-
truder that he was Spanish.

'I'm a friend of Matthew's,' said the man in the green
suit. 'I was playing him at pool last night.'

'He let you win,' Daniel said.

'As a matter of fact, he didn't.'

'That's unusual.'

The man pushed his glasses up his nose with his left
thumb and offered Daniel his right hand. 'Look, I'm Russell Rose. It's nice to meet you.'

Daniel shook his hand briefly. 'What brings you here?'
he asked.

'I have some business on the coast,' said Russell Rose,
trying to attract the attention of the waiter. 'It's a terrific
place, isn't it?' He had some gold teeth on the left of his

mouth which gave his smile a strangely lopsided look. 'What beats me is why is it that with the bars open all day and most of the night you never see anyone drunk in the street?'

'There's no need to hurl it down. It's there when we want it. It's just one of several things that Spain handles better than Britain.'

'You're happy here then?'

'Deliriously.'

'Good.' He pushed his glasses again with his left thumb. They had not seemed to be in need of adjustment, and Daniel realized that it was a nervous gesture.

'I have not been entirely frank with you,' Russell Rose said, still looking for a waiter.

'I didn't imagine for a moment that you had. You're a journalist, aren't you?'

'How did you know that?'

'I've seen one before.'

'Really? What are the identifying characteristics?'

'Gimlet eyes, unwashed hair, classless accent, a waft of alcohol even when they haven't been drinking and, of course, the knack of convincing complete strangers that they are old friends.'

'Very good, Danny. I recognize the man myself. Can I get you a drink?'

The waiter arrived now and Daniel said that he would have a beer. His first impulse had been to bolt, but somehow he felt that he could handle this man. He also always had two beers.

'What paper pays your wages?' he asked.

'The *News of the World*.'

'I thought they were more interested in vets who got struck off for interfering with their patients?'

'We're interested in the truth, Danny.'

'The truth?' Daniel laughed. 'Your sort of newspaper is to truth what Herod was to baby-sitting.'

Russell Rose was not to be deflected by this: it was much too early to stop being polite.

'Anyway, all the facts about your little coup have come into my possession by the usual nefarious means, and so I thought I'd fly down to see how you are getting on after your bunk. Of course, this coast is packed with people who left Britain in a hurry, but most of them are so crude. Armed robbery, murder, currency frauds. It's too boring for our readers. But what you did was so ingenious it's got appeal. After all, everybody has a bank account.'

'Even your readers?'

'So I'm led to believe. How is Leanda liking it here?'

'Leanda?'

'She's your wife. I've done my research.'

'She's very happy. She's at her Spanish class at the moment. This afternoon we will cool off in the pool. It beats dodging the rain in Fleet Street, Russell.'

'Wapping.'

'Oh, yes. You've moved. Or rather, bunked.'

'You were the one who bunked, Danny. I understand that you were a consummate bunker from way back. Expelled from school for non-attendance.'

'I was not,' Daniel said, shocked by the lie.

'Oh, well. I don't suppose you are going to turn up in the High Court in London to sue us for libel. You might not be a sitting target for the police, but you're a sitting target for the hacks. Some of them are quite prissy about people running off with someone else's money.'

'I bet they are. But you won't find a single person who has been hurt by it.'

Russell Rose now wrote something in shorthand on a San Miguel tissue from the dispenser on the table. 'Tell me, Danny, how long do you expect to be here?'

'There's nowhere else to go.'

'What do you do, apart from drink and swim?'

'Crosswords.'

'What's your house like? You're obviously not going to invite me round.'

'Fairly comfortable. Tennis court, swimming pool, that sort of thing.'

'Guard dogs?'

'No guard dogs.'

This is an anomic situation, Daniel thought. The word had come up in the previous day's crossword. There was no reason to continue talking to this man, but he didn't want to leave his beer. He decided to sit it out in silence.

Three sad-looking Spaniards walked by. There were a lot of sad-looking Spaniards – perhaps they were yearning for snow. He picked up the *Telegraph* and glanced at the front page. An opinion poll suggested that Mrs Thatcher would be calling an election at any minute. Daniel couldn't see how a government in power could ever be shifted with opinion polls telling them when to hold elections. Even with an unpopular government there had to be one favourable month in five years.

Russell Rose, feeling ignored now, stood up. 'I'll be seeing you, Danny,' he said.

'It seems highly unlikely to me,' Daniel replied, without looking up. But afterwards he wished that he had because Russell Rose pulled a small camera from his pocket and took a quick picture of Daniel at the table.

'Words and pictures,' he said. 'Words and pictures. It's all a newspaper needs.'

Mark Ward sat at his keyboard and looked for a song. A slight ache jogged across the frontal lobes of his brain, a reminder of a noisy night in Jay's that had been helped along by a barmy cow from Kalamazoo, Michigan, who had convinced herself that she was the main attraction. She was escorted by a docile and conspicuously toupeed geriatric from the same side of the Atlantic who had evidently been nurtured on verbal punishment.

Mark sat down to write songs with the casual addiction of the heavy smoker. It would take more than the lofty disparagement of Mr Conrad Gambardella of TPA Music to curb his production. (What did TPA stand for, anyway? Tin Pan Alley, he imagined. Tin Ear Alley, would be nearer.) Mark could write songs on buses, during earnest conversations or, if necessary, standing on his head, and the world was going to have to learn to like them because there would be no let-up on his side.

What he wanted today was a song so beautiful that the world would judge it irresistible, something so timeless that it transcended contemporary concerns, and was automatically endowed with a life expectancy at least as great as his. Something like 'You Don't Bring Me Flowers Any More', he thought.

He sat at the keyboard and doodled, reminding himself of alternative chord structures that he used without thinking. During his playing in Jay's he often amused himself with substitutions, sometimes forced on him by gaps in his knowledge. He had stopped playing the piano for a while when the guitar pushed it out. When he took it up again he had forgotten some things but had now improvised a New Orleans style of playing which saw him through many an awkward moment.

He began toying now with D major, transposing it to A major. That was nice – very guitarish, very folksy, and still, well, sophisticated. Changing from A to G with his left hand, he played lilting arpeggios with his right. Very nice. Interesting enough to sustain the one chord indefinitely. Somewhere along the way Mark had stopped doodling and now he was writing a song. Occasionally he would break the hypnotic quality by striking a G chord. There certainly wasn't anything brilliant going on, but it was

gentle and appropriate to the way he felt this morning –
gentle and slightly withdrawn.

He dabbled with chord changes but the basic premise
was enough. The one, the occasional change to G, would
be the hook line, the chorus, and the chorus would be the
title. He knew all that although he had no idea what the
title or hook would be. He began humming vocal scales
against the arpeggios. La la la la la la la. Up and down. Up
and down. His melody would not stray far from scales.

Mark liked to block things out so, after roughing out a
tune that was mildly reminiscent of an old Tim Hardin
song, he turned to the lyric, reminding himself of the likes
of McCartney, Stevie Wonder, Neil Diamond and Lionel
Ritchie. They had learned something from their pre-
decessors, Irving Berlin and Dorothy Fields. They all
dared to be corny!

He tried forcing some of his half-finished ideas into the
lines. Nothing really worked. There was an old disco song
that offered the dictum 'don't force it', as well as an alternative. But Mark couldn't remember what the alternative
was. Feel it? Feed it? Wait for it? Leave it alone? He
decided to leave it alone.

He got up, found some shoes and wandered down to
the port for a coffee. When he had coffee in Banus he
always went to the Salduba Bar on the corner so that he
could watch the new arrivals in the port and maybe spot a
friend. The coffee was expensive but the view was terrific.
A few yards along was the Sinatra Bar, where young
people gathered and hoped to be noticed. The wall there
carried dozens of advertisements for air tickets that were
for sale, placed by youngsters who had decided im-
pulsively to stay on the coast.

Stirring his coffee he did something that he usually
avoided. Instead of working intuitively, he listed what he
wanted from the lyric: one, a hook with universal appeal
and immediate understanding; two, a commonplace lyric;

three, something personal and passionate; and four, words that were sympathetic to the melody, gentle and softly persuasive.

Nothing came, and his headache didn't help. After ten minutes his thoughts had wandered off on their own, refusing to be corralled.

He was thinking about the lady from Michigan from the night before who had kept up a string of requests and then tried to join him in some of them. She had wanted the Scott Joplin rags – 'Maple Leaf Rag', 'Pineapple Rag' and, of course, 'The Entertainer' – but it was when she coaxed him into a Nat King Cole medley that she really let rip. 'Those Lazy Hazy Crazy Days of Summer' seemed to be her favourite song, although she did it a lot of damage, and she ruined 'Ramblin' Rose' for everybody in the bar. She had sat at the piano, spilling her drink and bullying her elderly escort until Mark had expected that she would be asked to leave. They were very tolerant of big drinkers in the piano bar, but a line had to be drawn if other customers became restless.

Eventually the man with the toupee, having failed to placate her with heated whispers, pulled himself off his stool and announced that he was leaving. She felt obliged to follow.

'You promise me the bloody world and then bring me to this dump,' she moaned. 'I wanna see the real Spain.'

'I never know what you want, honey,' the man said politely.

'Peace and quiet,' she said. 'A cottage by the sea.'

Sitting in Banus and watching the girls go by, Mark suddenly woke up. There was his line, his title, his song. A cottage by the sea!

> Shall I go ahead
> And build a cottage by the sea?

Deep in his chest, low in his throat, he hummed the

79

chorus line, the hook, setting his words against it. He took out the notebook that he always carried and tried some more lines.

Time will pass so quickly side by side
Chase a shaggy sheepdog through the pebbles at low tide
Would you like to come and live with me-ee . . .
In a little cottage by the sea?

No song that he had ever written had excited him like this. He knew that this was the hit song that he had been striving after. The tune was lovely and the words were perfect.

Despite his cynicism, or maybe because of it, he became infatuated with the song, visualizing the future of the couple in the cottage. The song had everything that he had listed: universal appeal, commonplace lyric, sympathy with the melody and it was almost embarrassingly personal. He would need a few drinks before he sang it in Jay's, of course, but he could always tell them that it was a little-known song by Lionel Ritchie.

FIVE

DANIEL'S craving for the normality of his past in England
had impelled him one morning to write for a copy of his
old school's magazine. He took it down to the pool as soon
as it arrived and lay on a sun-lounger in his swimming
trunks, absorbed in a trip down memory lane.

The magazine, called *The Elizabethan*, was a much more
professional job than when he had been at school; it even
had colour pictures. The school had bought some buildings for a larger science department. The new headmaster
was settling in. There was an appreciation of the most
famous old boy of all, the first Poet Laureate, Ben Jonson,
who had achieved something that was now beyond
Daniel's hopes: burial in Westminster Abbey.

Under a column headed Past Comments, he read: 'Eton
boatmen, Harrow gentlemen, Westminster scoundrels,
Winchester scholars.' He found this strangely reassuring,
as if he were fulfilling a tradition.

What interested him most, of course, was the news of
Old Westminsters, as the school called them. Sir Peter
Lazarus was to be a part-time member of the Board of the
Civil Aviation Authority. H. E. Pagan (1959–63) had been
elected a Fellow of the Society of Antiquaries. Some people
were obviously getting on with their lives in the way that
the school had intended. The roll call was a story of successes in many of life's little culs-de-sac.

A formal letter had arrived with the magazine inviting
news of Daniel's progress since he left school, but the
facts would not sit too comfortably in the glossy pages of
The Elizabethan.

81

Daniel Ward (1974–9) did a runner to the Iberian peninsula after nicking a million notes from the big four banks. Well done, Danny! We always had you down as an ideas man.

But reading the magazine, which had been intended to strengthen tenuous links with home, left him feeling more estranged than before. He jumped in the pool and swam up and down.

How it all came back to him! The smell of unwashed bodies in the school gymnasium, the cloistered existence and the Procrustean rules, the cold showers and the punishment run round Little Dean's Yard, the contempt of the boarders, the link with the Abbey and its awful accompanying feeling of living in the past, and its ghastly poetic traditions – not just Ben Jonson among the old boys, but Dryden and Cowper as well, for Christ's sake.

He climbed out of the pool and lay in the sun to dry. Graham Nash was due for a game of tennis. It was an exertion which today Daniel felt he could do without, but it was important not to break the routine of life among the exiles – their lives were made up of regular appointments, and sudden cancellations could cause inordinate dismay. Daniel understood this well enough: he had himself been so grateful for Graham Nash's appearance on occasions that he had wanted to offer him money.

He changed into his tennis kit and read yesterday's newspaper while he was waiting. The news was slightly unnerving. The headless corpse of an Englishman had been found in a remote valley not far from Mijas. He was thought to be the victim of a drugs gang for whom he had worked. Trafficking in hashish was a boom business round here, and the end of it was that you were a headless corpse in a dried-up river bed. Hashish grown by peasants in the mountains of Morocco was shipped across the Straits of Gibraltar in less than an hour and smuggled ashore on a moonless beach, usually sealed in silicone rubber to defy sniffer dogs. The drugs created a demand for money that had produced its own crime wave: the fortress which Daniel had created was to frustrate burglars, too. He heard a visitor buzzing now and went down to let in Graham Nash. He was glad his criminal days were behind him.

Graham Nash was a tall, athletic man of sixty who bounded round the tennis court with the eagerness of a twenty-year-old. It was a matter of great importance to him to attempt to return a ball even when there was little chance of touching it.

As usual they sat on the terrace afterwards drinking fruit juice.

'I've been thinking about money,' Graham Nash said, zipping up the cover on his racket.

'Very suitable for a retired bank manager, Graham.'

'And so should you. When you sold your computer firm, did you bring all the money here?'

Daniel wondered for a second what computer firm he was talking about. A liar needs a rat-trap memory, and his occasionally blinked.

'Yes, all my money is in Spain,' he said.

'Unwise,' said Graham Nash. 'I made the same mistake. Now they are in the European Community, Spain has promised to relax the exchange controls one day, but it could take years. In the meantime you can't get money out of this country.'

'I don't want to get money out of this country, Graham.'

'You never know. You might want to move somewhere else. And if you do move, you'll have to leave your money behind. It's been worrying me for some time. Supposing I have to go back to Britain for health reasons? Supposing Spain throws the Brits out?'

'What are you going to do about it, then?'

'I've opened an account in Gibraltar and I'm shifting quite a bit of my capital down there.'

'I thought you just said that you can't take money out of Spain?'

Graham Nash winked at him. 'You have to be a bit furtive, Daniel. Got any more orange juice?'

Daniel got up and fetched another carton from the fridge. He filled his visitor's glass. The idea of a former bank manager being furtive appealed to him.

'If they catch you they confiscate the money and fine you the same amount again, so the trick is to take small amounts often in case you get stopped.'

'And what's a small amount these days?'

'I take half a million pesetas in each shoe.'

'In each shoe?'

'That's how I take it over the border. They never look in your shoes.'

'Two and a half thousand pounds in each boot? Is that how they taught you to behave at the bank?'

'Needs must, Daniel,' said Graham Nash. 'There's a lavatory just over the border where you can transfer the money to your pocket.'

Something about this story cheered Daniel up. It confirmed a suspicion that he had always harboured, particularly since he set up home in lonely splendour at Mijas: when it came to money, *everybody* was artful.

Life was a matter of arranging little pleasures to look forward to, of fixing engagements that could transform an empty day and make it exciting in prospect, enjoyable in reality and memorable in retrospect.

They went to Gibraltar.

Five people in Daniel's Ford Escort was more than enough and they had to leave Lady in the flat. Mark, as the largest, claimed the front seat, and Matthew sat between Leanda and Kim at the back. The *carretera* was the most dangerous road in Europe, according to the eloquent though silent testimony of the 360 corpses that had been taken from it in the last six years – two fast lanes in each direction unseparated by any barrier and with the additional nightmare of cars slowing suddenly in the faster lane to attempt impossible left turns.

'Driving on this road is bad enough without £5,000 in your shoes,' said Daniel. 'I can hardly feel the pedals.'

'It's when your back wheels overtake your front wheels you have to worry,' said Matthew. 'Drive on, brother.'

To Daniel, opening a bank account in Gibraltar was a harmless precaution. He didn't know whether he would ever leave Spain, but it would be nice to have money available if travel became a possibility. It would also enable Leanda to spend money in England if necessary. To Matthew, a Gibraltar account seemed a good idea because it would earn more interest than the pillow. He would put it in Kim's name and it would enable her to buy abroad. To Mark, who didn't have £5,000 in the world let alone in his shoes, it was a day out to a place he had never seen. To Leanda and Kim it was a shopping expedition to buy those things that were not available in Spanish shops. At the top of Kim's list was English dog-food.

The geography of the coast gave the rain to the west and when they reached Estepona, and its Dominican monastery with a splendid Baroque façade, the land became greener than the scorched earth around Marbella. Soon they could see the Rock, stretching 400 metres into a blue sky and festooned by an assortment of electronic gadgetry. Amazingly, it disappeared again as they left the sea and drove inland towards San Roque.

'I forgot to tell you that I had a visitor the other day,' Daniel said as the Rock appeared again. 'A man called Russell Rose.'

'He came to see me, too,' Matthew told him. 'He said he was at Westminster with you.'

85

'Was he hell! He was from the *News of the World*.'

'What did he want?'

'What do you think? Copy. He was doing a bit of investigative journalism. He knew all about me.'

'How could he?' Mark asked. 'The bank never talked.'

'It sounded like an internal leak. Still, I bought the rag on Sunday and there was nothing in it.'

'I'm afraid they could hang on to a story like that for weeks,' Matthew said. He had spent a lot of time dealing with journalists. 'They'll use it when they need it. It's hardly topical. What did you tell him?'

'Very little. He was obviously going to make it up anyway if I didn't say anything. He had a few lies in his head before he met me.'

'Dad's going to love this,' said Mark. 'Some loafer at the golf club will bring the paper in when there are plenty of people about.'

The scene which this declaration conjured up in their minds brought the conversation to a close. At the Rock the queue of cars was so long that they couldn't see the end of it. They decided to park in La Linea and walk over the border.

Things went wrong for Daniel from the very beginning. Leading the way with a self-conscious gait designed to conceal the fact that he was concealing something, he had an unpleasant tremor at the first sight of what seemed to be an English policeman, a distinctive creature who had featured in too many of his dreams. He had forgotten that Gibraltar's policemen wore the same uniform.

The tremor, however, was a mild discomfort compared to what followed. The immigration official, a swarthy young man with an alarming squint, studied his passport for rather longer than seemed necessary, and then looked at his face and consulted documents that rested on his desk. He stood up and, while Daniel watched with mounting horror, put his passport into a photocopying machine.

It was handed back to him with a long, appraising look, and Daniel walked on, thoroughly shaken. He wanted to walk back the other way, towards the security of his car, but he knew that if suspicions weren't already aroused, his change of mind would achieve it. When the others joined him he could hardly speak. The money in his shoes, the English-looking policemen and now his passport copied by immigration convinced him that he had made an incredibly stupid mistake.

'They only did it to mine,' he said.

'It's a random check,' said Kim. 'They do it sometimes, I'm told.'

'He looked at me.'

'Well,' said Kim, 'he looked at me.'

They were crossing the airport runway which bisected the isthmus linking Gibraltar to Spain. The airport, and who could use it, was the subject of the latest Anglo–Spanish dispute. The Spanish claim seemed unanswerable – the runway was built on land that had never been ceded to Britain.

'Keep calm, Danny,' said Matthew. 'And keep walking.'

The town nestled at the foot of the Rock's western side. They came to it through dreary backstreets and a tunnel or two. The buildings seemed to belong to the fortress school of architecture, hardly surprising in a place which had endured fourteen sieges. Instead of statues, each street corner displayed a cannon, the triumphant ingredient in the Rock's blood-stained history.

Daniel and Matthew found a public lavatory and went in to transfer their pesetas to their wallets. Matthew couldn't stop laughing at the absurdity of what they were doing, but Daniel removed his shoes and pulled out the crumpled notes with an expression of utter wretchedness. Dumping the money was no longer the day's big event; getting off the Rock without uniformed company had suddenly replaced it at the top of his anxiety list.

In Main Street, the narrow, pedestrianized centre of Gibraltar, the shops sold expensive watches cheaply, radio equipment and perfume and little else. They looked at the cut-price goods on offer, but there was nothing that they wanted to buy.

The girls disappeared into a bank with the money, leaving Mark to laugh at his brothers in the street.

'Oh, the beautiful irony of it,' he said. 'The two of you have acquired so much money, and you can't even open a bank account, so the women get the money.'

Matthew shrugged. 'The women always get the money in the end, Mark. You will learn that when you get older.'

The girls came back into the street as cheerful as Mark. 'I've got five grand in the bank now,' said Kim. 'I don't need you any more. Cheerio.'

In a fit of homesickness they plunged into Marks and Spencer – here mysteriously called St Michael's – but it wasn't a branch that carried the food they all missed.

At the top of the street they found a public house called The Angry Friar, and went in. The friars, they learned, had left the Rock in 1704 and their Franciscan convent was now the governor's residence. Perhaps that was why the friar was angry.

Matthew bought beers for his brothers, beer with a British name but tasting slightly different, a gin for Leanda and an orange juice for Kim. Leanda's arm was round her husband now, but he sat staring at the table, evidently beyond consolation.

'You look like a man who doesn't know whether to do a swallow dive from the twelfth-floor window or just quietly cut his throat,' Mark told him.

'And is being tortured by the indecision,' Matthew suggested.

Daniel stared up at him, his face drained. 'You don't understand, do you? They're already examining a photocopy of my passport in London. The message will be back here in a nanosecond. I'll be arrested when I try to leave and I'll be on the next flight to London handcuffed to a policeman. I've had it. The game's up.' He picked up his beer and drank half of it very quickly.

'That is by no means certain,' Matthew said. 'According to Kim they quite often photocopy passports.'

'Of innocent people! So you never hear any more about it! I'm telling you, it's all over.' He looked as if he might cry. 'Why in hell I ever got talked into this trip, I don't know. The danger was obvious.'

'I certainly wouldn't want to take off from that runway,' said Mark. 'It's got water at both ends.'

'My God, they find it amusing,' said Daniel. He lit a Fortuna and stared blankly across the room. 'They've probably sent police out to look for me.' He hunched up his shoulders as if he could hide among the customers of The Angry Friar.

The jaunty atmosphere of a day out had now been replaced by a sepulchral gloom. It began to reach Matthew, who had been scornfully dismissive of his brother's concern only moments before. Now uneasiness crept over him too. There were warrants out for his own arrest and, although they hadn't photocopied his passport, the name Ward might cause bells to jangle in a computer-filled room in London. A picture of Matthew could already be on the desk of passport control in Gibraltar, along with a request to check who was in Daniel Ward's company when he thoughtlessly left the security of Spain to sample a piece of Britain in the Med.

He began to feel exactly as he had felt back in the hotel at Redbourn, fingering his false passport and making plans that would keep him free. He stood up suddenly.

'I've got it,' he said. He pulled Daniel by the arm. 'Come along, you public-school genius. It's no use waiting for the prefect to cane you. Follow me, kid. The answer's a boat.' He bent down and gave Kim a kiss. 'Leanda will drive you back. I'll see you in the bar this evening.'

'I hope so,' said Kim.

There was a small taxi-rank only yards away. They asked for the marina.

The taxi crept through narrow streets and a journey of only half a mile took ten minutes. Even in Gibraltar the building programme was frenetic; cranes loomed over half-built blocks just as they did in Spain.

'Driving a taxi in Gibraltar must be the most boring job in the world,' said Matthew cheerfully, but Daniel was too tense to talk.

The new marina was full of boats but, at first glance, it was difficult to see one that could help them.

'What are we going to do, hire one?' Daniel asked.

'Perhaps there's a day trip from Marbella.'

'Not very likely. It takes about six hours in one of those boats. Nobody is going to spend twelve hours on one for a day trip.'

'I think we've just had a piece of luck,' Matthew said after a while. Across the water he could see the little boat that took trippers out from Fuengirola. He had seen it often when he went down to watch the fish coming in. People were boarding it as they watched, and they walked towards it and joined the queue. Nobody was counting heads. They filed on and sat immediately and inconspicuously on wooden seats in the stern, their fingers crossed. They learned from the conversation around them that the boat had come down the coast yesterday; the trip, which took place only occasionally, was a night out in Gibraltar. Astonished at their good fortune, they sat in silence waiting for the engines to start.

The boat filled up but didn't move. A low cloud hung over the rock. The climate was different here.

Daniel was worried that somebody would recognize him and bring up the fact that he hadn't stayed in the hotel last night, but there were enough people on the outing for him to hope that no single one of them would know every face.

Matthew was worried by the sight of two policemen who had suddenly appeared in the marina and were now walking in their direction. They didn't have the normal aimless walk of a policeman – they seemed to know where they were going.

The boat's engines coughed into life.

Leanda and Kim dropped Mark off at Puerto Banus and drove on along 'the golden mile' to Marbella. The visual highlight of this stretch of the journey was the palace built on a man-made hill by the King of Saudi Arabia. It was a replica of the White House, only much larger. In the corner of the grounds was the first mosque to be built in Spain for centuries.

'I feel the urge to spend money,' Leanda said.

'What on?' Kim asked.

'How about clothes?'

The two hardly knew each other, but the alarm in Gibraltar had thrown them together today. Leanda found a side street in Marbella to park the Escort, and led Kim across the main road to a fashion shop called Giorgio. Kim had never been shopping with a millionaire's wife before and was overawed by the price tags laid out before her.

'Buy something,' said Leanda. 'This is your big chance. Matthew's pillow can stand it.'

'Not for me,' Kim said, looking at the silk dress that Leanda now held up. 'The sort of clothes that I am going to need are baggy T-shirts, flat shoes and track suits.'

'Get a designer track suit then.'

But in the street afterwards it was only Leanda who had spent money, on the silk dress and fashion jewellery and earrings to match it. They walked a few yards to the Charles Jourdan shop to try on some boots. Leanda found a pair that only cost £200. By the time they left to walk up to Orange Square she had spent a little over £2,000. It was only to be expected that when they sat at an open-air table she should order champagne.

'I think he'll kill himself,' she said.

'Who?' asked Kim, startled.

'Daniel. He gets very depressed.'

They had walked through a warren of twisting lanes to the old town of Marbella where flower-covered balconies hung over tiny gift shops, and half-open doors revealed shrub-filled patios. The lanes had been jasmine-scented but here in the small square, overlooked by a fifteenth-century town hall, it was the smell of orange trees that hung on the air.

'He feels cornered,' Leanda said. 'Paradise can be quite irksome when you can't go out.'

'What about you?'

'I'm not cornered, am I? But I do envy you your pregnancy.'

Kim looked at her elegant companion and thought: it's a perverse world. Here is a couple with a million pounds and a luxury home, and the husband is suicidal and the wife envies me.

'Try sex,' she said. 'It's caused lots of pregnancies.'

'A physical effort that is quite beyond my thirsty husband by the time we go to bed. The question is usually whether he can reach the bedroom before he reaches unconsciousness.'

Kim thought that this was more than she wanted to know. She said: 'Well, don't envy me. My pregnancy is hardly taking place in ideal circumstances, with my parents being a thousand miles away and the baby's father being married to somebody else.'

Leanda smiled for the first time. There was nothing

like a recitation of someone else's problems to lighten the burden of your own.

'What is your parents' attitude to all this?' Kim asked, reaching for the first time for the champagne. She was trying to avoid alcohol during her pregnancy, but she was feeling disturbed about Matthew. 'Did it come as a shock?'

'What? Daniel's little heist? My God, my mother doesn't know about that. She'd die. She thinks he made a lot of money out of computers. My father is dead. Fortunately, I sometimes think.'

Kim stared across at the clean, shiny statue of the King in the centre of the square. It had only recently replaced a rather grimy one of the fat dictator who had died, not a moment too soon, twelve years earlier. She was thinking that Leanda's secret from her mother could hardly survive a story in the *News of the World*, but she seemed to have enough problems without raising that painful possibility, and she now revealed a new one.

'My mother is coming out to stay with us in June,' Leanda said miserably. 'It should be hell. She was always fond of Matthew, by the way. He was best man at our wedding. But now that he's left his wife and fled to Spain with you, I dread to think what her attitude will be.'

'Does she know we're here? Couldn't we just avoid you during her stay?'

Leanda didn't want Matthew and Kim to avoid them; she wanted all the assistance she could find in keeping her mother happy. She looked at Kim's pretty face and realized that she envied a lot more than just the baby. Matthew wasn't a millionaire any more, and he wasn't public school, but he was livelier than Daniel. He got up and did things, like opening a bar, instead of sitting around in a neurotic trance. He didn't live in the past as many public schoolboys did, finding that life after eighteen was an anti-climax. He hadn't robbed a bank.

93

'I suppose we'll have to do it that way,' she said. 'But I hate deception.'

'Well,' said Kim, seeing a dainty lob that she couldn't miss, 'Daniel should be able to handle it.'

SIX

THE LETTER which was to change Mark Ward's life arrived a few days after the aborted trip to Gibraltar. It came, via an electric typewriter, on the usual highly ornamented notepaper with golden-and-purple curlicues traversing the top of the page and then running down one side of it in what seemed to be a wanton display of affluence.

Dear Mark Ward,

Fashions in music change by the hour and if 'Cottage by the Sea' isn't the new thing I'll give my Roller to War on Want. It is a beautiful song, both the tune and the lyrics, in no way inferior to McCartney's 'Yesterday'. I'm sending demos to the States today – complete with seagull noises! Leave it with me, will you?

Congratulations,
Conrad Gambardella,
TPA Music

Mark read the letter twice, seeking a catch. Good news had always been an unfamiliar commodity in his life, and the message was slow to sink in. But he grasped it eventually, threw the letter in the air and released a lonely 'Yippee!'

Life among the glitterati beckoned. He would be ready for their call.

He walked through the shower in a daze; it was like going through a car wash without a car. Afterwards he discovered that surplus wax and the shower's hot water had somehow combined to deafen him in his left ear which, closed to the outside world, could now hear perfectly what was happening *inside* his head. Cleaning his teeth was like the roar of traffic and drinking tea was Niagara Falls. Even turning his head produced a strange grating noise as if he had been put together not by a master craftsman, but by a subversive apprentice.

Too dazed to care about the temporary loss of one ear, he took his dirty shirts down to the launderette. When he had put his clothes in one machine, the soap in another and the money in a third he realized that the morning's post had seriously damaged his powers of concentration.

He left the shirts in the washing machine, this time with soap, and went down to the Salduba Bar for a coffee. The port was as crowded as ever, quite different in the morning sunshine, but just as busy. Coach parties now arrived in Banus, promising the tourists that they would rub shoulders with the stars. Mark had only ever seen one star in Banus, a sinister little man who played a sinister little man in a British soap opera, who had arrived here with a girl half his age. She had long, brown legs that were the talk of the port for two weeks, during which time she clung to the actor as if he had just been declared the undisputed winner in a competition that had combed continents to find the most wonderful specimen of manhood on earth.

Sitting outside the Salduba and drinking coffee, his ear popped and he could hear again. It was just as well, he thought. A one-eared song writer shared the career prospects of a one-armed boxer. He began to wonder how much money this new career might make him. When newspapers published lists of the nation's biggest earners it always seemed to be a battle at the top between song writers and royalty. Song writers were so rich that even when income tax had driven most of the country's talent abroad they could still afford to stay in Britain. They bought football clubs and islands and planes, and lived in Sussex.

Greatly cheered by this glimpse of the future, he tipped the waiter 200 pesetas and walked along the seafront to Jay's. He had to tell someone the good news.

The bar was empty in the mornings, although a few people were sitting on the banquettes outside, drinking coffee and looking wistfully at the yachts. Inside, Alvin was rehearsing a song.

'Hi, man,' he said, looking up at Mark through his big, trendy spectacles. 'I didn't know you got up this early.'

Alvin was playing 'Smoke Gets In Your Eyes' and seemed to be trying to imitate the Bryan Ferry version. He knew fewer songs than Mark and spent more time practising. Mark seldom appeared at Jay's before late evening.

'Have a look at this,' Mark said, offering Alvin the letter from TPA Music. 'It just arrived.' He wasn't sure that he was doing the right thing, but he had to show somebody.

'That's great, man,' Alvin said, looking disappointed. 'Let's hear it.'

He stood up and ushered Mark to the piano. While Mark sang, Alvin paced the room.

'A hit, a certain hit,' he said. 'Haunting and melodic. Not like your other stuff. It's just what Tom Jones needs to boost his career after the stuff he's been turning out. Why don't you send it to him? He might just bung it into his car cassette on his way home.'

'Don't you think his voice is too powerful?'

'Powerful and gentle. He'll wrap it round a song like that. He's your man.'

He sat down at the piano, the subject closed, and began singing old songs with his own words. 'Wurlitzer one for the money, two for the show. Won't you bring home Bill's bayleaf?'

Mark stood there wondering whether Alvin really liked his song or was only being polite. He obviously didn't want to discuss it any more. As he sat singing to himself in the gloom of the unlit bar his face looked unusually sad. Was he envious? Had Mark violated some code by inflicting his own song on Alvin?

He patted him on the shoulder. 'Thanks,' he said.

He walked out of the bar and into the sunshine. Alvin's enthusiasm for 'Cottage by the Sea' had strengthened this strange new optimism that he was feeling. Now it wasn't just Conrad Gambardella, that shrewd judge of popular music, enthusing over his typewriter. Two opinions were better than one. A quick reply to Mr Gambardella was the next little job after he had collected his shirts. He might even suggest that the cassette should find its way into the hands of Tom Jones.

Through the endless days of sun and torpor Leanda spotted an occasion that could give one day its significant moment: her twenty-sixth birthday. The milestone, which might otherwise have passed unnoticed, was marked by a dinner at El Capricho, a restaurant in the green-and-white-tiled Calle Los Canos. It had two forks, a culinary award which told you as much about its prices as its quality, and a terrace that looked down from the heights of Mijas on to a coast that was now, in May, bracing itself for a tourists' invasion that would exhaust and enrich it.

Kim's pregnancy had begun to show. She wore a loose summer dress that ignored her waist. Leanda wore her new silk dress, a dazzling concoction of purple and green, along with the jewellery she had bought in Marbella. Matthew had shut the bar for the evening, and it was Mark's night off.

He arrived in a taxi undecided whether to break the news about his song. His initial elation had been replaced by a cooler reality. The enthusiasm of a man whose judgement he had execrated for months did not guarantee the success he had dreamed about. Perhaps Alvin was only being friendly. Maybe other powers in the world of music would dismiss his offering as dross. Sitting at their table on the terrace he decided to keep the song to himself, worried that he might eventually look silly. He had always been a secret worrier – for much of his childhood he had imagined that he had an incurable illness which people were too kind to tell him about.

'Daniel is buying me a white drop-head Golf for my birthday,' Leanda announced. 'Isn't that sweet of him?'

'Sugary,' said Matthew. 'I used to buy Emma electric bath toys or scold's bridles, except when I lashed out on a set of crampons and a map of the Eiger.'

'I think he bought it in relief after his boat journey,' Leanda said.

'Was it bad?' Mark asked. He hadn't seen them since Gibraltar.

'Bad?' asked Daniel. 'Have you ever tried to be inconspicuous for seven hours? Those seats were not comfortable.'

Matthew told them: 'The nastiest moment was when we got back. We were the only people without any luggage and suddenly we stood out like two nudists in a bus queue. We got off the boat and disappeared a bit rapido. Do you remember Daniel's face in Gibraltar? What a picture that was! He could see himself hanging out of the high windows by his ankles with the Metropolitan Police belabouring the soles of his feet with cudgels!'

'I was a little aphasic, I must admit,' said Daniel. Aphasic had been the last answer he had got in the crossword that morning. 'I would rather not talk about it. Shall we eat?'

They all began with tomato soup because it had been specially recommended. It was unlike any tomato soup they had ever seen. It was made at their table and began with onions and mushrooms frying in a pan. Gin was

99

added and then set alight. Cream and chopped nuts followed and afterwards they couldn't understand why it tasted of tomato, but it did. It was the best tomato soup they had ever had. Mark's had disappeared long before the others had finished.

'Look at Cole Porter here,' said Daniel. 'Gourmet or glutton? You take him out to dinner and he gets soup on his eyebrows.'

'On *your* eyebrows,' said Matthew.

'We didn't waste time learning which side of the fork to eat peas from at our school,' said Mark. 'The faster you ate the more you got.'

'All those fat working-class boys,' Daniel said. 'All they ever learned at school was how to hurl food down their throats.'

'Have you met my little brother, the snob?' Mark asked.

'I'm not a snob,' said Daniel. 'If I was a snob I wouldn't be talking to you.'

'Boys! Boys!' said Leanda, who was ostensibly presiding over this celebration. 'Can we order wine?'

'The wine must come from Jerez and the women can come from anywhere,' said Daniel. 'That's an old Andalusian saying.' He seemed to be mildly drunk already.

It was the first time that the five of them had been together for any of their birthdays and perhaps to compensate for the missing years Matthew and Kim had bought Leanda a satellite television dish to enliven her winter evenings. Mark had bought her a book called *Cooking in Spain* which instructed her on how to produce 400 gastronomic experiences, from the banana cakes of the Canary Islands to walnut rolls from Galicia.

Leanda had arrived in Spain less prepared than any of them – she had received the least notice of this upheaval in her life – but she was adapting better than the others, pursuing interests in her methodical way as she probably would have done if she had been in England. She was the only one to set about learning Spanish and to study the country in which she found herself. She knew this wasn't England with sun. So now she knew the height of the Sierra Nevada, and she knew about the rich mineral deposits that lay beneath it. She could name the eight provinces of Andalusia. She knew all about the cotton and oranges and grapes that it produced, and that she was living in the middle of the world's largest crop of olives.

Tonight she was the only one to be eating a Spanish meal. While Daniel wrestled with a steak that made his fillings creak, she had chosen paella. Mark was working his way through three pork fillets – food was normally given a low priority in his bachelor rooms where the keyboard and not the cooker was the centre of activity. Kim was finding that her appetite was sadly affected by her pregnancy. The more she ate, the more there seemed to be on her plate. Was it being pumped up from below? How much had she to eat before she could see some plate?

Matthew, eating chicken, was admiring her face. It was a pretty face, mysteriously made prettier by pregnancy. Faces mattered to him more than anything else, he decided. He ate some chicken. No creature on earth had been exploited by men more than the chicken and it had a lot to do with the chicken's permanently angry expression. If it had looked sweet and helpless, the history of the chicken would be a very different story, as indeed would be the history of breakfast, lunch, dinner and salad. The coq au vin would have no history at all.

He saw the waiter, a small darting man with a moustache as black as soot, appear with a cake bearing twenty-six candles; Daniel had obviously stirred himself enough to do a little organizing today. When Leanda blew the candles out with one attempt, the waiter brought champagne, and Mark, the singer, led them in a chorus of 'Happy Birthday to You'.

When the cake had been passed round, and the champagne had been poured, Daniel, who had quietly disposed of a bottle and a half of Vina Real, felt the need to make a speech.

'A post-prandial stogie wouldn't come amiss,' he said, lighting a cigar.

'You're drunk,' said Leanda.

'Am I? I never know whether I'm drunk until I hear what I say. At Westminster they set a lot of store by public speaking, but of course one didn't drink a lot there. If you have a few drinks it's easier, or, to put it another way, more difficult.' He drank champagne. 'I want to pay tribute tonight to my wife. This is my wife.' He indicated Leanda with a wave of his cigar. 'The life that she is leading isn't quite what I led her to expect, but she copes with it with considerable aplomb. Sang-froid. Four and five. Anagram of road sign without the F.' He cleared his throat and thought for a moment. 'But Mijas is a beautiful place. What do we care if England has been turned into a land fit for Yuppies? What do we care if young men now think it is fashionable to wear jackets that don't fit them, and women wear shoulders that make them look like elephants? What do we care if the people who matter spend half their time shoving white stuff up their noses? Do they think we miss them? The crowded hospitals and the crippled schools. Do they think we care who wins the race between Aids and unemployment?' A tone of moral fervour, hopelessly inappropriate from somebody with Daniel's history, had begun to infuse his disjointed soliloquy. 'We've turned our back on all that. What we care about is . . .'

But what concerns he imagined that he shared with the others at the table were never revealed because his eyes closed even while he was standing and then he slid silently, like a launched ship, down his chair and under the table.

*

While giving the impression of being a dissolute, pleasure-seeking drunkard, the proprietor of Matt's Place, infected with the habit of a lifetime, never stopped working. He cooked snacks, shifted crates, polished tables, dashed to the supermarket for milk or food, chalked up notices that hung outside to entice sunburnt customers, wrestled with a recalcitrant coffee machine, dealt with numerous delivery men who arrived at strange hours carrying crates of Coca-Cola and San Miguel demanding, because of the bar casualty rate, cash now, and all the time held himself available for games of pool with restless customers. Most of these duties were shared with Kim, who otherwise sat behind the bar with Lady, keeping a meticulous note of who owed what. Lady had taken to the life of bar mascot and occasionally left her retreat to offer a damp welcome to customers she had grown to like.

Finding a hole in the evening between eight and nine, with customers being devoted either to early drinking or late drinking, Matthew introduced a happy hour of reduced prices which had no effect at all. On the day after Leanda's party he sat drinking Cruzcampo during this blank hour, listening to the conversation of his only two customers.

'Did Molly sell her villa?' asked one man.

'I don't think she can find a buyer,' said his companion. 'He didn't leave her any money, you know. Just the house.'

'I thought he had plenty of money. He used to be an estate agent, didn't he?'

'A barrister. He left the money to the children so she's dependent on them.'

'How awful. Why did he do that?'

'I don't think he wanted another man chasing her after he had gone.'

Vignettes like this drifted across the bar regularly, arousing in Matthew feelings of intense frustration. There were questions he wanted to ask, details he needed to know. Were the children sympathetic to their mother's position? Would she beg for ever? Had she legal redress? But sitting on his side of the counter Matthew knew when an intervention would not be welcome, and he did not plan one. That couple were his wages.

Instead he allowed his mind to drift to Leanda's party and its bathetic conclusion, and then to other birthday parties. He had held a fairly sensational one himself at the beginning of the year, just before the porridge hit the fan, a thirtieth-birthday breakfast in a private ornate room at the Dorchester. In retrospect, it was a farewell to affluence. A table was set in the middle of the room for thirty guests, and four men in white gloves were kept busy for a couple of hours serving a wondrous meal which had begun with Buck's Fizz, and went on to include bacon, mushrooms, tomatoes, kidneys, sausages, scrambled eggs and kippers. It was just about the last time that Emma had been civil to him.

He had always wondered how his being three years younger than his wife would affect things later on, but the marriage had not lasted long enough for him to find out. As usual, he thought, he had been ahead of his time. Today the younger husband was the new fad. Film stars did it all the time and talked about compatible sex drives and the prospect of a shared old age instead of premature widowhood.

The affair which had ended at one set of traffic lights had begun at another. 'I love you!' he had shouted at the auburn-haired vision in a white sports car alongside him in Bayswater. She turned her head away contemptuously, but he was already on his way to his first million and was not a man who was easily deterred. His life was not short of attractive girls, but this one fascinated him in a way that none of the others had managed. As the lights changed, she put her foot down and roared away. Matthew was driving a pink Lotus that morning and he switched into her lane and tracked her to the next lights. As they turned red and she braked, he rammed her in the back – gently, but not so gently that there wasn't some damage to discuss.

He approached her bearing money: in those first seconds he discovered her weakness. With the experience of many other unintended collisions, he judged the damage to her MG to cost about £200. He gave her £500 in £50 notes. As soon as she smiled, he invited her for a drink. Her face, not conventionally pretty, was handsome in a startling way with big eyes that made men look twice. Three months later they were married in the country, honeymooned in Bermuda and embarked on a five-year marriage which was ended by another incident in a car.

As he pulled himself another glass of Cruzcampo, Mark came in.

'Hiya,' he said. 'Where's Kim?'

'Walking the dog. Beer?'

Mark nodded and pulled a stool to the counter. The couple who had been deploring Molly's financial predicament chose this moment to pay and go.

'I'm worried about our baby brother,' Mark said when they were alone. 'After last night's embarrassment.'

'Why's that?' Matthew asked, pushing a beer across the bar.

'He's unhappy. You can see it.'

'I can see it but I can't do anything about it.'

'He's homesick. His life's empty. He drinks too much. At this rate he'll be an alcoholic in two years.'

'Sooner than that, I'd have thought. Frankly, I'm not that sympathetic. Want some nuts?'

'Well, I'm not very sympathetic either. Dad gave him everything and look what he's done with it. I work, you work, he does the *Daily Telegraph* crossword. But, somehow, I still feel responsible for him. Dad's not here, mother's dead. I always felt responsible for him. I was twenty when he was ten. I've always been a second parent.'

'I know you have. And after he'd been to Westminster he thought that we were both inferior beings. He didn't even try to disguise it, did he? I think he was actually ashamed of us and now he is trying to face up to the fact that we are ashamed of him. I remember once, when he had some friends from school coming round, he asked me to go out. He didn't want them to meet me.'

But Matthew remembered other things too – boyhood summers on Cornish beaches with Danny tagging along, the unwanted youngest, disrupting cricket in the sand. Matthew's desire then had been to compete with his elder brother at the games that they played. Daniel was an unwelcome distraction – there wasn't much a boy of four could teach a boy of nine.

'Think what he had during what they call the formative years,' Mark said. 'A dead mother, an absent father and two brothers who were too old to play with him. Doesn't it occur to you that we might be responsible for a lonely, drunken bank robber who only wanted to show his big brothers that he could do things too?'

Seeing the depths of his brother's concern, Matthew curbed the impatience he was starting to feel. 'That's setting it a bit high, Mark,' he said. 'An awful lot of little boys have been brought up with elder brothers and no mother, and even without the benefit of five years at one of our great public schools have managed to soldier along life's highway without nicking a million quid from the bank. He was a victim of circumstance. So is Prince Charles. So are you. If what you're saying is that if I hadn't made all that money he wouldn't have felt the need to rob the bank, you may be right. I remember how I used to look up to you. I know that elder brother thing. But it's hardly cause for me to get eaten up by guilt, is it? What was I supposed to say? I'd better stay poor or Danny might get it into his head to rob a bank?'

'What do you mean – you used to look up to me? How come I got dethroned?'

'Listen, your little brother was raised securely in the English middle class, he was provided with every little boredom-beater a kid ever had, from train sets to his own television, he was educated among the alleged cream of his generation, he married a remarkably loyal woman and he was rising quickly in a career which enabled him to buy a house in London in the first half of his twenties. His problems were simply non-existent. He didn't have to prove himself to anybody.'

'Yes, he did. His big brother was a multi-millionaire. Anyway, he's sitting on his patio now, drinking too much gin and staring miserably into his pool, wondering what to do.'

'As far as I am concerned he's sitting in his own luxury house on a sunshine coast, watching satellite television with a million pounds in the bank, while you and I work far into the night. I am not a puddle of tears, Mark, I am not a trembling jelly of compassion and, above all, I am not my brother's keeper. He should have gone on a shop-lifting spree at fourteen like the rest of us and got that something-for-nothing thing out of his system.'

It seemed to Matthew that Mark had never quite got used to the fact that his little brothers had grown up, left home and got married. He saw him now as a mother hen, absent-mindedly clucking over a long-deserted nest.

'He's invited us up for Sunday lunch and a swim,' Mark said. 'I want us to talk to him.'

'He won't listen.'

'We'll make him. We'll tell him that he's got to start doing something with his life instead of sitting on his own, feeling sorry for himself. Why doesn't he play squash or golf or buy a boat? Why doesn't he start a little business? They have computers in Spain, don't they?'

'Why doesn't he go home and face the music if he's so damned miserable?'

Mark finished his drink and stood up. 'I have to go and play the piano. I must say your lack of sympathy depresses me. You're on the run yourself, you know.'

'And I'm not sitting on my bum feeling sorry for myself. That's why I made a million and he stole it. Different approach.'

'But you'll come up on Sunday and talk to him?'

'Of course.' Matthew had come round the counter now and was busily brushing the pool table. After that the barrel needed changing. 'If you think joining a squash club is the cure for his ills you've got it all wrong. It runs a little deeper than that, Mark. Do you remember the one thing he always wanted as a boy?'

'Daddy's admiration.'

'You're right. I didn't think you would remember it. And that's what's destroying him. He's let Daddy down.'

SEVEN

A WHITE inflatable armchair, bought by Leanda in Marbella, bobbed about in the middle of the swimming pool. Kim sat straight-backed on its hot, wet rubber, trailing her legs in the water. She found that pregnancy and swimming went well together: the water took the growing weight and made her feel normal again. Mark lay on his back on the grass, daydreaming of an album that went triple platinum, while Daniel gave Matthew a brief tennis lesson on a court that was hot enough to deter the dog from interrupting them. Unlike Daniel, Matthew had had no tennis courts at his school, but driving up the winding hill from the coast he had passed Lew Hoad's tennis club. A few lessons from a man who had won Wimbledon twice should be enough to give his younger brother a match.

They had enjoyed a chicken salad on the terrace and Leanda was now busy making her own sangria in a Waterford crystal bowl. She spooned it into large glasses and carried them on a tray to her guests. Seeing the drinks, the tennis players abandoned their tussle and retired to the sunbeds round the pool.

'That was about as exciting as watching Swedes play tennis,' said Kim, from her floating armchair. 'I fell asleep twice.' She slipped off the seat and swam towards them. Lady, waiting to greet her at the edge of the pool, seemed to be considering plunging in herself.

'Why don't you take up golf, Danny? Or squash?' Mark asked from his recumbent position behind them.

Daniel took the sangria from his lips briefly to ask: 'Why would I want to do that?'

'To fill up your life,' said Matthew. 'It's your dolorous disposition that concerns us.'

'We're scared you might shoot what brains you have out,' said Mark.

'I'm all right, Mark, thanks,' Daniel said.

'No, you're not. You're miserable. You're not getting the most out of your life. You should be happy here. Most people would envy you. But your life isn't enviable.'

'When we were Catholics we used to believe that life was a waiting room,' Matthew said. 'But we're not Catholics any more. This isn't a waiting room. This is it. Man that is born of woman hath but a short time to live. You've had nearly 10,000 days already.'

Daniel got up and went over to the table where Leanda had placed the sangria and refilled his glass.

'Are you two having a go at me?' he asked.

'We want to see some happiness in your life,' Mark told him. 'Less sitting around and getting drunk.'

'I'm happy.'

'You're not, though,' Leanda said. 'I woke up one night and you were crying in bed.'

The disclosure embarrassed all of them, and Matthew asked hurriedly: 'Why don't you start a business? As a hobby.'

'And spend all night being polite to drunken customers? I've come here to relax.'

'You're relaxed as a newt half the time. It isn't good for you, kid. Anyway, I didn't mean a bar. That is the last place we want to put you. But what about computers? Stick to what you're good at and pursue it to death. The secret of success.'

Daniel, his glass newly filled, returned to his sunbed. 'In the first place, my Spanish isn't good enough to get involved in business. In the second place, I never shared your enthusiasm for work. I always thought there was something better to do with your time.'

'You don't seem to have found it.'

'Work as therapy, Danny,' said Mark. 'Anyway, when you were working nights and taking that course during the day you were working as hard as anybody in England.'

'And much bloody good it did me.'

'Why don't you go to Spanish lessons?' Kim asked him. 'You could go with Leanda.'

'I've had enough of classrooms, thanks. The truth is that the English are so bad at learning languages that the rest of the world has decided to learn English.'

'But not enough for you to start a business,' Mark said.

Daniel sat up on his sunbed and swung his feet round on to the grass. His eyes already looked faintly bloodshot from his drinking. 'Look, I'm very touched by your concern, but what you overlook is that although I may seem fed up here, I was thoroughly pissed off there. I hated the weather, the restrictions, the licensing hours, the petty-mindedness, the bureaucracy, the taxes, the jealousies, the fatuous television and the trivial press, the stupid obsessions of most of the people and their boring self-centred conversations. I hated the one-sided ratio of drudgery to fun. And do you know what I hated most of all? The bloody economy. During my entire life governments have protested that certain popular options were closed to them in the present financial climate. The present financial climate has now lasted for twenty-five years to my certain knowledge. Yet while hospitals close down and people wait for operations, they produce one and a half billion pounds to regain the Falklands without putting a penny on any tax.'

'And now you miss England,' said Leanda.

'And now I miss England. It's the little old devil called human nature. In fact I miss it so much that I am going off now to get the Sunday papers. They always arrive earlier than the others for some reason.' He stood up.

'Perhaps there's a depressive strain in my genes.'

He walked off, leaving them round the pool.

Mark stood up, shook his head, and dived in.

'I don't know what we can do with him,' Matthew said to Leanda.

'Short of erasing the past, neither do I,' she said. 'Still, I find the idea of Danny lecturing the British government on financial rectitude rather enjoyable.' She threw a ball to Mark and joined him in the pool.

Matthew pulled his sunbed towards Kim's and kissed her shoulder.

'How do you get the back of your legs brown when you're pregnant?' she asked.

'How is the small person, anyway?' he asked. 'Are you still getting the flutter?'

'The flutter is now a kick.'

He put his arms round her and wondered whether it was a boy or a girl in there.

'This is a wonderful sangria,' he told Leanda when the others climbed out of the pool. 'A perfect harmony of taste and bouquet.'

'Is it true that millionaires' wives clean their teeth with champagne?' Mark asked. 'I've always wanted to know.'

'Teeth?' said Leanda. 'We *bathe* in it. You both seem very concerned about my husband.'

'He's been concerned about Danny ever since he was born,' Matthew told her. 'It's a life's work.'

Mark explained: 'I had to help Dad. A family without a mother was no joke, Leanda.'

'Tell them the O'Connor story,' Matthew said.

'No, I won't,' Mark said. 'I've never told anybody that story.'

'Oh God,' said Kim, sitting up. 'You'll have to tell us now.'

'I'm not telling it. Matthew shouldn't have mentioned it.'

'What was it about?' Leanda asked. 'Perhaps I've heard it.'

'School,' said Matthew.

'Westminster?'

'No, before that.'

'I haven't heard it.'

'You're not going to hear it now,' said Mark.

'I'll fill your glass and get you an ice-cream.'

'It's not a pleasant story,' said Mark.

'I want to hear it now, and so does Kim.'

'A full glass, an ice-cream and a kiss from both of us.'

'We all have our price,' said Mark, kissing them. Thoroughly bribed, he sat on his sunbed and told the O'Connor story, pausing only to scoop strawberry ice-cream into his mouth from a silver bowl.

'When Danny was ten he was sent by our father to a prep. school to prepare him for great things. It was a school where the discipline was horrendous. The entire staff seemed to be made up of madmen and sadists, and sexual perverts as well, I shouldn't wonder. But the school had a wonderful record – around ninety-five per cent of their boys passed their exams and went on to the public school that their parents wanted. So Dad decided it was the school for little Daniel. It was an expensive place, but there was nothing flash about the buildings. Many of the classrooms were wooden shacks with just enough room for twenty desks. The shacks were dotted round the grounds and the boys had to run – in threes – from one shack to the next for each lesson. Anyway, there was one teacher whose name – shall I ever forget it? – was Seamus O'Connor. He was a sadist's sadist. The way he beat the boys was with a ruler. Not one ruler, but two. Not flat, but sideways. And not on the palm of the hand, but on the back, across the knuckles. Danny used to tell me about this, but I didn't believe him. He wouldn't tell Dad because he knew he wouldn't believe him either. Well, one day he came home and his knuckles were black and blue. And do you know why? He couldn't spell "scholasticism". Is that a word you have ever needed to spell? The only time I've ever heard it mentioned was by Danny when he showed me his hands. He said the boys were so frightened of O'Connor that some of them peed themselves in class. Well, I thought it was pretty rough, but then I forgot about it. I thought it was all part of Danny's rigorous training for the delights of public school. But then, a few days later, he came home and told me he wasn't going to go to school again. He was going to run away. We used to have these chats when he got home because Dad was still at work and I was home all day and out playing gigs in the evenings. It turned out that O'Connor had beaten him again. I forget what for. He had beaten him on the bruises of the first beating. Quite honestly, I felt sick. You couldn't even see his knuckles. The kid was ten, and I felt responsible for him. I promised that if he didn't run away and carried on going to school, Mr O'Connor would never hit a boy again. The words jumped out of my mouth because I knew he meant to vanish. It was a silly thing to promise, but I saw that Danny believed me straight away. He always believed me because I never lied to him. I had a gig that night in Windsor and right through I was wondering how I was going to keep the promise. It was a bloody nightmare, because of the look on Danny's face when I promised him. I told the boys afterwards when we were having a drink, and one of them came right out with it. He was the drummer, Jake, and he weighed about sixteen stone. "We'll go round there and catch him at it," he said. Another bloke in the band who was nearly as hefty as Jake said he wanted to come because his teacher used to beat *him* up. I've forgotten his name. Anyway, the following afternoon, the three of us – and I was twenty then, and big for my age – went round to the school. I got Danny to tell me what time he'd be in the right classroom and draw me a map showing which one it was. The three of us were eventually crouched down outside the classroom by an open window listening to every word. It was bloody uncomfortable and for twenty minutes nothing happened. I heard Danny parsing a sentence, and then some poor bastard got into trouble over a transitive verb. "Step up here, Smith," says this lovely Irish voice. "Both hands out, please." We heard the first crack and the boy's cry, and we crept quietly round to the door on all fours, and then just walked in. I went first as the spokesman, and my two henchmen stayed a pace behind me. O'Connor looked round and said, "Yes?" "That's a little sadistic, Mr O'Connor," I said. "Put your ruler down." I could see Danny's face white as snow, but his eyes were like saucers. O'Connor stared at me. "Get out of my class," he said. I honestly don't know what I intended to do. Lecture him? Reason with him? Threaten him? But I never had to decide because Jake pushed past me, picked up O'Connor and threw him about six feet across the room. O'Connor wasn't small, but he was a lot smaller than Jake. The other bloke, whose name I've forgotten, then hurled himself on to O'Connor on the floor and started to rip his trousers off. "Humiliate the bastard," he said. Jake joined him then and I started to get worried. We hadn't planned anything and this wasn't my scene at all. But some of these musicians are used to this sort of rag after a few drinks in the early hours of the morning, and the next thing I knew was that O'Connor was stark naked and hanging upside down from one of the rafters that crossed the room. They'd tied him up with his own trousers and he hung there naked, upside down and helpless. And during all this the boys never made a sound. "Let's split," said Jake. We headed for the door in the biggest silence you ever heard, but I turned back as we left and said, "Go back to your desk, Smith, and try to get the hang of those transitive verbs.'"

'What an extraordinary story,' said Leanda. 'What happened?'

'That's the end of the story.'

'There must have been some reaction. Did he ever hit a boy again?'

'Er, no.'

'Did he carry on teaching? Oh, come on, Mark. We've got to know what happened.'

'I don't want to tell it.'

'I'll tell them,' Matthew said. 'That night, in his bed-sit in Reading, Seamus O'Connor climbed into what we must assume was a hot bath and slashed both his wrists with a cut-throat razor. He drowned in his own blood.'

'He couldn't face the boys again, you see,' Mark said. 'It was hardly the ending I intended.'

'Couldn't he have taught somewhere else?' Kim asked.

'Apparently not. He was told that he would never be given the necessary references. It was the headmaster who had to untie him, and he wasn't very impressed. There was nothing in the brochure, you see, about teachers hanging naked from the rafters. It was a very élite school that leant more towards the aesthetic.'

'I bet Danny was pleased, anyway,' Kim said.

'I was his hero for at least a week. And here he comes.'

Although Daniel restricted himself to the *Daily Telegraph* during the week, an old family habit made him recklessly extravagant on Sundays, buying every paper he could lay his hands on. His father, who had little time to read newspapers on weekdays, had always taken several on Sundays when he had the time to look at them. 'Catching up,' he called it.

Daniel handed out copies randomly and settled down to read the *Sunday Times*. It was a quiet week for news. The ageing and increasingly *distrait* president of the free world was going to meet a man twenty years his junior who had replaced a series of collapsing geriatrics at the head of the unfree world. Coventry had won the cup. But the news that was getting the most attention in Britain was that Margaret Thatcher, encouraged by opinion polls that told her she had already won, had called a general election. Daniel was pleased. This was one of those empty alternate years with no Olympic Games or World Cup, and a general election was a welcome *divertissement*.

Mark, hoping for a lurid tabloid with its endless coverage of pop music, had been given one of the serious papers. He gazed at a headline which said: HUNGARIANS NEUROTIC – OFFICIAL.

'This isn't the paper I want,' he said.

'A bit intellectual for you, is it?' Daniel asked.

'I'll have you know that when I was a teenager I used to buy the *Financial Times* to make people think that I was educated,' Mark told him. 'Of course, you have to remember to hold it the right way up. You have to remember that the big type is at the top of the page.'

There was a redistribution of the papers and Mark was given the *News of the World*. Jumping through it in search of pop, he found himself staring at a double-column picture of his brother clutching a drink. The headline next to it, fitting exactly on all of its three lines, said:

DAN, DAN
THE BANK
SCAM MAN.

He suppressed an impulse to shout, knowing full well that the paper would be snatched from his hands before he could read it. He looked again at the picture of Daniel and recognized the bar in Mijas where it had been taken.

When he read the story, which was by-lined, 'From Russell Rose in Marbella', he imagined that he was his own father, reading it in his golf club while friends stood around waiting for a reaction.

A former public schoolboy who conned more that £5 million out of Britain's High Street banks talked to me last night about his life of luxury in the Spanish sun.

I caught up with twenty-five-year-old Danny Ward drinking champagne in the beautiful mountain town of Mijas, just a short Rolls Royce drive from the jet-setters' paradise of Marbella.

Ward, who was expelled from one of Britain's oldest public schools, Westminster, devised a complicated method of dishonestly boosting ten bank accounts, all in false names, before withdrawing the lot and fleeing to the so-called Costa del Crime.

He told me: 'I'm very happy here. I drink champagne, play tennis, swim, do the crosswords. It's better than rainy old Britain.

'My twenty-five-year-old wife Leanda is very happy, too. She's taking Spanish classes at the moment.

'Anyway, there's nowhere else for us to go.'

Ward, who was a computer whiz-kid before the bank scam, lives in a luxurious mansion in the foothills of the Sierra Nevada. It is guarded by a team of alsatians, and secret cameras pick up every visitor before he reaches the remote-controlled gates.

As he drank champagne last might and laughed at his financial trickery, Ward said: 'This is the life. Going to the office for peanuts is for monkeys.'

No bank spokesman would admit that the ex-public schoolboy had robbed them of millions. It is believed that they fear the scam could be copied.

But on the Costa del Sol a special task force of detectives has been sent in to clean up the crime-ridden coast.

From the luxury of their bolt-holes from justice, the gangsters plot major crimes, especially drug trafficking.

Scotland Yard has given Spanish police the names of a hundred men they would like to interview, but many of them, including Danny Ward, are protected because they arrived in Spain before the new rules on extradition which followed Spain's membership of the Common Market.

After reading the story, Mark took it to Daniel and pointed it out without telling the others. Daniel lay on the sun-lounger and read it in silence. He was shocked at the picture of himself, looking suitably furtive in the Spanish sun, he was shocked by the headline, but most of all he was shocked by the lies: He hadn't stolen £5 million, he wasn't drinking champagne, the interview wasn't last night, he hadn't been expelled from Westminster, there were no alsatians at the gate and the Sierra Nevada was a hundred miles away. Russell Rose wasn't 'in Marbella' but ensconced by now, no doubt, in a wine bar in Wapping wearing a white shirt to help his fading tan. But they always said that it was only when newspapers wrote about you that you discovered how inaccurate they were, and there was nothing he could do about it. As Russell Rose had said, he was unlikely to arrive in London with a writ for libel.

He passed the paper to Matthew without comment. Matthew knew more about journalism than his brothers and decided immediately that it was a very thin story, which probably explained its delayed appearance in the paper. Initially spiked, it had clearly been resuscitated in an emergency; some exciting piece of fearless prose had failed at the last moment to arrive and old notebooks had been combed in search of material that could fill a hole.

'What a bloody scumbag,' he said. 'I thought he knew you from schooldays.'

'My twenty-five-year-old-wife Leanda,' said Leanda. 'People don't even talk like that.'

'They do when they've been through a hack's notebook,' said Matthew. 'Did you make the remark about peanuts and monkeys? It doesn't sound like you.'

'No, and that's the point, isn't it? If I'd said nothing he'd have made it up as he made that up. There was nothing I could do or blame myself for.'

'I'm just glad I'm not in Dad's golf club this morning,' Mark said.

'And what about Mummy?' asked Leanda.

'Leanda's mother is coming out for a holiday this week,' Daniel told them. 'If she's seen the paper it should be a bit lively.'

'Does she read the *News of the World*?' Kim asked.

'Avidly,' said Leanda.

Three days later Mrs Plumridge flew into Malaga on an Iberia flight from Heathrow 'like an avenging angel', as Daniel was later to describe it. She had lived most of her life without boarding a plane and approached the ordeal with considerable misgivings – as far as she was concerned, it was better to arrive than to travel hopefully. But her recuperative powers had always impressed her friends, and by the time she had reclaimed her baggage she was her old self: a sizzling mix of bile, venom and self-confidence.

Fortified by a bottle of wine from one of the oldest bodegas in Rioja, Daniel studied the flight-information screen on the other side of customs. 'The eagle has landed,' he said. 'Sound the tocsin.' He had not expected to work eight down from that morning's crossword into his conversation so quickly. Either the wine, or a joke in that morning's *Telegraph*, had placed a foolish and badly timed grin on his brown face. The joke was appropriate, though. How long did the mother-in-law stay? A week, all but six days.

Mrs Plumridge emerged from customs in the company of two large suitcases balanced precariously on a trolley. She was a tall, angular woman with blue-rinsed grey hair and, even with the trolley, she moved with more energy than was to be expected from someone of her age.

'Leanda!' she cried, embracing and kissing her daughter. 'How are you, darling?'

'How was the flight?' Leanda asked. 'Give Danny the trolley.'

'Hello, Daniel,' said Mrs Plumridge. She stared at her son-in-law as if engaged on an abortive search for plus points in his personality. 'How are you?'

He knew immediately that she had read the *News of the World*. 'I'm fine. Are you well?' he asked.

'I'm on top form,' she announced as they made their way to the exit. 'Take me to your mansion.'

As Daniel drove them through the hills to Mijas, Leanda gave her mother a lecture on Spain in general, and Andalusia in particular, although hills were all she saw on the journey to the villa. Its opulence would have astonished her if she had not read the paper, but when they showed her to her bedroom with its own magnificent bathroom, she still looked round in silent amazement. The three-bedroom semi-detached that she had left that morning had been built fifty years ago to less demanding specifications.

They left her to unpack and wash, and told her to come down for a drink when she was ready. Waiting for her on the patio, Daniel became uneasy.

'Isn't she going to mention it?' he asked Leanda.

'Sooner or later.'

That was what worried him. At Malaga he had been ready for an outburst, but nothing had happened. Now it was to hang over him, an explosion waiting to happen and timed, no doubt, to go off when he least expected it. It would be impossible to relax for a week.

He opened the white wine that his mother-in-law enjoyed and put it in an ice bucket. He decided on a sensible martini for himself while Leanda prepared dinner. He took his drink to a table on the patio, sat down and stared at the coast. It occurred to him that Mrs Plumridge, booked in here for a week, would restrain herself for several days yet, rather than poison the atmosphere of her holiday. Nemesis postponed.

The *Daily Telegraph* crossword, interrupted by the trip

to the airport, lay unfinished on the floor and he picked it up. 'All is for the best in the long pass,' he read. An anagram of long pass, he decided. Oenophile, running across the grid, told him where the O went and he wrote in Pangloss immediately. He had read *Candide* at Westminster and thought that it was time he read it again. It was in tune with his current philosophy. What was so smart, it said, about looking on the bright side? Doctor Pangloss looked on the bright side and what happened to him? He caught such a virulent dose of pox that he lost an ear and an eye and the tip of his nose. He was almost killed in a shipwreck and again in an earthquake, and then he was hanged. So much for looking on the bright side.

Mrs Plumridge, washed, refreshed and changed into an olive-green trouser suit, stepped out on to the patio like a wrestler getting into a ring. Daniel tried to look on the bright side. This time next week she would be at Heathrow.

He had hoped at one time, in the distant past, that she would warm to him, but even when he was working fourteen hours a day to furnish a home she had given him the impression that his manifold deficiencies could not, with the best will in the world, be overlooked. He had thought then that his background and qualifications made him an exceptional candidate for the role of son-in-law, but the mind of a bride's mother was not susceptible to rational diagnosis. Her conversation had sometimes suggested that she had hoped her daughter would find a husband among the ranks of the city's Yuppies, the market makers, company analysts, bond salesmen and gilt dealers with their penthouse flats in Dockland and their jacuzzis and walk-in wardrobes. It had always been clear that he was not what she had in mind for her daughter when she had cooed over her bassinet.

'Where's Leanda?' she asked, striding across the terrace with her distinctive gait.

'Getting dinner,' he told her. 'Would you like some wine?'

In some ways she reminded him of a cassowary. The fact that a cassowary could disembowel a human being without even thinking about it did not in any way diminish the illusion.

She took the wine and sat down.

'No children yet, then?' she said. 'My, what a view!'

'It's breath-taking, isn't it?' said Daniel, grabbing the softer option. 'If it wasn't for that hill you could probably see Gibraltar on a clear day.'

'Don't you want any?' she asked.

'Yes, we do. They just haven't appeared.'

Their childlessness had begun to aggravate her quite early on in the marriage. What else was sex for? To have it, and not produce children, clearly struck her as reprehensible, even self-indulgent.

'Have you seen a doctor?'

'We haven't got that far yet.'

'You've been married about five years.'

'Indeed we have. Do you swim, Mrs Plumridge?'

People drowned in swimming pools.

'No, I don't and I regret it,' she answered briskly. 'When I was a girl swimming pools weren't so plentiful, and the seaside wasn't so accessible. You're very lucky. You have a lovely pool here. And lovely wine, I may add.'

'Are you an oenophile?' he asked.

'What's that?'

'A connoisseur of wines.' He had only looked the word up a few hours earlier: the *Daily Telegraph* crossword was earning its keep today.

'No, I'm not,' she said. 'I hardly drink at all.'

But he noticed that her glass was already empty and he filled it for her. The guests who said they hardly drank were always the fastest at emptying his bottles. By the time Leanda laid a very English meal before them, roast beef, she had had three glasses of Vina Esmeralda, and switched happily to a seven-year-old red Rioja for the meal.

'I didn't even know Spain made wine,' said Mrs Plumridge. 'I thought it was just sherry.'

'They've got more land under vine than any country in Europe,' Daniel told her.

'And you can afford to pay for it,' she said quite unexpectedly.

'Yes, I can,' he said, glancing at Leanda whose expression had turned abruptly to pure dismay.

'With your robbery,' she said.

They thought afterwards that it was the wine that had induced her to broach the subject tonight; her sober intention had probably been to wait a few days.

'Mummy, I don't think we want to talk about that tonight,' Leanda told her.

'You might not want to, dear, but it's best out in the open. I read the story in the newspaper. All my friends read it. How do you think it made me feel?'

'Pretty ghastly, I should imagine.'

'Ghastly isn't the word for it. I wanted to put my head in the gas oven.'

'Mummy, you haven't got a gas oven.'

'It's a figure of speech, Leanda. I was very upset. My daughter living with a crook! My daughter in the *News of the World*! I can't imagine what your dear father would have said.'

Leanda couldn't imagine what her father would have said, either, and Daniel, concentrating on eating his roast beef and keeping his head down, clearly had no idea. For a second he had contemplated joining this conversation. The phrase 'bourgeois morality' was at the forefront of his mind, but it sounded singularly inapt even inside his head. After all, he was a crook. He ate on, hoping that

Mrs Plumridge would be satisfied with having her say and that the storm would blow over.

This proved not to be the case.

'I have a solution,' she said, laying down her knife and fork. 'You must come home, Leanda.'

'I must *what*?'

'You must come home. We can tell everybody that you didn't know about the bank robbery until you read the newspaper, and that you then did the honourable thing.'

'Did the honourable thing and deserted my husband?'

'Did the honourable thing and refused to live on stolen money.'

Leanda looked at her mother and then at her husband, who was carrying on eating as if he had recently gone deaf. Whatever the shortcomings of life in Mijas, she thought, it had the edge on living with Mummy in her semi-detached.

'I can't do that, Mummy, and you shouldn't ask it,' she said eventually. 'My place is here, whatever Danny has done.'

'It's because wives think like that that we have so many crooks. If you made a stand it might bring your husband to his senses.'

'And what do you expect him to do? Fly home and go to prison for five years?'

'Well, he could return the money for a start,' said Mrs Plumridge, reaching for her wine.

'It wouldn't make any difference. There's no amnesty. He'd still be locked up and what would happen to me then?'

'You seemed to survive very happily before you met him.'

This was not quite true. Leanda's adolescence had been a sad stage in her life, a period of unrealized dreams, unsatisfying jobs and unsatisfactory suitors. She had married at the first opportunity, at twenty-one, and had no wish to turn the clock back.

'This conversation is stupid and I don't want to pursue it,' she said, standing now to collect the plates.

'And what about me?' asked Mrs Plumridge, her voice slightly raised. 'I have to live in a world of whispers and pointing fingers. Is that fair? What did I ever do to you?'

'Nothing, Mummy,' she said, somewhat chagrined. The anger she could take, but the hint of tears upset her. She disappeared into the kitchen before her mother could continue.

Mrs Plumridge looked across the table at her son-in-law, who was busily refilling a wine glass that barely needed it. He found himself starting to panic these days when his glass was half empty.

'Have you lost your tongue?' she asked him.

He shook his head but said nothing.

'Well, do you think it's fair on her? Her name blackened at home, quite apart from the fact that if she stays with you she will never be able to live in England again? I always imagined my old age with my daughter around. Grandchildren to buy presents for. Days out.'

He thought for a moment that she was going to cry, but only for a moment; his second thought was that she had probably never cried in her life. He felt it was his turn to speak.

'Mrs Plumridge, I thought you were here as our guest. I thought you were going to enjoy a holiday in the sun. I never guessed that your mission was to destroy our marriage, but since it is I'll move out until you've gone. I don't think it would be fair on Leanda to have the two of us under one roof for a week.'

Leanda, returning with ice-cream, asked: 'What?'

'He's moving out till I've gone, dear,' Mrs Plumridge

said. It was a development that she obviously welcomed. 'The home truths are getting to him.'

Daniel, ignoring the ice-cream, stood up.

'I'll see you when your mother's gone,' he said.

Leanda found it difficult to argue. 'Where will you be,' she asked, 'in case I need you?'

Daniel thought of the nearest friendly bar.

'I'll be at Matthew's.'

'Matthew?' said Mrs Plumridge. 'Is he down here as well? I'd love to meet him. I like Matthew.'

Daniel turned to her politely. 'He had to flee the country. There are ten warrants out for his arrest in England. The police want him for criminal fraud.'

'Good Christ!' said Mrs Plumridge.

Cruising down to the coast in his Ford Escort, Daniel, in old shirt and jeans, felt like a man who had escaped, not merely from the harridan who had evicted him, but also from the cosy restrictions of married life.

He was a bachelor again, a condition which, in retrospect, had been over for him too quickly, and he would regard himself as a bachelor until he returned to the marital handcuffs at Mijas.

Matthew was playing pool with the small Italian called Pepe. The stake was 5,000 pesetas and for once he was trying to win.

'How's Mother Plumridge?' he asked when his brother walked in.

'Lethal.'

'The *News of the World*?'

'I'm afraid so. It turns out that the demented old bat can read.'

He kissed Kim's hand across the counter and asked for a pint of beer.

'How many beds have you got upstairs?' he asked. 'I'm homeless. I'm what you call a displaced person.'

'We have a sofa,' she told him. 'It looks more comfortable than the bed. What happened?'

He told her, and Matthew stopped playing to listen. 'Sleep on the sofa,' he said. 'But you might have to share it with Lady.' At the mention of her name the dog came out from behind the counter to lick Daniel's hand.

Sylvia, the blonde German, was in the bar wearing the shortest of shorts. Daniel studied her legs gratefully until the pool was over. Judging by his quiet departure, Pepe had lost. Matthew collected the money from the edge of the table and put it in his pocket.

'He has a wonderful sex-life, that man,' he said. 'He tells all the girls that he has only six months to live and they tear off their clothes in sympathy.'

'The women he's had, he probably *has* only six months to live,' Kim said.

'What happens when they meet him six months later?' asked Daniel, curious at this insight into a bachelor's world. 'Aren't they suspicious?'

'He only pulls visitors.'

There were several customers in the bar now and Matthew had to change the barrel. While Kim served some visiting teetotallers with coffee, Daniel struck up a conversation with the lonely Sylvia who tonight had only vodka to keep her company. Her boyfriend was in Malaga jail, she told him, and she was having a dreary summer. All she did was ride horses. She struck him as being a silly little fun-seeker who had no idea what to do with herself. Her young face had been rearranged slightly by life's struggles – her eyes were too tired, her mouth was too hard – but her breasts refused to be ignored. Constrained by the prospect of a quick jump, he bore her stupidity with limitless charm. Being a bachelor, he remembered, wasn't all fun and games: the boredom quotient could occasionally go off the graph.

But when Matthew suggested a game of pool, it was Sylvia who left the bar.

'She's rejected my suit,' said Daniel.

'She's bespoken for,' Matthew told him. 'Listen, Mark was in earlier, and he's received a strange invitation to go back after Jay's closes to some Arab's place. He's an oil trillionaire and his home is one of the most fantastic on the coast. He asked if I wanted to go. Well, Kim's tired, so I'm going to close the bar early and shoot down there. It must be worth a look. Fancy it?'

'Will there be girls?'

'Why do you think the Arabs are here? The sunshine?'

They reached Jay's at two o'clock, but it was another two hours before Mark could leave. He had rounded off a noisy evening with a Fats Waller selection which had been so popular that nobody wanted him to stop, but he closed the piano, wished everybody good night, and made his way to the bar where his brothers were drinking bourbon. At his elbow was a small, smiling man with lots of black wiry hair and a neatly trimmed moustache.

'This is Mohammed,' said Mark.

The Arab smiled, shook hands and bowed as if they were the hosts and he an unexpected interloper.

His white Rolls Royce, with white leather upholstery, was parked immediately in front of Jay's, obscuring the view of yachts that had cost even more. There was no question of any of them getting into Kim's Scirocco.

Mohammed eased the Rolls silently forward, with Mark beside him and the others sitting like lords in the back. Even at this hour small groups still roamed the port, various nocturnal appetites still unsatisfied.

'I think you like my house,' Mohammed said, as if their approval would be a significant part of his day.

In the event, none of them ever forgot it. It stood behind high walls in the hills behind San Pedro, and approached in the dark it looked more like a fortress than a home. But the remote-control in Mohammed's car allowed them through first one gate and then another. After a third door had glided open at the touch of a button in the Rolls, they were in a huge garage crammed with at least forty of the world's most expensive cars – Rolls and Ferraris, Lamborghinis, Bugatti Royales, a 1925 Hispano Suiza and three Aston Martin Zagatos among them.

'First I will show you the cellar,' Mohammed said, leading them through several doors and down many steps. The cellar was a big, square room with a quarry-tile floor and walls about forty yards long. Each wall was covered in shelves and each shelf contained rows of Chivas Regal or champagne. They couldn't begin to guess how many bottles there were.

'Now here is an interesting thing,' Mohammed said. 'Follow me.' He pushed against one shelf unit and a whole portion of the wall swung back to reveal a corridor. He walked into it and the three of them followed. After about thirty yards there were two doors. One led nowhere, and the other opened on to more corridor which eventually came to two more doors. Again, one led nowhere.

'It goes on like that,' said Mohammed proudly.

'Where does it lead?' Matthew asked.

'It comes out in the hills one kilometre away. It is my escape route if my enemies come.'

They walked back down the corridor and into the cellar. Suddenly they were in a lift which took them up into the hall of the house.

Mohammed led them into his sitting room. Four girls were sitting on a giant sofa watching a video. Mohammed ignored them and went to the windows to turn on a switch. Floodlights revealed a swimming pool outside which was arranged on three levels with the water being pumped continually round and dropping in little artificial waterfalls between each level. The whole scene was beautifully landscaped and there were underwater lights in each pool at the corners of which stood marble statues of naked girls holding books above their heads.

'The heli-pad is on the other side of the house,' Mohammed said apologetically. 'I will get you drinks. Introduce yourself to the girls.'

'Who is this man, for God's sake?' asked Matthew. Looking out at the first pool he could see that it had a glass bottom. Beneath it was a snooker room.

'He belongs to one of the royal families in the Gulf,' Mark said. 'They have a lot of royal families out there, and even the camels are millionaires.'

'He's probably done a bank scam,' said Daniel, looking at the girls who continued to watch the video as if nobody had joined them in the room.

'All this and he's only here for a few months every year,' Mark said. 'He's got a horse farm in Connecticut.'

Matthew looked at the splendour of the pool and then over it towards where, not many miles away, Africa lay, agonizing over its latest famine crisis. He imagined the pictures of children with flies on their mouths, and thought of the extraordinary affluence here. Probably nowhere on the surface of the globe were total poverty and unbelievable riches placed quite so closely together.

Mohammed returned carrying Chivas Regal. In the light he was seen to be a short, muscular man with the shoulders of a boxer and the easy athletic grace of a professional sportsman. On the wall behind him, they now noticed, was a Picasso.

'Come on, girls,' he said. They all stood up instantly, as if they were paid by the hour and the time clock was now running. There were no great beauties among them, but none was ugly. Their nationality remained a secret until the end; they never spoke.

Mohammed stood under a crystal chandelier pouring drinks. Beyond him was a marble see-through fireplace. He went over to the television and changed the film on the video. Expecting a blue movie, they were astonished to find that they were watching the adventures of Sinbad.

The room was full of sofas and, when Mohammed sat on one, the prettiest girl sat on his lap.

'Arrange yourselves with the girls,' he told his guests, but for one of them it was already too late.

Daniel, the only one to have expressed interest in girls, was now slumped on one of the sofas with his eyes shut. A small dark girl wrapped her body round his, and ran her little finger over his cheek in a manner which suggested that further inactivity on his part would be highly unwelcome. But just a taste of the Chivas Regal at Mohammed's, on top of the bourbon at Jay's, following the beer and a couple of gins at Matt's Place, all of which had come after Martini and wine at home and an entire bottle of wine at Malaga Airport, had conspired to make him unconscious.

'Party time!' said Mohammed, and all four girls removed their clothes so quickly that it was clear that they had been wearing very little to start with. They posed naked in the centre of the room like the busty, marble caryatids that stood at the corners of the pool outside.

The pleasure created by this development among those guests who were still conscious was mitigated somewhat by the discovery that Mohammed was removing his clothes, too. He threw himself, not noticeably aroused, at the girl who had sat on his lap, and pulled her down on to the sofa with him. Staring boggle-eyed at this confluence of limbs, Mark found something reassuring in the discovery that, despite his incredible wealth, the only thing Mohammed really wanted was exactly the same as everybody else.

It didn't solve his own problem though, which was that this sudden commencement of something which, for him, required a more gradual approach, had left him unresponsive and embarrassed; and to tell his friend Mohammed that this was not how he did things would seem ungrateful and, for all he knew of social mores south of Turkey, hopelessly discourteous. He drank from his Chivas Regal and looked down at his unconscious brother, who had opted out yet again.

Matthew's reservations about the situation in which he found himself sprang from several sources. Immobilized by a small blonde who sat naked on the floor caressing his leg, a prelude, he imagined, to an ascent of his thigh, he had in mind an article he had recently read in the Iberian *Sun*, left by someone in the bar, on the latest sexually transmitted diseases, at the head of which was Aids. He didn't know whether these girls were professionals or, as seemed more likely, enthusiastic amateurs, but either way with habits like these they looked just the sort of thing a man should avoid if he didn't want to end up on the television news shaking hands with the Minister of Health from a hospice bed. And there were other deterrents. With an angry wife in England and a pregnant girlfriend in Spain, he felt that side of his life was complicated enough already.

Disappointment with the visiting studs had already driven two of the spare girls to Mohammed's sofa where he now struggled enthusiastically among three of them towards some distant goal, possibly a place in the *Guinness Book of Records*. The fourth girl still seemed to be hoping that Matthew's leg led somewhere. Her right hand, running up and down the inside of the leg, had now found that there was more of it above the knee, a discovery that seemed to encourage her. Matthew concentrated on a Rembrandt he had suddenly spotted above the marble fireplace.

'We ought to go,' said Mark. 'We ought to get Danny up-right.'

Matthew bent down and picked the girl up off the ground.

'We have to go,' he said, kissing one breast.

133

The girl smiled as if he had promised something memorable.

'Go, not come,' Mark told her. 'Our brother is not a well person.'

He glanced over at the sofa where a profusion of arms and legs sprouted from the silk cushions. 'Thanks, Mohammed. Good luck,' he said. He wasn't quite sure what the appropriate remark was; the situation had been carelessly neglected by the books of etiquette that he had sometimes consulted during an uncertain childhood.

Mohammed's head emerged suddenly from the mêlée.

'You go?' he asked. 'There are many bedrooms.'

'Danny's ill. We must take him home.'

'OK. Ring the bell in the hall. Hassan will show you out.'

His head vanished, a disappearance that was followed by a squeal.

A huge handbell that looked as if it ought to belong to a town crier stood on a table in the hall and Matthew enjoyed ringing it. It summoned immediately from one of many doors a dark-skinned gentleman who escorted them without speaking through doors and then gates until they were standing in the road. They could see the lights of San Pedro half a mile away and they began to walk.

'We'll get a taxi to Banus from there,' said Mark. 'What a bloody odd evening.'

Daniel revived in the air and marched unsteadily between them.

'What was odd about it?' he asked. 'The last thing I remember was talking to a German girl in Matthew's bar.'

'Memory gaps,' said Matthew. 'The first warning sign for the alcoholic.'

EIGHT

ON 11 JUNE the British public was invited to find an umbrella and go out and vote. It was the wettest summer for many years.

Sitting under a blue sky, Daniel decided to create a small link with home by holding a general election party in the garden. A radio on the patio, tuned permanently to the BBC's World Service, would relay results to those who were interested. For a while it would be just like living in England, except that their skin would be brown and their clothes would be dry.

Mrs Plumridge's holiday had ended prematurely in a tangle of recrimination. Balked in her attempt to persuade her daughter to return to England, and stunned by the discovery that Leanda's brother-in-law was also in flight from Britain's wonderful police force, she was finally made to feel guilty about driving Daniel from his own home. After four days she decided to go.

'This is no place for me,' she said over breakfast. 'I'm going to ring the airport and change my ticket.'

'It's your own fault, Mummy,' Leanda told her. 'You could have had a wonderful holiday.'

'I'm afraid there was no chance of that with the company you keep.'

Later that morning Leanda drove her to Malaga in her white Golf, and she disappeared through passport control in a flurry of disapproval. Leanda was both saddened and relieved. She could get off the tightrope.

Daniel returned home looking dreadful. Four days seemed to have aged him four years. His eyes were sunken and bloodshot, his complexion blotchy. His hands shook when he attempted unsuccessfully to complete the *Telegraph* crossword.

'Too much drink and not enough sleep,' he explained, slumping on a sunbed on the grass.

'I always said you weren't cut out to be a bachelor, dear,' Leanda told him. 'It's a gruelling life and you don't have the self-discipline.'

Daniel was reluctant to agree with her, but he thought that there was something in it. If he felt like this after four days, what on earth would he be like after four months?

'A coffee would help,' he said. 'If you brought me the phone as well, I'd be even more grateful.'

Lying in the sun in the peace of his own garden he began to revive. Perhaps he would try a day or two without alcohol and see how other people felt.

Leanda returned with two cups of coffee, a plate of biscuits and the cordless phone.

'I thought I should ring Graham Nash and apologize for not being here for tennis,' Daniel said. 'He's very strong on reliability.'

'He never came,' Leanda said. 'I was going to tell you. It's the first time he's failed to turn up, isn't it?'

'Perhaps he's ill.' Daniel rang his number. 'We'll have a party on election night,' he said while the number was ringing. 'Make a list of people we could invite.' He raised a finger as Graham Nash's voice came through.

'Graham? It's Danny. Two things. You failed to turn up for tennis and I wondered if you were OK. Two – we're having a party on election night and hope that you and Sylvia can come.'

Graham Nash's reply was preceded by a long silence. When he finally spoke his voice was strangely formal, as if he were back in the bank-manager's office, refusing an overdraft to an improvident customer.

'We feel you misled us,' he said, 'and have been misleading us for a long time. Sylvia saw the *News of the World* at a friend's house, and it came as a shock. As you know, I used to work in a bank and I can't be seen associating with people who rob them. There will be no more tennis and I'm afraid we won't be coming to your party.'

Daniel's uncertainty about how to reply to this was short-lived, because Graham Nash had replaced the phone.

'The bastard,' he said. 'The sanctimonious turd. He won't even admit to buying the *News of the World*. It sells more copies than any paper in Britain and nobody, apparently, ever buys it.'

'What did he say?'

'There will be no more tennis is what he said. More fool him. He needed the company more than I did.'

'I always found it odd, anyway, watching a bank manager play tennis with a bank robber,' Leanda said. 'Sending out invitations to a party could be a painful experience. Let's scrap it.'

'Certainly not.' But Graham Nash had depressed him more than he had shown. Friends were a precious commodity on this coast: the supply was finite. He finished his coffee and decided, after all, to have a drink. He went into the bar and ran his eye along the bottles: Glenfiddich, Glenlivet, Glen Orange. For the want of something to do, Leanda appeared to have arranged the drinks in alphabetical order.

He took a large Teachers to the pool and began to make a list of people, some of whom he scarcely knew, who might be inveigled into attending a summer frolic. There were forty names on his sheet quite quickly, and he wrote out the invitations at once, before the whisky could affect his handwriting.

Graham Nash, it emerged, was an exception among the exiles, perhaps conditioned by a lifetime of suburban respectability in the bank. Others had no compunction about drinking free champagne, whatever the source of the money that paid for it, and some were not even inhibited by the fact that they had not received invitations.

At least sixty people gathered on Daniel's lawn on election night, grateful to be involved in a British occasion. The recent past of some of them was every bit as dubious as the host's.

A small, bespectacled man called Mr Jones, who looked like the under clerk in a beleaguered and disaster-prone enterprise, was in fact a former Midlands solicitor who was the present owner of at least £5 million, cash that was passing through his sticky hands on its journey from vendee to vendor in a property transaction in Manchester. Overcome by the responsibility of guarding such bounty, Mr Jones became attached to the money and couldn't quite bring himself to pass it on. Within hours of discovering this weakness in himself, he was sitting on a British Airtours charter flight out of Manchester and heading south over the Pyrenees. He now owned a villa in Marbella.

A hard Scotsman with red hair, called Garton, had arrived uninvited in a white Rolls Royce with a wife who looked like Dolly Parton, and so was called Dolly Garton. The origins of his fortune were obscure, but there was no shortage of rumours, the most prevalent of which said that he was the mastermind in a headline-grabbing episode three years earlier when a security van had been ambushed in Paisley and subsequently blown up. A five-inch scar down the side of his face suggested that he had probably not spent his money-making days at a desk in the city.

Another man, with the unlikely name of Fraser Marriott, had used the columns of various Sunday newspapers to let hundreds of holiday homes in France. Cheques from travel-starved readers, desperate to reserve a stone farmhouse in the Dordogne, a château in Normandy or even a gîte in Brittany, flooded in to his rented flat in Islington. At the time that Fraser Marriott put his advertisements in the newspapers, he didn't even have a house in England, but now he owned a penthouse suite in Puerto Banus.

The disapproval which guests like these may have produced in the law-abiding majority who attended Daniel's party was discreetly veiled. Live and let live was the motto round here, and those who had been brought up to embrace less charitable views clung firmly to another conviction: provoking men who had five-inch scars on their faces did not necessarily lead to happiness.

Among the majority of the guests, those whose appearance would not cause a *frisson* at Scotland Yard, were Rob Beaton, one of the few commuters in the area, a money broker who flew to London from Gibraltar every Monday to sell dollars to Switzerland or yen to New York and returned on Fridays looking several years older; Carl and Paula (or Paul and Carla) who ran a hairdressing salon used by Leanda in Marbella; the retired couple who drank in Matthew's bar; a retired publican from Hackney, called Stan, who had the ventricose waistline of a professional darts player and who never drank less than a gallon of San Miguel every day; and Steve Finch, another boozy veteran of the sunshine existence who liked to discuss gilt-based investments over Scotch. His much younger wife, Alison, in a blue trouser suit, exuded a thoughtful gravity that was strangely at odds with her high-spirited spouse whose carefree personality, fuelled no doubt by the exponential curve of his wealth, could enliven any room. When somebody bored him, he allowed the drink in his mouth to trickle down his chin while at the same time feigning tremendous interest in the torrent of words that was coming from his increasingly perplexed tormentor.

The guests had been asked on arrival to pose in the privacy of a side room for a Polaroid picture of one small part of them. It was an idea of Leanda's, who wanted more from a party than people standing around drinking. All pictures – hands, ears, damaged elbows, post-cartilage knees – were numbered and displayed on the terrace, with a bottle of Dom Perignon on offer for the person who could link the most pictures to the correct guests.

The Scotsman, Garton, had produced his left hand, which Daniel then noticed was short of a finger. His Dolly Parton wife had offered a breast, released with a struggle from a bra like a hammock. Rob Beaton had offered the top of his head, revealing a baldness not normally seen by shorter humans. Stan the publican displayed his legs, which were surprisingly thin given the weight that they carried. Fraser Marriott produced a naked bottom, a message perhaps to his many dissatisfied customers. There were three moustaches, two of them on men.

Some of this did not meet with the approval of Leanda who with Kim had been busily preparing a seafood barbecue, after a tour that morning of the local fish markets.

'Have you been taking pornographic pictures?' she asked. 'That wasn't my idea at all.'

'Only when they insisted,' Daniel told her. 'You'd be surprised what people want you to photograph.'

'Nice place you've got here, Danny,' said Garton. 'Wanna sell it?' He looked as if he might take it anyway, even if it wasn't on the market.

'No, thanks. I like it.'

'Read about you in the papers. Nice one, son.'

'This isn't the normal cocktail-party conversation, is it?' said Kim when Garton had gone. 'Have we got any killers here?'

'I dread to think,' said Leanda. 'Thank God my dear mother has gone home. There are some fairly unprepossessing examples of the human race on this lawn.'

'I've been reading that all the parties here are attended by Princess Soraya, the Duchess of Seville, the Maharani of Cooch Behar and somebody called Count Rudi von Schoenburg.'

'Well, ours isn't.'

When the first results came in, confirming that Mrs Thatcher would be the first Prime Minister for more than a century to win three consecutive elections, it became clear that the criminal vote was solidly Conservative, sharing a common interest with the politicians in self-reliance, private enterprise, money-making and, above all, independence from the welfare agencies; and those who were surviving here on a pension had hoped, with very little confidence, for a Neil Kinnock victory. Many of the guests who fell between these positions, who were honest and affluent but out of touch with British political life, had believed initially that the new Prime Minister would be called David. As the extent of the Alliance disaster dawned, a lot of them found good things to say about Margaret Thatcher.

'Spot a bandwagon, jump on it. That's what I say,' said Stan, the publican. 'I've been agreeing with my customers all my life.'

'But you must believe in something?' Daniel suggested.

'If I do, I can't remember what it is.'

Matthew was floating in the pool. A night off from the chores of the bar was a precious occasion. Paul and Carla (or Carl and Paula) from the hairdressing salon were in the water, too. She had the sort of legs, he thought, which made sex maniacs send job applications to monasteries, and her face, hidden beneath an array of cosmetics that were sold in her salon, betrayed no hint of a tan. After three months of trying, the unrelenting Spanish sun had produced no more than a red nose.

Mark, who had arranged a late arrival at the piano bar, sat on the edge of the pool with his feet in the water.

'Have you noticed how women stop talking to women when they find a man to talk to?' he asked.

'This also applies to men,' Matthew said. They looked across the lawn to how the party had split up: women were mostly talking to women, men to men.

'The funny thing is,' said Mark, 'that when women all get together they think themselves in a ghetto, but when men all get together they think that they are enjoying themselves.' He slipped into the pool and began to swim towards the deep end. He liked to sound like a misogynist – it concealed his search for a woman. But he wasn't going to find one at parties like this. Guests were invited in pairs and, despite the occasional drama, they stayed in pairs.

Leanda and Kim were calling now to let the guests know that food was available. Beside a tureen of gazpacho, prawns, crayfish and red mullet were laid out alongside lobsters that had been prepared earlier, salads and bread rolls.

'It's terrible news,' said Rob Beaton, who was now stationed permanently alongside the radio. 'Roy Jenkins is out, Shirley Williams is out, Bill Rodgers is out. The gang of four is now a gang of one. What happened to the middle ground in politics?'

'Thatcher took it when Kinnock vacated it,' said Daniel. 'That's why she'll win in 1991 as well.'

'Poor David Owen,' said Kim. 'He's the only politician I ever fancied.'

'What I want to know,' said Leanda, 'is why all his lot part their hair on the right-hand side. Most men don't. Is it part of the Alliance uniform? I saw all their pictures in the paper this morning and they all had right-hand partings. Steel, Owen, Hughes, Alton, Cartwright and that bloke with the lean and hungry look – Maclennan. It's absolute death for a politician. The only one who did it was Ted Heath.'

'It's a factor which has been stupidly overlooked by the serious political commentators,' said Rob Beaton.

'Didn't Adolf Hitler part his hair on the right?' Matthew asked.

'He fits the theory,' said Leanda.

142

'I should have thought that Hitler was one of the most successful politicians of the century,' said Rob Beaton. 'He took over his country, saved it from economic collapse and damn nearly took over the world.'

'He was successful until he was unsuccessful,' said Leanda. 'And when he was unsuccessful he didn't bugger about at it.'

'I must write to *The Times* about this,' Rob Beaton said. 'I think you've illuminated something.'

'Blessed are the politicians, for they shall promise the earth,' said Matthew.

Steve Finch was discussing his favourite subject beside the bougainvillaea. 'What you need is a £25 million base,' he told Fraser Marriott. 'It's much easier to turn £25 million into £50 million than it is to turn £4 million into £8 million. That's why the rich get richer. How on earth do you turn £5 into £10?'

'Put it on a horse,' suggested Fraser Marriott.

'Well, there's a pretty forlorn venture unless you know the trainer.'

'In my experience, knowing the trainer is the fastest way to lose money on horses. He'll tell you how hot his animal is, but what about the rest of the field? What are their trainers telling their friends?'

'Well, there you are then,' said Steve Finch. 'I steer clear of horses myself, not being attracted to poverty. But you give me £25 million and I'll double it without you bothering to get out of bed.'

'Problem here, Steve,' Fraser Marriott said.

'You don't have £25 million?'

Fraser Marriott shook his head, as if embarrassed by this suddenly exposed deficiency.

'If you haven't got the readies, kid, I can't help you,' said Steve Finch, with a wink. Fraser Marriott stared at him, not knowing whether he was joking or not.

A few feet away Garton had identified one picture in

the picture competition, and was berating his wife for her sauciness.

'Leave it out, doll. This is a nice party. People don't want that sort of thing here,' he told her. 'Danny's got class. He went to public school. He was even in the *News of the World*.'

Mr Jones, the discredited lawyer, had sticky fingers again, this time through eating his salad. He sat close to the radio, occasionally writing a result on his napkin, as if in the hope that a party might be swept to power which had high in its manifesto the promise of an amnesty for absent villains, free flight home thrown in.

Stan, the publican, was testing the water with Alison Finch. He knew that she was much too bright for him but he found her face irresistible.

'What a swell party this is,' he said.

'All it lacks is Bing Crosby,' she replied. 'Where's your wife? I never see her. Is she agoraphobic?'

'Probably. I'm claustrophobic, which must be why we seldom meet. No, she's a good girl. Doesn't mind three in a bed.'

Alison Finch reared slightly, like a nervous horse. This was more information than she wanted. She gazed at the crowd on the lawn.

'When you look at the human race in action, you can only wonder at the time and money devoted to rearing babies,' she said.

Stan was both discouraged and encouraged by this. He recognized misanthropy when he heard it; on the other hand, babies were definitely connected to sex.

'You have no children?' he asked.

'My consort – my flatulent and flaccid consort – refuses. Unfortunately, I was married before I discovered this prohibition.'

Stan spotted, or thought he spotted, an opening here.

144

'He's no good in bed then?'

'He's very good. I put him down about eleven and he sleeps all night.'

'But I expect he was good when he was younger? What happened the first time he got into bed with you?'

'As I recall, he farted twice and asked for the hot-water bottle.' She emptied her glass and left him in search of a refill.

Daniel was shuffling through the entries in the picture competition. Some guests, accidentally or deliberately, had avoided the camera, but there were forty-two pictures on display and most of the guests had spent some time studying them. Few had more than ten correct guesses, but Alison Finch had twenty-eight right.

She took the bottle of Dom Perignon without a smile.

'This will keep me going tomorrow, when I haven't got yours to drink,' she said.

'How did you manage to win?' Daniel asked her.

'I study people. Tell me, who did the beautiful pair of hands belong to? That was the most interesting picture there. They looked like a pianist's.'

'You're right again. They belong to my brother, Mark, who plays the piano in Jay's.'

'I must meet him.'

Daniel looked round. 'He's gone to work, I'm afraid.'

Steve Finch came over.

'Has my wife won champagne?'

'Darling, I want you to take me to Banus one evening. Danny's brother plays the piano there.'

'Do they let you in with a tie on?' asked Steve Finch.

'Who have you been talking to?'

'Everybody. Fraser Marriott. What a waste of fresh air he is. No *savoir faire*. Most people haven't got anything interesting to say but they keep on talking because silence embarrasses them. He's like that. Still, it's a lovely party,

Danny. There's an old Spanish proverb which sums it up.'

'What's that?' Daniel asked.

'How agreeable it is to do nothing, and then to rest afterwards.'

In an uncharacteristic mood of optimism, Mark had added Jay's telephone number to his reply to Conrad Gambardella and informed him hopefully that he could be reached there after ten o'clock. There was no phone in Mark's Spartan apartment, nor need for one.

One evening, working his way through a few Randy Edelman numbers, he received a message from Alvin that London was on the line. He had just moved smoothly from 'The Uptown Up-tempo Woman' to 'Concrete and Clay', and he indicated to Alvin that the caller should hold. Interruptions were always a disaster at Jay's; it was much easier to keep a crowd going than pick them up after a break.

Eventually he left the piano and asked Alvin to take over.

'You'll like it,' he told him. 'A very beautiful girl has just come in and sat at the piano.'

'I noticed her,' said Alvin. 'What a little cracker, man.'

He slipped on to the stool and launched himself on 'If a Picture Paints a Thousand Words', a song he appeared to be singing exclusively for the small, dark-haired beauty who faced him across the piano.

The telephone was on the wall in a small room at the back where customers sometimes sat when the main bar was crowded.

'Mark Ward,' said Mark.

'Conrad Gambardella, Mr Ward,' said a deep voice in his ear. 'I couldn't hear you singing "Cottage by the Sea".'

146

'I'm saving it,' said Mark. 'It's nice to hear from you.'

'I'm the bearer of glad tidings, Mr Ward, or may I call you Mark?'

'Please do.'

'Tom Jones loves your song, and says it's what he's been looking for for five years. He's going to do it as his next single, and then on an album.'

Mark was listening to words that he didn't believe.

'That's wonderful,' he muttered.

'That's money, Mark. But it's a terrific song.'

'When will this happen?'

'He's doing it now. It'll be out within three months and I think it's going to be his first big hit for years.'

'Tom Jones,' said Mark. 'Blimey.'

'Are you ever in London?' Conrad Gambardella asked now. 'We should meet.'

'Maybe in December. I have to work.'

'Well, you'll be able to give that up soon. I'm sending you a contract for this song, and another I'd like you to sign if you're planning to turn out any more songs like "Cottage by the Sea". Have a look at them, and if you have any questions I'll fly down and see you. The royalty split with TPA is seventy-thirty in your favour, and then there's the question of which publishing company handles the song. Tom Jones could insist that his does. I don't know . . .'

It was getting too complicated for Mark. The first news item was so vast that his mind wasn't ready to absorb the subsequent information.

'Listen, are you sure?' he said. 'A Tom Jones single? There's no doubt about it, is there?'

'Don't worry yourself, Mark. It's all for definite.'

'Well, thanks. I'm dazed.'

'What about the contracts?'

'Send them.'

He hung up and leaned against the wall. His wildest

dream had just become a reality and there was no one to tell. He went to the bar and bought a whisky, giving Alvin a signal that meant 'keep playing'.

The bar was more crowded than ever and would stay packed now until October. The visitors became more unruly as the summer wore on. Last night a man had sat drinking at the piano from ten until three, when his wife had walked in and emptied a piña colada over his head. He had been expected home, apparently, at eight. Another man had insisted on singing 'Bye Bye Blackbird', a semi-tone flat, wrong words and no rhythm. A black Londoner had sworn that Alvin knew a song that he did not know and had been removed, with furious opposition, from the premises.

But Alvin was enjoying himself tonight. He and the girl were exchanging lover's smiles, despite the fact that they had never met. As Mark watched, she ordered a Bloody Mary for him, having seen that that was what he drank, and had a waiter deliver it to his side at the piano. He held the drink up in salute, and sang 'Annie's Song' just for her.

Mark sat at the bar in a world of his own, imagining Tom Jones wrapping his powerful voice round 'Cottage by the Sea' and yet sounding gentle. It couldn't fail to be a number one hit the way he would do it. It couldn't fail to make Mark rich. The fantasy took him to the places that he had never had the money to see: California and the Caribbean, Australia and Hong Kong. He had always wanted to travel and had been quietly irked for a year or more by the fact that his brother had a million pounds and couldn't move, while he was free to fly anywhere in the world and couldn't afford a ticket.

He looked across at the girl who was obsessing Alvin. She wasn't very old, probably not even twenty, and looked Spanish. Her dark eyes sparkled. She wasn't a hooker, and yet she was young to be so flirtatious. Even those girls who imagined naïvely that there was some show-biz glamour in a piano bar seldom sent a drink to a man they hadn't met. But she couldn't take her eyes off him. She listened to his songs in a cocoon of pure delight, smiling, applauding, occasionally mouthing the words that he was singing, and encouraging him all the time with a look that should have caused a few wrong notes.

Mark had a few admirers but none had evinced devotion like this. He ordered another Scotch, to the barman's surprise; he was known as a small drinker in this alcoholic shrine, but tonight was different, tonight was the night that would change his life.

A signal reached him now from Alvin that he wanted a break after his next song. It was 'Fool on the Hill', and he sang it as if he was keen to reach the end.

'. . . back from a protracted struggle with the Spanish telephone system, a warm welcome again please for the star of Puerto Banus, Mark Ward!' Alvin stood up and whispered to Mark: 'I'm going to crack that little darling.'

'Good luck.'

Mark sat down. 'Ladies and gentlemen, I could sing you some Beatle hits or even some Rolling Stones hits and in a minute I will. But first, for the very first time, I'm going to sing a song called "Cottage by the Sea", because I wrote it and I've just heard on the electric telephone that Tom Jones is going to record it.'

There was a lot of applause at this news. Even Alvin – heading unknowingly towards a traumatic encounter – stopped to clap.

> When you're just a little bit older
> Scarves and bright shawls round your shoulder
> Is this the place you'd like to be-ee-ee
> Shall I go ahead and build a cottage by the sea?

It was a preview, a first test of the public's reaction, although most of them didn't know whether they liked a song or not until they had heard it at least twice. But they took to Mark's song very quickly and so many shouted 'Encore!' that he sang it again. And then they stood and clapped and shouted, 'A hit! A hit!'

Overwhelmed by this reception, Mark felt tears come to his eyes. He looked across to Alvin and saw that he was crying, too. For a fleeting moment he imagined that his colleague had become emotional about the way the customers had welcomed 'Cottage by the Sea', but then he saw that the girl had gone, and a quite different scene had been playing itself out only a few yards away. He had to wait in some frustration until the next interval to find out what it was.

Alvin had fetched himself another Bloody Mary, and the Coca-Cola he knew the girl was drinking. He then edged his way through the crowded room to where the girl sat at the far end of the piano. She wasn't looking at him now, but nervously listening to the other pianist, a big Englishman, who was introducing a song that he had written. She was disappointed: she wanted to hear the hit songs that she already knew.

There were no free stools at the piano and Alvin had to stand between her and a gently perspiring German lady who was wedged on the next stool a yard away.

'Thanks for the drink,' he said. 'I've brought you one.'

The girl seemed very nervous, as if she had never imagined that things would come to this. Perhaps she was younger than she looked.

'Thank you,' she said.

She was a Spanish girl who spoke good English, he realized.

'You're a very beautiful girl,' he told her.

She looked at him then in a cool, appraising way, running her eyes over his hair, his mouth, his shirt and finally his rather ostentatious glasses.

'I didn't know you wore glasses,' she said.

The remark mystified him. He said: 'Do you want to come outside for some air?'

For a moment he thought that she wasn't going to answer. Then she said, very quietly: 'Before you say anything else, there is something that you should know.'

'What's that?' he asked. This wasn't quite the smooth passage that he had been anticipating during the last half hour at the piano.

'You're my father,' she told him.

Alvin was a non-stop talker, but for a moment no words came. He remembered the summer of 1970 very well, the hotel where he had played the piano, a waitress called Maria. They were both twenty. He had returned to America not even knowing that she was pregnant.

'Your mother is Maria?'

The girl looked happy again. 'I'm glad that you remember her.'

'How is she?'

'She's fine. Married to a man in a bank. I have two brothers.'

'How did you know I was here?'

'Mother knew. She said I could come and see you. I've always been curious about my father.'

'Well, of course.'

'But now I must go. I'm not allowed out late.'

'Well, hang on. What's your name?'

'I'm supposed to look at you, not talk to you.'

'Where do you live? Don't go yet.'

But the girl ignored his questions, kissed him suddenly on the cheek and walked out of the bar.

Alvin stood at the piano with tears in his eyes and watched her disappear through the crowd, reluctant at first to follow in case her parents were waiting outside. The daughter I have always wanted, he thought. He put his glass down and pushed his way through the customers, but when he finally got outside the girl had vanished among the evening strollers and he was left gazing at the unresponsive water.

NINE

MATTHEW took Lady for her evening walk to the Sala de Juego, where rows of Spanish fruit-machines waited like robot muggers to impoverish the tourists. For a short time in England, in countless bars, he had conducted a clandestine relationship with the American cousins of these rapacious little monsters, convinced briefly that his dedication and experience would persuade them to yield up their hoard of gold. He memorized their reels and nudged in winning lines, but at the height of his success he was only winning £10 in an evening. When he worked he could make thousands.

Walking back along the front he found himself thinking about his wife – she had been around during the fruit-machine craze. 'A mindless activity,' she had called it. He had fancied himself briefly at roulette, too, devising sure-fire systems that he imagined, at the moment of invention, would get him banned from every major casino. Emma had disapproved of that as well. Placing a £10 chip on a roulette table was a hundred times worse than pushing a tenpenny piece into a fruit-machine – Emma's mathematics had always been faultless, and there was only one suitable recipient for his extravagance.

Their first Christmas together he had bought her a £10,000 ring which he had put into a balloon and then blown up. The balloon hung above her head all day while she sullenly wondered where her Christmas present was. He would never forget the expression on her face when he had burst the balloon with his cigar in the evening, and the ring had fallen into her lap. It was a greed that he found deeply unattractive.

Watching the last of the sunbathers gather their towels, he was glad all that was behind him. He didn't know what was in front of him, but he was happy to forget the past. Bachelors with their girlfriends were quite different from married men with their wives, he told himself. You could spot the difference at 400 yards in a fog, let alone across his own small bar. The bachelor was animated, enthused. The married man slumped silently, his hash settled, his goose cooked, his money spent, his sexual options reduced to no option at all. In his bar the couples who hardly spoke to each other were the married ones.

In his bar at the moment, Kim sat talking to Sylvia about life in Malaga jail. Sylvia had visited her boyfriend that afternoon with the usual vodka-filled orange, and was concerned at how ill he looked. Kim could not guess what diseases a man might contract in prison, and didn't want to try. She had her own health to worry about. She thought that she was probably six months pregnant now and she never saw a doctor. If she had been in England, life would have consisted of frequent visits to doctors, nurses, maternity hospitals and scanning machines that would have told her not only what her baby now weighed, but also the precise date of its arrival.

She stood up and walked across the bar; standing was sometimes more comfortable than sitting.

A woman came in carrying a large suitcase. She looked at Kim who was now bending in an exercise that sometimes relieved her discomfort.

'*Estoy embarazada*,' Kim said, by way of explanation.

'Well, don't be embarrassed,' said the woman.

'No, it means I'm pregnant. Sorry. Didn't realize you were British. Can I get you a drink?'

The woman left her suitcase near the door and sat on a stool at the bar.

'I'll have a lemonade,' she said. 'I've been drinking on the plane.'

Kim gave her a Sprite. 'Holiday?' she asked.

'Sort of. I've got to find a place to stay.'

'The Florida is nice,' Kim told her. 'Are you alone?'

The woman leaned back on her stool. She had a pale, tired face with beautiful big eyes, and auburn hair that had obviously been looked after by a good hairdresser.

'Quite alone,' she said. 'I had a husband once, but he left me.'

'Leaving you with nothing?' suggested Sylvia.

'I wouldn't say nothing. He left a losing betting slip on the Grand National, a signed photograph of Henry Cooper, a Fleetwood Mac album, an extraordinarily offensive letter from the income tax people and a pair of socks.'

'That's men,' said Sylvia. 'Where is he now?'

'Well, he can't be far away,' said the woman. 'This is his bar.'

Matthew had always collected coincidences, but even he was startled to see Emma sitting at the bar in her Jaeger suit. He had been thinking about her as he opened the door, and there she was. Only Lady was delighted.

'Emma,' he said.

'Hallo, Matthew. Congratulations.'

'What on?'

'I hear you're about to become a father.'

He walked past her to Kim and kissed her on the cheek.

'Is everything O K?' he whispered.

'Fine. A bit of a shock.'

'Quite.'

He addressed his wife over the bar. 'What brings you here?'

'I thought I'd have a holiday.'

A holiday? he thought. Here? What was wrong with somewhere east of the Urals, at the back end of nowhere?

There were lots of places she could have chosen. Tristan da Cunha. Baffin Island. Dronning Maud Land, promising gaiety and romance in the Southern Ocean.

'Also, I want to talk to you,' she said.

'How did you know I was here?'

'I rang your father.'

Of course, he thought. His father, with his quaint ideas about marriages being meant to last, would have passed on his whereabouts gladly, in the hope that a reconciliation might follow. His father was a man of honour. Who knew what agonies he was enduring at the way his sons had developed?

Matthew observed the huge suitcase which loomed alarmingly by the door and marvelled at his situation. Here was the wife who had created all his problems, posing as a friend. And here was his girlfriend, six months pregnant, looking hurt. And he was in the middle. Men in this situation were usually found soon afterwards hanging in a shoe cupboard. He should have disappeared into the clamorous crowd down here as soon as he arrived, and not bought a business. Putting his name up outside a bar had made him a sitting duck.

He took Kim to one side. 'I'll have to take her out for a meal. Find out what's going on. OK?'

She gave him a look which seemed to carry fear, anger and surprise all in one brief expression, and then she nodded.

Hungry himself, he took Emma to the Beefeater, which barbecued fillet steaks like nobody else. It was crowded as usual, but they got a table outside in the alley.

'I'm still your wife, Matthew,' was her opening remark when the waiter had scribbled their order. 'And I have no money, and nowhere to stay. I thought you might put me up.'

'We have a one-room flat over the bar, Emma. One bed. A pregnant woman and a dog. What do you mean – no money?'

The dangers that he could see clearly now seemed to multiply as he considered them.

Problem one: if she went to the local authorities and told them that she was his wife, she could claim half ownership of the bar. Problem two: not knowing what had happened to his marriage, he had described himself as single on the plethora of forms he had signed during the transaction. A dishonest statement on a public form was not something that the Spanish enjoyed. He could soon be sucking vodka-filled oranges in Malaga jail. The impulse to throttle this materialistic cow would have to be stifled. Kid gloves, he told himself. Propitiatory gestures.

'The tax man has taken all the money, Matthew,' she answered. 'And my solicitor has failed to get a penny maintenance out of you.'

'Well, who set the tax men on us?' he asked.

'I was distraught. I was foolish.'

'You were vindictive, Emma. You've created your own problem. What about the business?'

'I've been voted out. Once your forty-two per cent was split between the three of us, the other two had sixty per cent.'

He worked it out. Fourteen per cent for each of them took Emma's twenty-six per cent to forty, and the sixteen they each had to thirty.

'Well, you've still got the shares. You still get the profits even if you don't work there for a salary.'

'There are no profits. The tax thing has ruined it and the firm misses you.'

'I always knew it would.'

'Don't you miss it? Look at you now. You used to be immaculate in your splendid suits and Turnbull and Asser shirts. Now, in old shirts and jeans, you look like a hippie. What have you done?'

'I've eliminated stress from my life, Emma. At least, I thought I had.'

'Running a bar? It's so plebeian.'

He recalled the matrimonial gulag to which she referred so fondly and his blood ran cold. Now she was back again to enfilade the new utopia he was struggling to create.

'It's honest toil, Emma. One of your great faults was that you never knew where money came from.'

'It's hard when you once had so much.'

The steaks arrived with chips and house wine. Crowds milled past, some of them searching in vain for an empty table at the Beefeater.

Pouring wine for his wife, Matthew looked for changes in her now that she had dealt with the changes in him. The intervening months had brought about a certain edginess, as well they might have done, and she had probably lost a little weight. The eyes which he had once thought beautiful seemed now, in the present tense situation, merely intimidating. But the red hair was as sensational as ever – there was no neglect there, whatever the financial position.

He looked at her and tried to guess her intentions. Would she stay and bleed him dry? Did she understand that half the bar could be hers? Had she arrived in the hope that her marriage was not dead?

'When's the baby due?' she asked, grimacing at the house wine.

'September, we think.'

'Well, that tells me something.'

He shouldn't have named a month.

'It's funny that we never had one,' she said. 'Kim seems a nice girl, and I've spent months hating her.'

'A hectic business life isn't conducive to having babies. You have to relax to become pregnant. And, yes, Kim is a nice girl. Listen, where are you going to stay?'

'On the beach?'

'I'll put you up in a hotel.'

He pointed at the circular towers of a hotel at the end of

the alley. The El Puerto was a lively place, full of package holidaymakers. He didn't imagine that she would want to stay there long.

'How much money did you take out of England, anyway?' she asked.

'Not much.'

'Enough to buy a bar.'

As in the old days, most of her remarks seemed to hit a painful spot.

'Well,' he said, 'I do have a millionaire brother living up in the hills.'

'How is he? They. Is Mark still here?'

'They're both fine except that Danny drinks too much.'

'Your father was very upset by the story in the paper.'

'I was hoping he wouldn't see it.'

'I gather that somebody took great pleasure in producing it at the golf club.'

Matthew could imagine, but didn't want to. The pangs of remorse that arrived when he thought about his father could mar a day.

'How come you fetched up here?' Emma asked.

'We drove south and ran out of land. The car wasn't amphibious.'

'That isn't true, is it? You'd already put Lady on the flight to Malaga.'

'So I had. How did you know?'

'The police knew that much.'

He forked his last chip. She was beginning to unnerve him with her innocent, information-collecting ways. The less that she knew the better, until he could find out which way she was going to jump.

'You must have had a false passport,' she said, pushing her plate away. She picked up what was left of her wine and drank it with distaste.

'As a matter of fact, I did.'

'It's amazing how quite respectable people can slip

easily into the criminal life. It certainly fooled the police. They knew you'd gone because of Lady, but they couldn't figure how you got out.' She put her empty wine glass on the table and looked at him. 'I suppose you want a divorce with a baby on the way.'

'I thought you were already seeking one?'

'I changed my mind.'

He saw then that she was here to get him back. She had always been a great one for second thoughts.

'I'm not interested in divorce,' he said, 'seeing that I would never get married again.'

'What about Kim?'

'She's still married, and just as disillusioned with the idea as I am. Look, I ought to be getting back. Moving barrels of beer around when you are six months pregnant is not a good thing.'

'Well, if we're still married, Matthew, you have responsibilities.'

He called the waiter over and gave him a 5,000 peseta note.

'Come and look at the hotel,' he told her.

When the waiter had brought his change they walked the few yards down the alley to the seafront. There was a small fairground on the beach side of the Paseo Maritimo, and scores of children were riding ponies and toy motor-bikes, and driving bumper cars.

The El Puerto, only a short walk along the front, was a sand-coloured hotel built in two circular towers. It reminded Matthew of Centre Point in London, despite its roundness.

They went in and picked their way through a noisy crowd of half-dressed holidaymakers who were shouting to each other in half a dozen languages, and eventually got the attention of a reception clerk.

'How long shall I book?' he asked her.

She thought. 'A week. I might not like it.'

He gave the clerk her passport, and wondered whether her 'it' meant the hotel or the visit itself. Might she demand a better hotel, a luxury £500-a-week haven with Buck's Fizz for breakfast which, she would soon discover, abounded on this coast? Was this going to be one of those open-ended visits that never found an end? He wrote his name and address on a form and signed a document which said that he promised to pay the bill.

That seemed to take care of everything and, anxious to get away, he turned to say goodbye. But she slipped her arm in his.

'I'll come back to your bar for a drink,' she said. 'I've forgotten my suitcase.'

Mark slept fitfully through a night that was punctuated by vivid dreams. 'Cottage by the Sea' soared in public esteem. It was impossible to avoid on the radio, and difficult to avoid in the street where it drifted out from those shops which used music to generate trade. Garrulous disc jockeys with ten-word vocabularies lauded his song with adjectives that few understood. Strange young men who earned their livings writing about the arcane world of pop music flew out to interview him in the steamy heat of a Spanish disco, and then flew home again to pass on the priceless secrets thus acquired in the carefully sculpted prose of a semi-literate anthropoid ape. Singers without a song, and comedians searching for the right note on which to end their tired acts, took up 'Cottage by the Sea' and found a warm public response they had previously missed. The song rocketed to number one in the charts, and stayed there despite the efforts of the finest musical talents on both sides of the Atlantic to dislodge it.

It was a night which made waking up an anti-climax. He boiled an egg and tried to untangle the reality from the dream. Was Tom Jones really going to record his song or had he dreamt that, too? A coffee brought him to full wakefulness, and he knew that that part, at least, was true. But the dreams were hopelessly overblown. Whatever success was coming his way was arriving too late for the fickle world of pop. Now that people who couldn't sing became rich shouting lines you couldn't hear, what hope was there for a beautiful tune which had words you were supposed to listen to and find moving?

By the time he took his morning stroll in Banus he had begun to feel hopeful again. The people who wandered along the water's edge, enjoying their brief annual date with the sun, looked like record buyers to a man, and not just any old disc. They were people of taste and discernment. They were his public!

He decided that it was time to break the news; perhaps congratulations would make it more real to him. After an afternoon siesta, and an early evening mixed grill in El Gaucho, he rang Daniel and Leanda and invited them to meet him at Matt's Place.

'I have some good news,' he told his brother.

'You never have good news, Mark.'

'Well, I have some now. Be sure to bring some of your ill-gotten gains.'

'This is expensive good news, is it?'

'Matthew has champagne in his cellar that he has been saving for just such an occasion.'

Cruising up the coast in a taxi soon afterwards, he looked forward with some relish to telling his rich brothers that, even without an education, he could earn big money, too. It was the sort of situation that he had rehearsed many times in his head.

The Rolls Royces and Cadillacs swept down the golden mile where every developer in Europe seemed to have some plan for improvements. Beachfront apartments sprouted among the trees, placards offered ten-year mortgages with 300 days of sunshine every year thrown in at no extra cost.

Perhaps the flamboyant life that was permanently on offer here to other people would soon be the sort of thing that he could afford from his back pocket: the luxury villa, the private pool, the rooftop solarium, the jacuzzi bath. Security, privacy, comfort and a first-rate investment as well.

When the taxi dropped him on the front in Fuengirola, his tip was absurdly generous: he was already behaving as he imagined the rich behaved.

The tableau which greeted him through the window of Matt's Place destroyed his picture of the future and returned him to earth with a bump. He saw Matthew in the middle of the room with Kim on one side and Emma on the other. He thought for a moment that he was dreaming again. It was a long time since he had seen Emma and she was the last person he expected to see here now. He stopped for a moment and wondered whether to go in. The expression on Matthew's face suggested that this was not the best place for a celebration this evening, but he had come this far and decided that other people's problems were not going to spoil his evening.

'Hiya,' he said. 'Your very best champagne, *camarero*.'

'Good evening, Mark,' said Emma formally. 'How are you?'

'Champagne?' Matthew asked. 'What do you know that I don't know?'

'I'm rich, brother. At least, I'm going to be. Bring on the bubbly, *por favor*.'

Matthew disappeared into the cellar below the bar and Mark turned to Emma.

'What brings you here then?' he asked.

'I came to see my husband.'

'You only left him with tuppence. You don't want that as well, do you?'

She gave him a cool look and picked up a gin from the counter. 'I don't think remarks like that will be very helpful in the present situation,' she said.

He turned to Kim who sat looking miserable on the other side of the bar. Getting a party off the ground in here tonight was obviously going to be something of a challenge.

'O K, kid?' he asked.

'As well as can be expected,' she told him. 'I'm getting a lot of backache.'

'Isn't it wonderful?' said Emma. 'Matthew going to be a father!'

'Absolutely terrific,' said Mark. 'I love babies. Particularly if they belong to somebody else.'

At that moment Daniel and Leanda walked in.

'Good lord, it's Emma,' said Leanda.

Watching this awkward reunion, Mark thought that the embarrassment quotient was almost excruciating. Emma was embarrassed to be there with pregnant Kim in the background, Daniel was embarrassed by the newspaper publicity he had received, Leanda was embarrassed to meet Emma in front of Kim and Matthew was so embarrassed by the whole business that when he returned with three bottles of Moët et Chandon he placed them on a table in the middle of the room without saying a word and looked like a man who was trying to find the exit.

'A holiday, is it?' asked Daniel.

'A sort of holiday, Danny,' said Emma.

'You could have gone to Crete.'

'Matthew isn't in Crete.'

'Ah,' said Daniel. He turned to his brother. 'Open the champagne, Matthew. I'm paying, apparently.'

Matthew opened the first bottle and moved away gratefully to serve four Scandinavians who had come in for a game of pool. He winked at Kim, who stared unhappily back. She fondled Lady with one hand, and noted the Scandinavians' bill with the other.

'I can see you live it up on this coast,' said Emma. 'Is it champagne every night?'

'And every morning,' said Daniel. 'You're dead a long time, see?'

'It's nice to be able to afford it.'

'You were never far from a bottle when we were in England, I seem to remember,' Leanda said.

'That was then. This is now.'

'How long did you plan to stay?'

'I haven't decided,' Emma said. 'Are you all enjoying yourselves here? I thought Danny looked very contented in the paper.'

'Everybody saw that bloody newspaper,' said Leanda. 'I always imagined my friends improving their minds with the serious Sundays, but there they all are, delving into other people's dirt.'

'Reading about other people's misfortunes is how they cheer themselves up,' said Mark.

'I don't call having a million quid a misfortune,' said Emma. 'You should see my current account.'

'Never mind, Emma. At least you can fly to England without a policeman saying hallo at Heathrow,' Leanda told her.

'Well, so can you,' said Daniel. 'You can go on a shopping spree in your beloved Harrods, if you want.'

He scowled at Mark to show his displeasure at the company he found himself in, but Mark had already made up his mind about this evening. Emma's unwelcome arrival had filled other heads with other things and cheated him of his moment of glory. He said he had to go to work and left the bar.

'What is this evening all about, anyway?' Daniel asked when Mark had gone. 'Why are we drinking champagne?'

Matthew was sitting behind the counter with Kim.

'I've no idea,' he said. 'He didn't tell us.'

TEN

THE MORNING that he woke up face down in a ditch, Daniel began to feel that his life was not all it should be. It only took an hour or two of drinking champagne by the pool later that day for him to reach some decisions about how it could be improved.

The most important of these was that Leanda should have a baby. If ever a family needed a child to give it unity and purpose – not to mention a little useful work – it was his.

'I want you to come off the Pill,' he told her when she joined him in the sun.

'I'm not on the Pill,' she replied. 'I gave it up months ago.'

He was surprised. 'You did? Why?'

'Is a nun on the Pill? Listen, most nights the question isn't what you are going to do in bed but whether you'll manage to climb into it.'

'Well, last night I didn't.'

He had called into Mijas to buy a newspaper and, as Leanda was visiting a Dutch woman she had met at her Spanish class, he had stayed on for a drink or two. Or eight, as it had turned out. He was sitting outside Los Arcos and watching the children play in the main square when Steve Finch sauntered past with his *Financial Times* and felt the need to discuss budget deficits, global economic upswings and Mrs Thatcher's privatization programme.

'I have a night off,' he said, ordering them both whiskies. 'My wife has gone down to Banus to watch your brother play the piano. Not my sort of thing at all.'

Whisky was not Daniel's favourite drink if he was out

on a bender, but eight slipped down without any trouble at all. Discussing which great British service would eventually provide the biggest profit to its new investors was the last thing he remembered.

'You have decided that it is time to have a family, have you?' said Leanda. 'Do you think you are up to it?'

'The responsibilities of fatherhood?'

'No, the mechanics of procreation.'

'You're very funny, dear. One day somebody is going to throw you in the pool.'

'My, we *are* getting physical today.'

But she was laughing happily, because she wanted a child as well.

'We made love once,' he said. 'I'm almost sure we did.'

They were both laughing now.

'I would describe you as more couchant than rampant these days,' she said. 'The copulation explosion seemed to miss you.'

'It's the men who have headaches now, I read.'

But her remarks disturbed him. Could he attribute his languid libido to alcohol, or had he already reached the stage when sexual intercourse became a duty rather than a pleasure?

That evening he didn't drink at all. He found one of the videos that Mrs Plumridge had brought them at their urgent request, and spent two hours watching British television that Britain had seen a month before. It was an eerie sensation that made him feel, once or twice, as if he were back in England. Tree-planting in Scotland, Contraception for Kangaroos – was British television getting worse, or had his malevolent mother-in-law alighted on the most tedious programmes out of malice? A news bulletin arrived with items that were now history: the general-election campaign, an air crash, a report on Aids and an explosion in Ulster, which provoked a surly, fat-faced man to talk about the 'Rooman Cart-licks'. How it

167

all came back to him! Watching this stuff, he discovered, was a cure for homesickness. Only an episode of *Dallas*, which Mrs Plumridge had provocatively included, left him wishing frustratedly for more.

Leanda loved soap operas. To her they were more real than real life, and their absence from hers was the greatest single deprivation that she faced. It had to be an American soap opera, with the money and the power that the Americans enjoyed looking up to; she enjoyed looking up to it, too. Who would want the living standards shown in a British soap opera? While the Americans looked at the stars and dreamed of success, the British looked at the mud and rationalized failure.

'I'm going to have a shower,' she said. 'I've left you something in the bed.'

'Is it a woman?'

'No, it's something you'll notice.'

He went to his own bathroom and had a shower, too. The idea of having a child had grown on him during the day – a boy, a girl, it made no difference. Walking at one, talking at two, beating him at chess at three. He had even reached that awkward moment when the little thing had asked where Daddy got his money from, but there would be plenty of time to prepare for difficult questions like that. He decided on a dab of Armani eau pour homme.

What Leanda had left him in the bed was a good-luck card.

She came in wrapped in a pink towel like a one-piece bathing costume and he suddenly remembered how sexy she was. He had forgotten that already: there was no greater passion-killer than marriage. He kissed her brown thighs as she stood by the side of their four-poster bed. She had the legs of a model.

'Will you remember how to do it?' she asked. 'First thing is, you need an erection.'

'I remember that bit. I had one in '84.'

'I don't remember that.'

'I was on a bus.'

He pulled her into bed with him as she laughed and the towel was left on the floor. They rolled across the bed locked in each other's arms. He had read somewhere that it was dangerous to lie underneath a woman – it overloaded the left ventricle of the heart. That was how Attila the Hun had died. But when he was on top his face became buried in the pillow and he couldn't breathe. He did quite a lot of breathing when he made love. Once he tried it side by side and nearly broke it off. Sexual intercourse was a difficult undertaking, and there were no evening classes.

His face was now against the side of her head.

'I've got one,' he said. 'I've got one.'

'One what?'

'You know. What I had on that bus.'

'Well, for Christ's sake don't lose it. They're like gold dust round here.'

Sex had always been funny for them, an orgy of pants and laughter, and tonight it was again. He eased himself on to her and thrust and thrust and found what he was looking for and thrust some more; there was no hint of gratitude.

'One more time then,' she said when he stopped. 'Let's do it properly this time.'

'Christ,' he said, feeling wonderful. 'That was just a warm-up lap.'

Matthew was in bed with Kim. She lay on her side while he rubbed her lower back. The nights were disturbed now by her attempts to get comfortable and her frequent need to go to the bathroom. Only Lady, sprawled out on the old Spanish sofa, woke refreshed every morning, demanding a walk on the seafront.

The disappearance of sex from his life had passed almost

169

unnoticed by Matthew, who never closed the bar before three o'clock and arrived in bed exhausted. No matter how many times Kim woke him, he was soon asleep again; often the dream survived the interruption.

'Rub it lower,' she said. 'Here.'

He massaged her back gently and suddenly she fell asleep. He lay there wondering again what sex the baby would be. Nearly all his friends had started with a daughter, a phenomenon they attributed, after a recent survey, to alcoholic consumption. Of course, there would soon be a new survey attributing it to sugar, or lead in the air, or remote-control devices for television sets. He had instigated a few surveys himself in the interests of consumer research.

The prospect of a baby was beginning to fascinate him. He had always been strangely depressed by the diminutive and red-faced replicas of his friends, reminding him of his own mortality. But the period of a human pregnancy was long enough to become adjusted to the idea that you were going to become a father too. He was looking forward to it, although he remembered that back in England when a friend was a father-to-be it was the single men who expressed envy on hearing the news; those who were already fathers maintained a tactful but ominous silence.

'It won't stop kicking,' she said, suddenly awake.

He ran his hand across her stomach and felt the sudden bump where an arm or a leg was protesting from within. The bump came and went and came again.

'Energetic little sod,' he said. 'Soon be shifting barrels for us.'

'If you still have a bar,' Kim said.

He rubbed her back again. 'Don't you worry about Emma, Kim. I'm going to have her dropped off by the fishermen. She should be washed ashore in Naples in a few weeks time. They're quite used to that sort of thing there and won't even bother to try to find out who she was.'

'What *are* you going to do?'

It wasn't only the baby that kept Kim awake these days. Emma hovered, a spectre at the feast, haunting her now with fears that Matthew could be taken from her and transformed reluctantly into the person he had once been.

'It's very difficult,' he admitted. 'I've got to go on being nice to her. If she turned nasty she could ruin me again.'

'It's ridiculous. You can't go on like that. How long for? When does it end? It's not fair on me.'

'What can I do? I can't buy her off with the money I've got left.'

'But she knows you have money. She keeps trying to find out what you paid for the bar.'

'I'm in a cleft stick.'

'It *isn't* fair.'

'It's quite fair,' he said angrily. 'I committed the unpardonable folly of marrying the bitch.'

They lay in silence for some time, but the concerns raised by their conversation prevented sleep.

'You forgot to tell me what your father wrote,' he said finally.

A bright blue envelope had arrived that morning from Preston Bissett, near Buckingham, where Mr Raynsford was the clerk of the local council. With three daughters, all of whom had caused him trouble in one way or another, he had taken the break-up of her marriage and her flight to Spain with equanimity. A letter signed by both parents, and possibly coloured by a poor view of her choice of husband, had arrived wishing her luck soon after she arrived.

But now, in the throes of pregnancy, she had felt obliged to let them know that their first grandchild was on the way. It wouldn't arrive in the circumstances which they had probably imagined over the years, but she thought it her duty to tell them. A strong religious faith, which had carried her confidently through adolescence, had dwindled in the face of the realities of adulthood to a vague desire to stay honest with her friends and relatives, if with nobody else.

Dear Kim, *her father had written in his immaculate handwriting*,

It is naturally disturbing to your parents to learn that you are expecting a baby by a man whom we have never met and you are not married to, but we have a television set and are not unfamiliar with the way the world is going. We look forward to meeting Matthew Ward, despite his chequered past. Robert telephoned your mother last week to inquire about your whereabouts. It seems that he is anxious to get a divorce, although I can't imagine that he is contemplating matrimony again. I hope that when your divorce is through, you and Matthew Ward will be married. Your mother assures me that there is no social stigma attached to illegitimacy these days, but I can assure you that there are legal complications for which your child won't thank you. Whatever you decide, be assured also of your parents' love.'

'He said he hopes we get married,' said Kim.

Mark was in bed with Alison Finch. It was difficult to say who was more surprised.

She had arrived at Jay's alone soon after ten, wearing white slacks and a yellow silk blouse. There was a big handsome man with a lot of curly black hair singing his heart out at the piano, and she ordered an icy, dry martini and took a stool there. By the time he had sung 'She', 'Moon River' and 'The Way We Were', she had established an eye contact that unsettled him.

He saw a beautiful woman of about his own age, with lovely eyes, a sensual mouth and an expression which conveyed, more than expressions normally manage, a pure intelligence. She was dressed cheerfully but stylishly. He took her for a tart.

'A stunning lady,' said Alvin, when they changed places.

'She's not your daughter, is she?'

'Don't mention that. I'm still having nightmares.'

Mark went over to the bar for a San Miguel and by the time he had been served the woman was beside him. He turned to give his usual performance, which offered the politeness to the customer that was much encouraged at Jay's, along with a firm impression that a wife and six children were waiting for him at home.

'Alison Finch,' she said. 'You must be Mark. I can tell by your hands.'

'My hands?'

'They were photographed at your brother's party. I won the champagne, by the way, but you had gone.'

'I remember you,' he said, remembering. 'You were with your father.'

'Husband, actually.'

'Sorry.'

'Not at all. There is a twenty year age difference.'

'Let me get you a drink. It looks like a Martini. You know Danny, do you?'

'My husband discusses money with him. Money is what my husband is interested in. Will you sing 'The Hungry Years' for me?'

He did and now they were in bed.

She had stayed until the end and shown no desire to go home and so he had invited her back to his tiny apartment for coffee.

'What's a nice man like you doing, living alone?' she asked, pretending not to notice the untidiness which surrounded her.

'It is strange, isn't it?' he said. 'I think I'm ahead of my time. Only a few years ago a man who hadn't got married was regarded as sexually odd. Now he's regarded as mentally bright.'

'Quite right, too. Marriage is a dead duck. Do you know what Balzac said about husbands?'

'Balzac? I've heard of him. We musicians get a lot of time to read.'

'He was a French writer.'

'Which one was Balzac and which one was Flaubert?'

'Well, Balzac was Balzac, and Flaubert was Flaubert.'

'That clarifies it.'

'Balzac was older.'

'And what did he say about husbands?'

'He said the majority of husbands reminded him of an orang-utan trying to play the violin.'

'And that accords with your view of things, does it?'

'I got married at twenty to a man who was forty, and now I'm thirty and he's fifty. I prefer bachelors who play the piano since you ask.'

'Black or white coffee?'

There were two upright chairs that properly belonged to a dinner table, and a low table between them that was covered with sheet music. He tried to shift some of this to make way for their cups.

'You sing beautifully,' she told him. 'Do you write songs as well?'

'As a matter of fact,' he said, delighted that somebody had at last asked him, and doubly delighted that it was her, 'Tom Jones is about to record my latest.'

'Phew!' she said, impressed. 'That *is* something.'

'I could be looking for a larger home.'

'You need it,' she said. 'There's hardly room to make love in here.'

'It's so long since I made love to anybody I hardly noticed.'

'Would you like to make love to me?'

'To see if there's room, you mean?'

'Yes, we'd better find out.'

174

'It's as well to know,' he agreed. 'It could be useful when the new occupant arrives.'

His bed was only four feet wide, but she cuddled up so closely to him that although he took up most of it, it didn't seem to matter. Alison Finch's mouth, so inviting to contemplate, was bliss to kiss.

'A hard man is good to find,' she said, finding one.

'Did Balzac say that as well?'

'It sounds like Mae West. A man in the house is worth two in the street, and all that.'

'Alison Finch,' he said. 'What a discovery you are!'

'I should have married a creative person in the first place,' she said quietly. 'You give my husband books and he cooks them.'

'Is he rich?'

'Immensely.'

'How did he manage that?'

'Inheritance, investment. That's all he ever did. He turns money into more money without getting out of bed. A quick jaunt through the financial pages and a couple of phone calls before breakfast. That's why we're here. "You only need a telephone," I told him. "They have telephones in Marbella and you'll pay less tax on your unearned income.' so we bought a house at San Pedro and we've been here eight years.'

'The hungry years?' he asked.

The headboard began to bang rhythmically against the wall.

'I think the hungry years are over.'

ELEVEN

AN IDEA that had originated some weeks earlier, and was intended to guide Daniel towards interests more rewarding than drinking until he fell over, took them one hot morning to the golf course at Los Monteros. The Rio Real course was the most beautifully manicured on the coast with picturesque greens and views of the sea. The water hazard was the river which gave the course its name; it kept reappearing, inviting disaster, but contributed to the setting which made it worth the 4,000 pesetas green fees.

'The troubadour looks a bit perky this morning,' said Matthew when they had reached the fourth. 'What happened to the morose brother we knew and loved?'

'He's found a woman,' said Daniel. 'There's a zip in his stride which suggests leg-over to me.'

'Well, his sex life is high up on a list of things I don't want to hear about,' Matthew said, looking for a wood.

Mark drove off and was satisfied with his shot. The ball bounced up the fairway and seemed to be going in the right direction. They had come under the Malaga–Gibraltar road to reach this hole, a long, tedious par-four where you struggled if your drive was weak.

'As a matter of fact, Tom Jones is going to record one of my songs,' he told them. 'That's why you were drinking champagne the other night, but the arrival of Emma pushed it into the background.'

They were full of apologies now, and dropped their clubs to congratulate him. Mark smiled happily. His cheerfulness this morning had nothing to do with 'Cottage by the Sea', but the song was enough to throw his brothers off the scent which they had correctly picked up.

'Will you be rich?' asked Matthew.

'I'm expecting a fortune,' he told them.

'Am I going to be known as Mark Ward's brother?' Daniel asked.

'I think when fame arrives I might stay buttoned on the subject of my brothers.'

'Perhaps you could buy my missus off,' Matthew suggested. 'She's following me around like a private eye.'

Daniel put his ball on the tee and gazed at the prospect. Then he drove off quickly and smiled at the others.

'I'm on the green from there,' he announced.

'If you didn't drink so much you could be a good golfer,' Mark told him. He yearned to be good at the game himself, but sporting success had always eluded him. A frame-winning break, a set-winning serve, a punch that took a title – those were the things that he had dreamed of as a boy, but all he had ever done better than most was play the piano.

'You've got a problem there with Emma,' said Daniel as Matthew was about to drive. Matthew scowled at the gamesmanship, but drove anyway. The ball vanished somewhere to the right.

'You can beat us both without those tactics,' he said. 'I haven't got a problem. I'm going to drown her.'

'Why don't you take her across to Tangier and sell her?' Mark suggested. 'Some fat sultan in his tent might make you an offer you can't refuse.'

'And the following week she would walk into my bar. It's like trying to lose your shadow.'

At the fifth tee they could see the sea again, and on the eleventh they found pomegranates growing. Daniel's lead had extended to the point where there was no longer a competition; the course was a par-72 and he was going to get round in under 100. His opponents were distracted by women, one by love and one by hate, but he didn't know that as he forged ahead in the searing sun.

In the Stud Bar afterwards – named after the footwear allowed, not the sexual proclivities of the customers – the drinkers were sunburnt, cosmopolitan and rich. 'Do you know the Pierre on Fifth Avenue?' a man asked, but when Mark turned round to tell him that he knew the pier at Southend he saw the man was talking to Kevin Keegan.

'Will you still mix with us when you're rich?' Matthew asked Mark.

'Not if I can help it.'

'Big brother makes it at last,' said Daniel. 'But I still think there's a woman in the scenario somewhere.'

The desire to talk about it was too strong now that they were sitting down with a beer. 'You're quite right,' he told them. 'I've met a lady.'

'I thought nobody could ever replace Jean Simmons in your affections,' said Matthew. 'Who is she?'

'Is this marriage?' Daniel asked. 'You double your costs and halve your freedom.'

'Well, I shall soon be able to afford it, won't I?'

Matthew and Daniel looked at each other and shook their heads in mock horror.

'Shall I tell your big brother, or will you?' asked Daniel.

'You don't get married when you can afford to get married, Mark,' said Matthew. 'You get married when you can afford to get divorced. That's why the very rich get hitched so often. Marriage is something that they can afford. No one else can, but they do it in their blind stupidity. Learn from the mess I'm in.'

'Another thing,' said Daniel. 'Women are different from men. They don't want to talk about the things that we talk about. They will tell you, if you ask them, that they don't waste their time talking about things they can't change, like politics and sport.'

'They talk about things they can change, like husbands,' said Matthew.

Mark finished his beer and stood up.

'What a droll duo my little brothers are! The married misogynists! I don't feel in need of advice from either of you. I'm the one who likes women – remember? And we successful song writers can't sit here chewing the fat with the criminal fraternity when there's a beautiful woman to meet.'

He walked out of the bar with a wave.

'He's a new man,' said Daniel. 'He's changed.'

'I know,' Matthew said. 'And he's going to be a star.'

The defection of his tennis partner created a void in Daniel's life that he quickly filled. Steve Finch had once revealed, during a brief absence from the financial pages, a fondness for chess, and they agreed to play one game a week, at five o'clock every Tuesday. The move from the tennis court to the chess board was a good idea: most days it was too hot for tennis.

They sat in easy chairs on the patio with drinks on the table at their elbows and the chess board on a foot-high marble table between them. Steve Finch took chess almost as seriously as he took his investments and knew a lot about the game. He knew the difference between a Sicilian defence and a Nimzo-Indian, and would occasionally pass along the information that Petrosian had once made a similar move. Daniel was delighted to hear it. He had lost very few games of chess in his life, and to find a worthy opponent out here was a happy discovery.

One evening they sat in their usual silence, sipping sangria and staring at the board in solemn concentration. Daniel loved the game – two people sitting head to head for more than an hour without speaking, the ultimate in un-sociability.

Steve Finch's bishop swept across the board and took Daniel's king's rook pawn. 'Bobby Fischer played that move in the first game in Iceland in 1972,' he said.

'And lost the game,' said Daniel, moving forward the knight pawn to trap the bishop. 'A poisoned pawn.'

'I know he lost the game, Danny, but you're not Boris Spassky, are you? Fischer forfeited the second game as well by not appearing and was two–nil down after two games yet level after five. Unbelievable. They don't play chess like that any more.'

Daniel moved his king towards the bishop that he would eventually take. Steve Finch seemed unusually talkative tonight. He also looked bothered. He drank his sangria and examined the threatened bishop.

'I'm worried about my wife,' he said.

The remark took Daniel by surprise. He was, as usual, engrossed in the game. Was Steve Finch preparing an excuse for the defeat which now seemed likely?

'Why?' he asked. 'Is she spending more than you're earning?'

Steve Finch shook his head, and then sat back is if he could see no hope on the chessboard.

'No, she's got a man. At least, I think she has. Have you heard anything?'

'Heard anything?'

'Gossip. About her.'

The sound of pennies dropping in his head seemed so loud that he imagined his opponent could hear them. One thing he could remember about the night that he slept in a ditch was that Alison Finch had gone to Puerto Banus to hear Mark play the piano – that was why Steve Finch had been drinking whisky with him. And now Mark had a woman!

He wondered whether his expression betrayed these internal conclusions. He also wondered whether Steve Finch already had suspicions in that direction and was deliberately raising the subject with Mark's brother.

'Where would I hear gossip?' he asked. 'From the

barman in Casa Pepe? As a matter of fact, gossip is one of the things I miss most on this coast.'

He poured them both some more sangria and lit a cigar. The smell of jasmine and orange blossom was soon replaced by something more pungent.

Steve Finch leaned forward again and moved a pawn.

'Somebody is going to know, and I'm going to find out,' he said. 'It's happened very suddenly. I always assumed she was happy here.'

'What makes you think she's got a man?'

'Oh, it's quite clear. Firstly, she's out a hell of a lot which she never was before, and, secondly, she goes round the house singing.'

'Really? What does she sing?'

'Something called "Cottage by the Sea", mostly. Heard of it?'

Daniel shook his head. 'The most recent song I know was written by Gilbert and Sullivan. You're older than her, aren't you?'

'Twenty years,' said Steve Finch briefly. 'It's never seemed to matter.'

The carefree personality who allowed alcohol to dribble down his chin when he was trapped by a bore had disappeared. He watched Daniel remove his bishop from the board, but his mind wasn't on it.

'You think your marriage is all right, but you never really know,' he said. 'Perhaps I've been too preoccupied with making money.'

'I always thought that was the man's role,' Daniel said, studying the board. He wasn't going to let this victory slip from his grasp whatever the distraction.

'It's the man's role, but it's not enough for the ladies,' Steve Finch said. 'I was married once before and she left me because I was obsessed with money. Or so she said. She flew to America with a man who reputedly had an eight-inch willy, so I was never entirely sure of the motivation.'

'Didn't I hear that Alison wanted children and you didn't?'

'Where did you hear that?'

'She mentioned it at my party to somebody.'

'I thought she'd got over that. Maybe she hasn't. I don't know. I never pretended that I understood women.'

He leaned forward again and looked at the board. Then he knocked his king over.

'You can have this game,' he said. 'I'm afraid I'm not in the right mood to give my best. What I'm going to do is drive down to Fuengirola and wander about. Perhaps I can catch her with somebody. I've got to get it sorted out. I don't fancy living here on my own.'

'Why don't you talk to her? That's what married couples are supposed to do. I read it in a book.'

'I haven't got anything to go on yet. I need evidence, not suspicions. Do you want to come down with me?'

'I'll stay here, Steve. Leanda is going to do me a lovely dinner when she gets out of the jacuzzi. It's what being married is all about.'

Matt's Place was crowded. They came out of the shops, or up off the beach, or down from the showers at their hotels, and although eating would figure on the evening's programme somewhere, it was drink that was at the centre of things, even for people who rarely saw the stuff at home.

They stood in groups of three, four or five, boasting about the stress-filled occupations that had paid for this trip – the rodomontade induced among strangers by several pints of Cruzcampo was tediously repetitive. Matthew fancied introducing a rule that would forbid any customer to utter more than 200 consecutive words without anybody else speaking; he had heard too many conversations ruined by women of both sexes.

He was cornered himself by a middle-aged woman who

evidently had no friends and had selected the barman as a suitable audience for her life story. The banality of her conversation made his head ache. The signs which should have alerted him to the presence of a non-stop talking woman – the frequent puffing of a cigarette, the ever-moving hands, the deep, horizontal lines scored across the forehead – had all been missed, and now he was trapped.

'He liked red wine and I like white wine, so we used to drink rosé,' she said.

From a thousand ideas in his head he couldn't pluck one reply. Whether she wanted it or not, her conversation excluded participation. Only her entertaining line in mala-propisms kept him conscious: her first husband had been 'a pillock of society', his brother was educated at 'either Eton or Harrods'.

Eventually he saw an excuse to move. A man had put his pint of beer down on the pool table.

'Excuse me,' he told the woman. A look of alarm flitted across her face. He went round the corner and asked the man to put his beer somewhere else. The group glowered at him as if his request was unreasonable. If you added their IQs together it wouldn't make two digits, he thought.

He was beginning to wonder whether he was cut out for this work. It required an enthusiasm for the human race which he now knew he did not possess. He went to the window to see if Kim was returning from the supermarket. In true Spanish fashion, they were so impressed by her pregnancy that they sent a boy back with her to carry the shopping.

Deserted in mid-stride, or bored on her own as all bores were, the woman had gone when he returned to the counter and he was able to look at the English newspaper that a customer had left earlier. A cricket match had been stopped at midday because of bad light. Looking out at the bright evening sun he found it almost impossible to imagine. A sixteen-year-old motor-cyclist who had killed a woman of thirty-two in a sex attack was ordered to be detained for five years. He thought of the prison sentence which his Q C had implied was coming his way and threw the paper angrily to the floor.

His anger was in no way softened by the sight of Emma threading her way through the crowded room. She took the recently vacated stool at the bar.

'I've brought a bill from the hotel for you,' she said. 'I'll have a gin.'

'Are you going home then?' he asked hopefully. The one fact which might have persuaded her to leave was the one thing that she didn't know when she flew out – that Kim was expecting a baby. However, it turned out that this had not decided her to cut short the visit.

'I'm staying on. I like it here,' she said. 'But the hotel want a weekly settlement.'

He poured her gin and concealed his feelings.

'How's Kim?' she asked.

Why? Have you put a spell on her? he wanted to ask.

'Fine, thanks,' he said, taking her bill. He bent down to the safe below the counter where he kept a sizeable float. All the tradesmen were paid in cash. He handed her just over 30,000 pesetas and she put it in her bag.

'Is the gin on the house?' she asked.

'Why not?' he said. 'What have you been doing?'

'Relaxing. Enjoying myself. Shopping.'

'You're not entirely penniless then?' he said.

'I'm not that stupid, am I, Matthew?'

'No, you're not,' he agreed.

A man came into the bar and took the stool next to her.

'You're Matthew,' he said, offering his hand.

Matthew shook the hand knowing that he had seen its owner somewhere.

'Steve Finch. I was at Danny's party.'

'Ah, yes. I remember.'

'You don't remember my wife? Give me a whisky, will you.'

Matthew reached for the whisky bottle. 'I always remember the wives. It's the men I sometimes forget. Yours is a very attractive little number in a blue trouser suit who won the picture competition.'

'That's her,' said Steve Finch, looking relieved. He took a huge swig of whisky. 'Have you seen her lately?'

'Tonight do you mean? No.'

'Since the party?'

Matthew shook his head. 'Should I have done?'

'I don't know whether she's been in here or not. I don't know where she's been, as a matter of fact. But she's out gallivanting somewhere and I'm rather keen to find out where. Bit of a blow to one's *amour propre* when you don't know where your wife is.'

'You've lost your wife?' Emma said. 'I've lost my husband. Life's like that.'

'Not yet I haven't,' said Steve Finch grimly. 'She'll be back tonight. The question is: where will she have been?'

'My guess is with a man,' said Emma. 'There's nothing so treacherous as folk.'

'This is my wife,' said Matthew quickly, in case Steve Finch took it into his head to knock her off the stool.

'His estranged wife,' said Emma. 'Hence my cynicism.'

'You know what it's like then,' said Steve Finch. 'I didn't get your name?'

'Emma,' said Emma.

'I thought you were pregnant?'

'It's his girlfriend who's pregnant,' Emma told him. 'This also helps my cynicism.'

'Well,' said Steve Finch, 'we've all got our problems.'

Kim appeared at the door, accompanied by a small boy carrying two large carriers of food. She scowled at Matthew as she nodded at Emma's back.

'Hallo, lovely,' he said. 'Have you spent a fortune?'

'He never called me lovely,' Emma told Steve Finch. 'Not even when I was.'

'She's definitely pregnant,' Steve Finch said. 'People seem to have pretty chaotic private lives these days.'

'You've noticed?' said Emma. 'Welcome to the 1980s.'

TWELVE

WHEN ANNA kissed an anarchist she planted bombs not flowers, thought Mark as he watched a somnolent lion basking in the sun. He was planning a song that he would call 'Revolt'. It began with words in his head that would be transferred to paper later and joined by music after that. He knew that it was the sort of thing that people were singing eight or ten years ago, and not at all the type of song that Conrad Gambardella would be looking for to follow 'Cottage by the Sea', but he had always swum against the tide. He was swimming against the tide when he wrote 'Cottage by the Sea'.

The lion stood up to take a closer look at him. Alison had suggested that they meet at the zoo – her husband hated them. It was the only one on the coast, a small zoo that lay in the shadow of Fuengirola bullring. Its star was an extrovert gibbon who swung from branch to branch of its home on an island in the pond that was the centre of the zoo. Peacocks strutted freely through the gardens, but the monkeys were the main attraction: baboons, chimpanzees, mandrills and marmosets.

It seemed to Mark to be an odd place to keep a tryst, even if zoos were not among Steve Finch's enthusiasms, but he learned, as he strolled among the leopards and the pumas, that Alison had wanted to be a vet until a change of heart at ten. In the event, she became a secretary in the city, where she met her husband in the throes of his first divorce.

They had coffee at a snack bar and wondered what to do with their day. Life so far had consisted of love in the afternoon and Jay's in the evening, but love was not an option today, Alison had told him, and the streets were full of eyes that would be surprised to see them together.

'Let's go to Malaga,' she said. 'The train ride's lovely.'

To avoid the eyes, they got a taxi from the *zoologico municipal* to the station. Trains went up the coast from Fuengirola every half hour, and they were soon enjoying a scenic view of the coast that ended only temporarily at Torremolinos where the train plunged underground to the station.

'We can't go on meeting like this,' said Alison. 'To coin a phrase.'

'What can we go on meeting like?' asked Mark.

'It's so furtive. We don't want our social life to be restricted to bed and the zoo, do we?'

He smiled at her. She had the sort of voice, he thought, that a man wants to hear on the next pillow.

'I suppose, at a pinch, we could skip the zoo bit,' he said. 'I must admit that this is a new role for me. I've never taken out another man's wife before, or had to look over my shoulder when I'm out. It's rather exciting. I'm a character in a movie. One arm round the lady, one eye on the door.'

'This skulking aspect gives it extra spice, does it? It gives it a zing you would miss if we just met openly in the town?'

'You give it the zing,' he assured her. 'The furtive aspect is not of my making. I'll come and knock on your door if you like. Ask Mr Finch if his wife can come out to play.'

The train reached Malaga Airport and half the passengers climbed out with luggage.

'I think he suspects something. I never used to go out this often. I used to read a book by the pool. It's made him restless. But he hasn't quite plucked up the courage to ask what the hell is going on.'

'Leave him. Come and live with me. Put him out of his misery.'

'Is your fridge crammed with low-fat champagne-rhubarb-yoghurt?'

'Down where the other half lives we only have cans of San Miguel in the fridge, and sometimes we run out of that. We have books you can read but not a pool to read them by. Do I make it sound inviting?'

'Damn nearly irresistible, actually. Get up. We're here.'

Malaga was more the real Spain than anywhere down the coast. Most tourists never reached its centuries-old streets but the beggars were still there, perhaps finding the natives more generous. The city's bustling history went back to the Phoenicians, but its proudest boasts today were that Picasso was born there, and it had the lowest rainfall in Europe.

Alison headed for the modern department store, El Corte Ingles, in search of a two-in-one perspex cruet set, but Mark wanted to see the city.

'All department stores are the same to me,' he said.

'But their prices aren't,' said Alison, brandishing her cruet set. 'Shall we have some *tapas*?'

They found a *tasca* in a back street that served wine from barrels, and they ate the small portions of several dishes: lean ham, meatballs, prawns, Russian salad.

'I'm still hungry,' said Mark when they returned to the street.

'You're supposed to be,' Alison told him. 'They are to whet your appetite.'

'What we need is an authentic Spanish restaurant.'

They found La Alegria in another sidestreet, a big, airy restaurant whose customers seemed to be entirely Spanish. They were shown to a table in a corner, and handed large menus. They ordered paella.

'When Anna kissed an anarchist she planted bombs not flowers,' said Mark. 'It's the first line of my new song. How does it go on from there?'

'How about, "She used his stick of dynamite to while away the hours"?'

'Not bad. Perhaps you should do the words and I'll stick to the music. We could be the next Rodgers and Hammerstein. Actually, it's meant to be a song about disaffected youth.'

'The terrorist as heroine? I don't think that's you, Mark. You've got to carve a niche. There's got to be such a thing as a Mark Ward song. 'Cottage by the Sea' is one of the sweetest songs I ever heard. I doubt whether your man in London is expecting you to follow up with a song about bombs.'

'Until my man in London starts sending me large cheques he can keep his opinions to himself.'

He was distracted suddenly by the back of a woman's head at a table twenty yards away. The auburn hair and its style convinced him that the woman was Emma, but it was difficult to be sure because of the customers in between.

'I do believe that's my sister-in-law over there,' he said. 'Matthew's angry wife.'

'Emma? I've never seen her.'

'She's the redhead, and she's with a man. How interesting!'

Alison tried to look but her view was blocked.

'It must be fascinating to have two brothers on the run. Doesn't it make you feel out of things?'

'I've always felt out of things. They always had good jobs, money, wives. I was an embarrassment to them.'

'Now they've got their revenge – they're an embarrassment to you.'

The waiter brought their paellas and a bottle of wine. He poured a little out for Mark who indicated that he wanted both glasses filled without a tasting session.

'If Emma has got a man, it could solve Matthew's problem,' he said. 'Perhaps she'll get off his back. I wonder who the chap is?'

He drank some wine and looked across at his sister-in-law. The back of her head obscured the man's. But suddenly she was gathering things from the table and putting them into her bag. Then they both stood up.

Alison took one look and turned away, hiding her face with her hand.

'I'll tell you who she's with,' she said. 'My husband.'

Some people who thought they were alcoholics actually had neuro-chemical imbalances that made normal drinking impossible. Daniel read this in a magazine one morning as he toyed with the idea of a vodka. There was an hour to kill before he walked into Mijas to get the papers, and an hour was difficult to handle. Too short for chess, too long to ignore, and there wasn't a crossword in the house. The previous afternoon he had filled a similar gap in his life by putting olive oil on a plate by the pool and seeing if he could fry an egg in it. He could, and was doubly gratified to hear on his radio that in London it was still raining.

He returned to the article. Was heavy drinking an illness or a weakness? It certainly ruined lives and destroyed families. In America, it caused half the road accidents, seventy per cent of the drownings and thirty per cent of the suicides. Nearly half the homeless were alcoholics. In that great republic across the water, eighteen million people had a drinking problem, but the message was getting across: drinking was on the decline. When the bottle was your only friend there wasn't much to look forward to apart from blackouts, memory gaps, vertigo, delirium tremens and a toxified liver.

Leanda came downstairs and sat in an armchair opposite him. She was wearing one of his blue short-sleeved shirts and white shorts. Despite the tan which she had carefully built up over the months she managed to look quite pale. She rubbed her back.

'My period's started,' she said. 'Isn't that a shame?'

'And I had just got used to the idea that we were going to have a baby,' he said, standing up. 'I think I'll have a drink. Do you want one?'

'No, and nor do you.'

For two or three days he had hardly drunk at all, telling himself naively that he was preparing for his new role of father. If Daddy was plastered, changing a nappy became an examination in origami. With no alcohol to haul him towards sleep, he had laid awake for hours discovering the misery of insomnia while the cicadas hummed through the night. But now he saw no reason not to drink, and he poured himself a large vodka.

An hour later he had switched to Victoria beer and was sitting outside Casa Pepe with the *Daily Telegraph* lying unopened on the table in front of him. He was surprised at how disappointed he was that there would be no baby. He had allowed himself to picture the child by the pool, the ball games, the swimming lessons. For the first time for months he had something to look forward to.

He drank some beer and saw Steve Finch approaching, waving a *Financial Times*.

'It's chaos at home,' he said sitting down. 'The Alliance are tearing themselves apart, the Labour Party is dead but it won't lie down, and Thatcher is there for ever. A good time to buy shares, Danny. The world is going our way.'

'It might be going your way, Steve. I don't buy shares any more.'

'You've got the capital, no matter where it came from. You've got to invest it.'

'I get a laughably small interest at the bank. What do I care? I'd really like to be in England with it now. Think of the fun you could have with a million quid. Starting firms, building empires, making films even.'

'But if you were in England you wouldn't have the million quid.'

'That is my problem.'

Steve Finch had taken Daniel's publicity without blinking. He knew bigger villains on this coast and was a civil man. Daniel had concluded that his obsession with the idea that people should make lots of money was so huge that he hadn't room in his head to consider individual methods, let alone pass judgement on them.

'Let me buy you a pint,' he said.

A waiter took his order and went back inside to the bar. A coach pulled up and dispersed a noisy horde of tourists who set off immediately on a two-hour quest for meretricious baubles.

'How's Alison?' Daniel asked.

'Who?' said Steve Finch.

'The lady you married.'

'Ah, well,' said Steve Finch, 'there have been developments there.'

'She's got herself a man?'

'No, I've got myself a woman. Strictly *entre nous*, as they say on the other side of the Pyrenees. I have met a remarkable woman who is right up my alley, pally.'

'You sound remarkably chirpy about her, Steve. Who is she?'

'As a matter of fact, she's your sister-in-law.'

'Emma?'

'That's her. A woman of sterling qualities. I met her in Matthew's bar when I was looking for Alison, and we've been meeting since.'

The idea that both members of the Finch family were now romantically involved with his relatives tickled Daniel, but he also realized that he would have to start being careful about what information he revealed to different people. His perception of Emma, for instance, as a greedy and ruthless woman who would shop her husband in a fit of pique would not be the sort of thing that Steve Finch wanted to hear, and the news that it was his girlfriend's brother-in-law who was wooing his second wife would be almost as hard to accept as it was to follow.

'Emma's a lovely woman,' he recited. It seemed to roll off the tongue quite easily.

'She is that,' said Steve Finch.

'What's the news on Alison?'

'Well, there I've drawn a blank. Nobody I've asked has seen her with anybody. I'm being circumspect. I watch. I wait.'

'She'll probably catch you out before you catch her out.'

'No chance. I pick my places carefully. We had lunch in Malaga the other day. It's safe, see? How's Leanda? You don't seem to have the same domestic problems that others have.'

'She wanted a baby, but all she's having is a period.'

'That's what I mean. You have different problems. Alison said she'd be out tonight, so I'm taking Emma to Ana Maria's. That's another safe place. Alison hates flamenco. Why don't you bring Leanda along?'

Daniel thought about this for some time. He saw a puzzle and a solution. 'That would be nice,' he said. 'Would it be OK if I bring my musical brother Mark? He's always wanted to see some flamenco and has never quite got round to it. He's got a new girlfriend that he'll probably bring with him.'

'Let 'em all come,' said Steve Finch. 'It'll be a nice evening. Do you want another drink?'

'Why not? Two pints is coitus interruptus to a serious drinker like me.'

Mark opened the thick envelope with loving care. The padding was bulky but he eventually penetrated its depths and had his hands on a flat, finely grooved piece of vinyl, a miracle of twentieth-century merchandizing, a ticket to fame and prosperity, a seven-inch black disc with a colour-ful label and a hole in the middle, a record. COTTAGE BY THE SEA it said in capital letters and, im-mediately underneath, in small letters in brackets: (Mark Ward). Below the hole, in the same capital letters as the song's title, it said TOM JONES.

He held it in his hands for some time, turning it and feeling it and rereading the label as if words had never been arranged so interestingly; and then he leapt across the room and put the record on his old Fidelity record deck, and sat back, feet up, to listen.

There was no doubt, he had to admit to himself, that the song had benefited from the singer. Tom Jones had delivered it perfectly and wrung the last ounce out of the hook line which contained the title. He played it again in a glow of satisfaction.

It occurred to him as he listened that there was a letter around somewhere, and delving into the envelope again he found a note from Conrad Gambardella.

Dear Mark, *it said*.
Here is a rushed first copy of the record. Your complimentary copies will follow next week. The release date is Tuesday, 25 August, and we hope it will be in the charts before the end of the month – and then go upwards! Thanks for signing the con-tracts. Your copies plus £5,000 advance against royalties are being sent separately. The word is that one or two big names have already fallen in love with the song and are keen to do their own versions. What colour Roller do you want?

A PS asked where his next song was.

There was only San Miguel in the fridge to accompany this good news but Mark opened a can, put the record on again, and sat down to enjoy both. The record was spinning for the eleventh time when there was a knock on the door.

He got up reluctantly, not wanting to break the spell. It was Daniel, accompanied by a strong smell of beer.

'Is that it?' he said, listening.

Mark nodded, and Daniel walked through and slumped into a chair.

'Play it again from the beginning,' he said when it had finished.

They listened in silence to the record.

'Well, it's a hit,' said Daniel. 'A smash hit. Congratulations.'

'I'm glad you like it,' Mark said. 'I hope you're right.'

'Alison Finch likes it. She sings it round the house.'

Mark was nonplussed. 'How the hell do you know that?'

'Her husband told me. He's trying to find out who her boyfriend is, but he's drawn a blank.'

'Whereas you fed two and two into your computer?'

'And the Amstrad said it was four. Have you got any beer in this dump?'

Mark fetched a can of San Miguel and a glass. 'How long have you known?'

'Almost from the beginning. She said at my party that she wanted to hear you play, and then I knew that she had come down to see you one night when I was drinking with Steve. Then I heard that she had a new man, and you had a new woman. I didn't need Sherlock Holmes even before he told me that she kept singing a song called "Cottage by the Sea".'

'He's taking Emma out.'

'I know. But how did you?'

'You're not the only detective in this family. We saw them together in a restaurant in Malaga.'

'He thought he was safe there.'

'So did we.'

'Got any more of this interesting chemical?'

Mark fetched them each a can of beer and was relieved to see that the fridge was now empty. After this, Daniel would have to sober up.

'What brings you here, anyway? You don't get to visit the workers very often.'

'I want to know how serious you are about Alison,' Daniel said, pulling the top off his beer.

'None of your business, little brother.'

'I need to know.'

'Look, I'm a rising star in the pop firmament. I don't have to sit here being grilled by a bank robber.'

'It's somebody as devious as me who you need. Do you want the lady? I'm here to help. I'm here to deliver her into your hands for good, and, at the same time, perform a great service for my other brother.'

'It sounds a tall order to me.'

'A public-school education, Mark. We know how to manipulate people, put them where we want them, like pawns on a chessboard. And a pawn can take a queen.'

'Is that an allegory or a metaphor?'

'I'm just a humble bank robber, Mark, not a grammarian. What are you doing tonight?'

'What I'm always doing, earning a living casting pearls before swine.'

'That one's a cliché. Even a bank robber recognizes that. You can get an hour off?'

'If necessary.'

'Bring Alison Finch to Ana Maria's.'

'And what will I find there?'

'Steve Finch with Emma, me with Leanda.'

'Terrific.'

'It's the answer, can't you see? Steve Finch is gunning for Alison's mysterious boyfriend, but if he is sitting there with his arm round Emma it rather takes his bullets away. And if we can drive Emma into Steve's life, Matthew is going to be mightily relieved, isn't he? One hour in Ana Maria's will resolve five people's problems. By tonight this dingy apartment will be Alison Finch's new home. Perhaps you ought to clean it up a little. Remove the top layer of fluff. The change in lifestyle could be a bit traumatic for her.'

Ana Maria's was in the old part of Marbella, at the top of the town. It stood in the Plaza Santo Cristo and looked from the outside like a row of tiny, old houses, no longer inhabited. But inside walls had been removed to create one large room with dim lighting, and simple tables and chairs round the edges. Customers had to order their drinks as they went in and the entrance fee was contained in the price of the drinks. Ana Maria's didn't open until midnight.

Five empty chairs standing in a straight line in the middle of the room were suddenly occupied by three men and two women. Their arrival was greeted with applause. The women wore the sweeping, ruffled gypsy dresses which were the hallmark of the flamenco; the men wore slim, Cordoban suits. Sometimes a man danced, sometimes a woman, who would sing as well. Sometimes they danced together, but all the time the ones who weren't dancing played the guitar or the castanets or clapped their hands. The rhythmical clapping and primitive singing inspired strong and deep emotions in some of the customers, who clapped and wailed too.

'This is quite something, isn't it?' said Steve Finch, who was doing a bit of clapping himself. He was sitting at a table with Emma, Daniel and Leanda, and there were two empty seats awaiting the arrival from Jay's of Mark and his new girlfriend.

'Look what they put into it,' said Emma. 'The passion and the feeling.'

'I'm feeling like another gin,' said Daniel. 'It's hard to get served in here.'

'Drink mine,' said Leanda.

The dancer, a small man with lots of black, curly hair,

had discovered that while he was beating out an extraordinary salvo with his feet, his fly had burst open. He turned, in the arrogant flamenco manner, and with his back to the audience did up his trousers while continuing to dance. Tumultuous applause greeted this feat, which embarrassed the dancer who thought he had got away with it.

A woman now stood and sang about the intricacies of love and death in a slow, piercing voice. Her applause was just dying down as Mark and Alison Finch came in through the door at the far end of the room.

'Here's Mark,' said Daniel. 'He managed to get away then.'

'He's with Alison,' said Steve Finch, staring incredulously across the room.

'Oh, my God, so he is,' said Daniel. 'I never realized that his new girlfriend was your . . . Oh, my God!'

'Let's keep calm,' said Steve Finch.

'I'm embarrassed,' said Emma.

They came across the room all smiles, followed by a waiter who was carrying their drinks.

'Hallo,' said Alison. 'Hallo, Leanda, I met you on election night. Hallo – you must be Emma?'

'Yes, hallo,' said Emma.

'I saw you in Malaga in La Alegria. With my old man there.'

Alison was dressed far more casually than usual, in old jeans and a tartan shirt. To Steve Finch, the clothes seemed to be making a statement.

'*Flagrante delicto*,' he said, but amid the clacking of the castanets nobody seemed to hear him.

Daniel ordered more drinks from the waiter who had followed Mark to their table, and wondered whether he should introduce Steve Finch to his brother. In a normal social situation this introduction was overdue, but this wasn't a normal social situation.

'How are you, Emma?' Mark asked. 'Enjoying your stay?'

'Very much,' she said without looking at him. She seemed to be more confused than anybody.

'Well, this is cosy,' said Leanda, who had been prepared for tonight by her husband. After falling into a drunken sleep at six o'clock, he had jumped up, bright-eyed, at nine and talked of 'bringing things to a head'.

Alison, spotting the missing introduction, now leaned forward and tapped her husband on the knee.

'Steve, this is my friend Mark. Danny's brother.'

He looked at her and then at him and shook hands. '*Chacun à son goût*,' he said. In the stress of the moment he appeared to have lost the capacity to talk English.

'Pleased to meet you,' said Mark.

Watching this, Daniel wondered where his plot was leading. British reserve and politeness had taken over. Steve Finch, caught with Emma, had been neutralized, and could not indulge in the angry scene that his situation demanded. And Mark, who was too big to hit anyway, was more interested in the music. He listened to it intently, as if a Spanish flavour might surface in his next song.

The dancer with the newly buttoned trousers was now plucking attractive ladies from his audience and dancing briefly with each; it was surprising how women, whose previous dancing experience had been a much more sedate event, took to flamenco enthusiastically, stamping their feet and clapping their hands over their heads, delighted to shed some inhibitions at last.

The man picked Alison. Steve Finch had said that she hated flamenco, but she hurled herself into it with tremendous fervour, finding the evening itself, perhaps, as much as the dance, an occasion for excitement and relief. Mark clapped with her, but Steve Finch stared balefully at the spectacle.

'Funny it should be your brother,' he said to Daniel.

'I'm as surprised as you are,' Daniel said. 'Mark isn't a womanizer.'

'It's a pity they caught me with Emma. It spiked my guns.'

'What are you going to do?'

Steve Finch looked as if this was the most difficult question that anybody had ever asked. He glared at his wife, twirling happily on the dance floor.

'He's going to marry me,' said Emma. 'I'm sick of living in a hotel.'

Steve Finch looked at her. 'If that's a proposal I might very well accept it,' he said. He took Emma's hand and smiled at her, and then looked at Daniel. 'Do you think your brother wants to marry my wife?'

'I wouldn't be surprised,' said Daniel.

'My God, she'll have to get used to a different standard of living,' said Steve Finch. 'A pianist in a piano bar?'

'She'll adapt,' said Emma. 'Women have to.'

THIRTEEN

DANIEL stepped out on to his patio the following morning to see a television camera trained on his house. At first he couldn't believe what he saw. Two cars and a Dormobile were parked across the road and at least six men and a girl with a clipboard stood drinking coffee by the vehicles. The camera, on a tripod nearby, was pointing at his front door.

He stared at this scene for a moment, feeling bewilderment and then anger. What right had these overpaid layabouts to intrude on his privacy? An Englishman's home was his castle, even if it was a villa in Spain. The anger built up in him as he imagined further uncomfortable publicity. It seemed to him that he had nothing to lose by smashing the camera.

In the road the director, the reporter, the cameraman, the assistant cameraman, the sound recordist, the assistant sound recordist, the lighting man and the girl with a clipboard and a stopwatch had finished their coffees and returned the cups to the back of the Dormobile. The ninth member of the entourage, who was known as Grips and was paid to carry things, had so exhausted himself persuading their three Spanish drivers to carry things that he was still fortifying himself with cheap Spanish brandy in the back of one of the cars.

'Come on, dears, let's do the stand-upper now,' called the director, a short, excitable man in very short shorts that suggested a sexual ambivalence he wasn't trying to disguise.

The reporter, a tall bearded man called Dermot Drysdale, looked at the notes he had made, memorized his introduction, and stuffed the papers in his pocket. He had suggested this trip himself, seeking an escape from Britain's rain, after coming across an old copy of the *News of the World*. In London it was the journalists' silly season, which meant that real news was hard to find. It was always in August that somebody was about to reveal the Loch Ness Monster, or cross the Alps on a skateboard. If such things happened in any other month, journalists were too busy to notice.

The assistant cameraman had written SCENE THREE TAKE ONE on a clapper board.

'Action!' shouted the director.

Dermot Drysdale, looking very much like a man who was at the centre of things, was suddenly talking to the camera in a stern Midlands accent.

'Here in Marbella, where there are 300 Rolls Royces but the police have only three patrol cars, a blind eye is turned to how people got their money. In the villa behind me, for instance, lives a young Englishman who stole several million pounds from Britain's high street banks and now lives a life of relaxed pleasure in the sun. Daniel Ward, a computer expert, arrived here in a hurry two years ago and the banks are helpless to get their . . .'

'Here he comes,' shouted the director excitedly. 'Get that camera off the tripod!'

Daniel, held up only temporarily by the necessity of opening his electronic gates, was now marching down the road towards Dermot Drysdale, who was not new to this sort of thing. He abandoned his report and went for the interview. It could all be put together afterwards.

A radio microphone, no more conspicuous than a tie pin, was fixed to his tie, and he also had a hand microphone. He turned to face the advancing Daniel.

'Mr Ward, have you any plans to repay the millions you stole in London?' he asked neutrally. There was no need for the censorious tone used by less experienced reporters; the facts would speak for themselves.

'Why don't you piss off and get a decent job?' Daniel shouted.

That was all right, thought Dermot Drysdale. They could always bleep out 'piss'.

'The money,' he said evenly, 'that doesn't belong to you?'

It was clear now that Daniel was not going to stop for a discussion. He was still coming forward.

Dermot Drysdale started to move backwards in the hope of getting more words out of his prey before the violence broke out.

Behind him, the cameraman, his Sony video camera now on his shoulder, started to go backwards down the road too, guided by the sound recordist who was behind him with a hand on each of the cameraman's hips.

But Daniel walking forward moved faster than a television crew walking backwards, and his first punch, a long swinging left, hit Dermot Drysdale painfully in the eye. He was near enough now to throw a right hook that dumped the television reporter in a ditch at the side of the road.

It was the camera that he wanted to destroy, but his way was barred by the man they called Grips, who was now in his element: flying fists were much more to his taste than making television programmes with a bunch of nancies. He threw a punch at Daniel which caught him high up on the forehead. Daniel stopped. He had made his protest and was outnumbered. Dermot Drysdale had achieved a wobbly perpendicular and was looking for his microphone in the ditch.

'Cut!' said the director. 'Great stuff!'

Daniel turned and walked back towards his villa. He felt a lot better. It was a funny thing, he thought. When he arrived he had expected a visit sooner or later by the police, but the only people who hunted him down were journalists.

In the road Dermot Drysdale was worried about his eye. How could he film if it turned black?

'Voice over,' said the director. 'The story of what Ward did against shots of his villa, and we've got a good mug shot of him now. But let's film the sign off before it does go black.'

'It's already too red,' said the sound recordist. 'It looks as if he's been out on the piss.'

'Why don't I do it with one hand over my eye?' suggested Dermot Drysdale. 'Give it a bit of atmosphere.'

'Lovely idea,' said the director. 'Set it up.'

Dermot Drysdale covered his left eye with his left hand and peered at the camera with his right eye. 'Dermot Drysdale, *World News*, Marbella,' he said.

Their caravan had rolled on, perhaps in search of further excitement, when Daniel left the villa later that morning to buy his newspaper.

Sitting outside Casa Pepe with his glass of Victoria beer, he fingered the bump on his forehead and felt inordinately pleased with himself. Journalists lectured the public, castigated the politicians, berated the stars of stage, screen and sport, and now they had put themselves in charge of law and order. Another twenty years and they would be running the country.

He picked up the product of this omniscient clique and scanned the headlines. The world was being its usual charming self. In the Middle East, Israelis were tear-gassing mosques; in Haiti, voters were being shot dead in the polling stations; in Afghanistan, Soviet SU-17s were bombing villages; in America, men of arguable guilt were being tied to chairs while white cyanide crystals were dropped into pans of sulphuric acid beneath their seats; in Ethiopia, a million starved while the government ate; and the world did not yet know, he thought, what was happening to black men in the privacy of South African police stations.

Beside this catalogue of horror, his sin seemed venial, and a feeling of innocence and resentment overwhelmed him. Why me? he thought. Why me? Well, it's you because you stole £1 million, he had to remind himself. It's you because you practised deception and dishonesty on a scale that would undermine civilized life in Britain if the rest decided to follow your example. It's you because you are hopelessly, fatally, irretrievably flawed. It's you because you're a thief.

A long way short of convinced by this ruthless assessment, he turned to his favourite corner of the paper. He read: confused, vague, without a fit, I am all about the one that got away. Eight letters. It was obviously an anagram, but which letters would make it up? On the corner of the page he wrote down vague without an 'a', fit and I. He saw then that the answer was 'fugitive', and decided not to do the crossword that morning.

The following week Leanda received the first letter she had been sent by her mother since Mrs Plumridge flew home. It said that she had seen Daniel behaving disgracefully on *World News*.

'It was the second item, after the crisis in the health service,' she wrote. 'TV man catches one on the Costa del Crime.'

On the day that 'Cottage by the Sea' was released, Mark swung through the wavebands of his portable radio in search of a programme that might be playing it. He picked up stations from Moscow to Morocco but didn't hear his record. He decided to ring Conrad Gambardella at his London office. Alison, not yet accustomed to his strange working hours, lay sleeping in their small bed; he left her a note and walked to the port.

'Lovely to hear from you, Mark,' said Conrad Gambardella. 'Today you start earning money.'

'Has the radio played it yet?' Mark shouted. He was using the wall phone in Jay's, and a Spanish girl was hoovering the carpet by his feet.

'We've got a check on that – hang on,' said Conrad Gambardella and, for a minute, the line went quiet. 'Great news, Mark,' he boomed suddenly. 'It's been on Radio One twice and Radio Two once. That's way above average at this stage, but of course Tom Jones is Tom Jones.'

'Let me know what happens, will you? I feel a bit cut off down here.'

'Don't feel deprived, kid. It's still raining in London. We'll keep you up to date with a weekly report. Got any more songs?'

'I'm working on them.'

He wasn't working on them. Since Alison moved in on the night of the fateful visit to Ana Maria's, he hadn't written a word. Life had been too much fun to contemplate that sort of effort. In Alison's Renault they had used the free hours of the day to do things that had never interested Steve Finch. They had driven to Ronda, built on the edge of a gorge, Nerja, with its amazing underground cave, 800 metres long and only discovered in 1959, and to the Alhambra at Granada. They had laid on the beach like tourists, which Alison, perhaps to allay his fears, had said was a lot more fun then lying on her own by a pool. Most evenings she joined him for at least a part of the time at Jay's, but she was also engaged on cleaning and redecorating the apartment.

'Don't bother,' he had told her. 'When I get some money I'm going to buy us something good.' But he didn't argue when she persisted. It was probably a flat that only a musician could live in.

When he left Jay's he walked along to the Salduba for some breakfast. The harbour was a forest of masts, and it was one of those scorching days when even hardened sun-bathers would think twice about lying too long in the sun. Already the temperature was in the eighties.

He ordered a coffee and tortilla, and imagined housewives in Luton putting down their dusters to listen to his song. Of course, to the housewife it would be Tom Jones's song, but then most of them thought that Frank Sinatra wrote 'My Way'. The unsung creative artist in his dust-caked atelier had no place in public esteem. Well, he should worry. The royalties would be safely lodged with Hambros in Gibraltar and the tax man would never hear of him either.

Through the crowd of morning strollers he could see Alison approaching. She was dressed in white today, white blouse, white trousers, white sandals.

'Hallo, lover,' she said. 'I was just thinking as I walked along the front how nice it is to sleep with a man who doesn't wear pyjamas.'

'Men don't wear pyjamas any more, do they? I thought they died with vests and flannels.'

'Steve wears pyjamas. And vests.'

'Has he got a flannel?'

'He has, actually. And ties and braces.'

'Steve is a man from the 1940s. Does he wear sock suspenders?'

'He doesn't go that far. How about a coffee?'

Mark ordered one. 'Danny wears socks in bed in the afternoon,' he told her.

'Why?'

'It's quite interesting. If he has drunk a lot at lunchtime, which isn't unheard of, and wants to sleep it off, he leaves his socks on. He says you wake up after a deep sleep, it's dark, your watch says six o'clock. Is it morning or evening? Should you get up and look for breakfast, or is it time to prepare for dinner? The next question he asks himself is: have I got my socks on?'

'The answer lies in the socks.'

'Exactly. If he has his socks on, he knows that it's evening.'

The coffee arrived. 'There's something vaguely eccentric about your brother,' said Alison, stirring in the sugar. 'Have you rung London?'

'Three plays by ten o'clock. Housewives are already humming it.'

'That's wonderful, Mark. How are we going to celebrate?'

'A little surprise,' he told her. 'We are taking my brothers and their respective partners to Toni Dalli's. By a long-standing arrangement I have a night off.'

Toni Dalli's Oasis Club on the golden mile was on everybody's itinerary at one time or another. It was in the evenings that the rich abandoned their wonderful homes and came out to enjoy the good life: champagne in the night clubs, not beer in the bars. They took over Regine's, or the Beach Club at the Marbella Club, and discussed yachts, helicopters and private jets during a restless search for sparkle and glamour. Among their number were playboys, gigolos, sheiks, husband-hunting heiresses, footloose widows, sporting stars coping with very early retirement, impoverished aristocrats with obscure titles, film producers with no films to make, tycoons with second homes in the sun and other burly and mysterious residents of the sub-tropical paradise who had left their bodyguards and Dobermanns back at a walled-in villa in the hills to keep an eye on the safe. Some of these came to Toni Dalli's.

The Oasis Club was built like a Moroccan palace. The evening, half food, half music, was stage managed by Toni Dalli, a one-time opera singer who had himself enjoyed a brief moment of pop stardom a long time ago. At the drop of a sombrero he would sing the song now to the diners, the younger of whom were more familiar with the tune from an ice-cream commercial shot in Venice.

He had a surprise for them the moment they sat down at a large round table in the corner.

'Ladies and gentlemen, we only have live music here, as you may know,' he said into his microphone, 'but tonight we are making an exception. I would like you to listen to a new record, released today, by Tom Jones, because it was written by one of our guests tonight who you may have seen singing in Jay's: Mark Ward – he's over there in the corner.'

Polite but restrained applause greeted this break with tradition, and then the sound of Tom Jones filled the club.

'How did he get that?' Mark asked, mystified.

'I gave it to him,' said Alison.

The extraordinary reaction to the record convinced them all that Mark had a hit. The applause was immediate and loud, and then all the guests stood up and continued clapping. Mark stood and waved and then sat down.

'There's your juke-box jury,' said Matthew. 'A standing ovation.'

'You must be very encouraged by that,' said Kim. 'It was amazing.'

'Do you think the Performing Rights Society will get some money out of him for playing it?' Mark asked, but secretly he was thrilled. It was the first public reaction to the record.

When the waiter brought the menus, Daniel urged everybody to eat expensively.

'Mark has never bought us dinner before,' he explained. 'Are you giving up your job, Mark, now that you're rich?'

'No, I'm not,' said Mark. 'And I'm not rich yet.'

'He's a belt and braces man,' said Matthew.

'And so would you be if you had spent most of your time with your trousers round your ankles. My life has been one long financial problem.'

'I'll have corned beef and beans and a can of beer,' said Matthew. 'I have pesetas.'

'Four bottles of Moët et Chandon,' Mark told the waiter.

'And four ice buckets,' said Alison.

Leanda turned to her, curious about the social upheavals which had passed, frustratingly, with barely a comment. 'How does it feel to have Matthew's wife living with your husband?' she asked. 'It must be strange?'

'Bliss,' said Alison.

'What's going to happen?'

'I've no idea. I suppose the next communication will come from a solicitor, or don't they have divorces in Spain?'

'I'm sure they do,' said Kim.

'Well, he'll fix it,' Alison said. 'He'll want to marry Emma. He's too old to live in sin.'

'So am I,' said Kim.

Four men with striped pantaloons were strolling among the tables playing mandolins. The songs were Spanish one minute and a song that had begun life on Broadway the next. When the customers had finished eating, these strolling players dragged ladies from their seats and danced them round the floor, banging them occasionally with a tambourine.

Mark sat back, having had more champagne than he had ever had in one evening, and thought that it was the finest night of his life. Alison at his side, his record out today and, for once, he and not his brothers was the host. If envy was an admission of inferiority, tonight he could look them in the eye.

He pushed aside the half-eaten Tennessee Grasshopper which he had ordered out of curiosity. It turned out to be a mint mousse with a chocolate top, but all he really wanted was champagne. He filled his glass and watched the others drinking and laughing. Daniel was telling them about the visit of a television crew, and how he had hit a reporter, but Mark was too absorbed in his own success to listen. One of these days the television people would be flying down here to talk to him.

He wished that his mother were alive to see him now. The others might have broken her heart, but he would have made it up for her. Although this was the finest evening of his life, thinking about his mother he was reminded of the happiest moment. He was eight and Matthew was three. He had gone to bed early because he felt ill. His mother came up to the bedroom later to see how he was. She was a short, pretty woman. She felt his forehead and took his temperature. She looked a little worried. 'You won't be going to school tomorrow,' she said. When she had tucked him up and left the room, he climbed out of the sheets and jumped on the bed with joy.

That was the happiest moment of his whole life.

Matthew lay on the beach surrounded by holidaymakers who were evidently exhausted by donkey safaris and chicken barbecues. He had seen too little of the sun, he decided, and was now posing as a holidaymaker himself. He bought an ice-cream from the man who kept shouting *helado*, and gazed around at the topless girls beneath the parasols. Kim found the heat oppressive now and rested in the afternoons in the flat.

Hundreds of bodies, red, white and brown, lay not so quietly in the heat, most of them covered by an oil or a cream which promised to protect them from a sun which at this time of the year could remove their skin in an hour. He lay there, turning a deeper brown himself, and listened to the conversations that came at him in many languages from the surrounding sunbeds.

'Do you know Donkey Dobson?' asked a girl of her big-breasted neighbour.

'The wally with the willy? Intimately. We went to Corfu last year.'

'What's it like?'

'Very popular. Attracts a lot of people.'

'I meant his willy.'

'So did I.'

Matthew would have liked to hear more of this but a large group of Dutch women, who had arranged their sunbeds like a witches' coven, had decided to burst into song. The Dutch sang, the Scandinavians played ball games or threw themselves into the murky waters of the Mediterranean, and the Germans read books. Even the Spanish had discovered their own beaches now. Ten years ago the last thing you would expect to find on a Spanish beach was a Spaniard, but now they were everywhere.

Matthew had always preferred the sun to the snow, no matter how crowded the beach, or how beautiful an Alpine ski resort might look on a poster. It cost a fortune to kit yourself out for the ski slopes, he always said, but you could get a pair of swimming trunks for three pounds.

The sea was full of pedalos and people failing to stay upright on their windsurf boards. Where there was space, bathers bobbed in the water trying to cool down. On the beach the seasons were ignored as football and cricket were played side by side. Unruly children sprayed sand over sunbathers as they rushed by in pursuit of friends.

It was hard, thought Matthew, to identify this playground with the real Spain that lay to the north, a country whose history had been one of unrelieved triumph until the sixteenth century, and disaster and disappointment ever since. Six hundred years under the Romans and 700 under the Moors had produced a country unlike any other and he yearned to explore it. It was a country of startling contrasts, of deserts and snow-covered mountains. Along with the sun-baked beaches was the most southerly ski resort in Europe. It was a country of volcanoes and forests, with wild bears, wolves, lynxes and the only wild camels in Europe. The highest road in Europe was in the mountains above Granada. It was only an hour or so away and he had never seen it. Nor had he seen the hut-dwellers in the hills, or the gypsies of Andalusia who lived in caves but had refrigerators, and he had missed the *feria* in Seville. He must be the only person who had not seen the fortress palace of the Moorish kings which was so close, and all he had seen of the different Spain of Catalonia, which had once been a separate republic within the Spanish state and no doubt would be again, was during his hectic southward dash in the Scirocco. A journey which would have made a fascinating couple of months had been completed in a frantic twenty-four hours. The Spanish had had the best builders since the Romans, and there were amazing bridges and cathedrals that could not be seen anywhere else on earth. But he hadn't seen them.

More and more he thought of selling the bar and seeing the country. But the bar had paid for their summer, and if he sold it he would be using his capital which was still earning no interest in Daniel's safe. Life was moving in the wrong direction when you had to live off your capital, but his talent for making money was hampered by his living in a country where he didn't know enough about the language or the rules to do the things he was best at.

Lying on his sunbed and watching a boat tow a water-skier through the bathers, he wondered whether to buy a *finca* in the hills and run some sort of business from there. If he bought ten pool tables and put them in the right bars they would each make him £50 a week. That would be a start. Why not twenty pool tables, making him £1,000 a week? A small home industry, printing rude messages on the front of T-shirts, was also a possibility. Making money had never been difficult for him. Most people were so busy going to work that they never had the time to get rich.

Kim had suggested moving back from the coast. She wanted a rural backdrop for her baby. She fancied making money, too – out of the soil. She had a list of things she thought she could sell, including beetroot and mushrooms.

Perhaps he would get married again. Eighty per cent of men were married before they were twenty-four. What percentage were married twice before they were thirty-four?

Kim was keen to extract at least a promise of marriage since receiving the letter from her father. Sharing a home with her had proved to be such a painless experience that he could almost consider it.

He closed his eyes and listened enviously to the story of Donkey Dobson.

AUTUMN

'It has always seemed strange to me,' said the Doc. 'The things we admire in men, kindness and generosity, openness, honesty, understanding and feeling, are the concomitants of failure in our system. And those traits we detest, sharpness, greed, acquisitiveness, meanness, egotism and self-interest, are the traits of success. And while men admire the quality of the first, they love the produce of the second.'

– John Steinbeck, *Cannery Row*

FOURTEEN

MATTHEW and Lady walked briskly along the seafront. It was more than four miles from end to end, but he had never found the time to do it in one outing. Eight miles would take him at least two hours on his own, and it would be cruel to do the walk without the dog, whose diversions and investigations en route would probably double the time needed. Nevertheless he was walking more than he ever had before and feeling very fit because of it. The Scirocco, which was little used, had been lent to Daniel, whose car was undergoing repairs, and they had been pleased to lend it – it needed the exercise.

It was the usual sunny evening. A solitary white cloud sat on the peak of the Sierra de Mijas like a lady's hat. Tourists patrolled the seafront, grateful for such heat in September. Antonio's beach bar were doing their *espetones de sardinas*, fresh sardines washed in sea water and speared on thin reeds, grilled on an open spit on the beach. Often Matthew left the bar in the evenings to buy some.

The trouble with all this fresh air and exercise was that it had caused a revival of his sexual appetite, a long unsatisfied yet curiously dormant commodity during the months of Kim's pregnancy. He was distracted now by a young girl who sauntered by in white shorts. She was only about fourteen, but her eyes showed that she knew why men looked at her.

It was at this stage of women's pregnancy, he reflected, that husbands appeared before magistrates, arraigned for bizarre sexual peccadilloes involving girls on buses, or provocative young wives in the deserted aisles of a supermarket. The sanest man could make a fool of himself when confronted by a pretty girl, let alone a man whose immediate sexual history did not differ markedly from the Pope's.

A car went past very quickly, hooting angrily at a cyclist who wobbled off the *paseo maritimo* and stopped to wave his fist. Five seconds later there was a sound that Matthew had never heard before: a brief, loud, dull bump followed by an eerie silence. Then the screaming started.

Looking up the road he could see that the car had driven straight into the back of a coach that was braking to turn right. It was more than a hundred yards away but he could see that it was a yellow Scirocco and he broke into a run, shouting to Lady to keep up.

By the time he arrived at the car the crowd that had gathered had pulled out two girls with blood on their faces, but the driver seemed to be trapped. The driver was Daniel and his face was covered with blood, too.

The bonnet had been pushed up enough to smash the windscreen and jam the driver's door, and the steering wheel was a funny shape.

They laid the girls on the pavement, which collected bloodstains quickly. The girls lay there, conscious but not talking, and Daniel sat in the car with his head in his hands, not talking either, while two men tried to wrench his door open. When Matthew joined them at the window Daniel didn't seem to realize that he was there.

Somebody must have phoned immediately for an ambulance because it arrived surprisingly quickly. With it was a small police car containing two of the municipal police force.

Matthew went over to the girls, who were being lifted silently on to stretchers. One of them decided that she didn't need a stretcher and was helped to the ambulance, where she sat down and burst into tears.

He went back to Daniel in the Scirocco. Four men were rocking the car now in an attempt to free it from the coach. The steering wheel seemed to be preventing Daniel's release on one side and the jammed door on the other.

It soon became clear that while the ambulancemen were interested in the girls, the police were interested in Daniel. They stood by the Scirocco, monitoring the frenetic attempts to release him, while he sat in the car seemingly unaware of the activity outside.

Matthew walked over to the ambulance where the girl who had been crying was now drinking something from a mug, and holding a cloth to her face.

'Are you English?' he asked.

The girl shook her head slowly and Matthew went to walk away.

'Scottish,' the girl said.

'What happened? That's my brother, and that was my car.'

'He's pissed as a rat,' the girl said.

'Where did you find him?'

'Drinking in Benalmadena. He wanted to show us his brother's bar.'

'Is he hurt?'

'I hope so.'

He went back to the car. It was obviously a write-off. Both front tyres were flat, he now noticed. If it had been one of those cars that had the engine in the back, the collision would probably have taken Daniel's legs off.

The police, with more experience in these matters, had taken over the job of releasing him. They were using some tools on the door which suddenly sprang open.

They bent into the car and helped Daniel out. He leaned against the vehicle with glazed eyes that were either the cause or the result of the accident, and clutched his chest. Matthew knew that the municipal police did not yet carry breathalysers, although they were due to get them. Only the Guardia Civil conducted breath tests, and they weren't here.

The two policemen helped Daniel to their car. Matthew walked over to them. He was trying to remember what the Spanish was for brother. Was it *hermano*, or did that mean sister? But his attempt to talk to the policemen was brushed aside: they had got their man and soon he was sitting in the back of their car. One policeman joined him there, and the other switched on the engine. The car and the ambulance disappeared together, and the crowd that had gathered began to disperse, although some still stayed to examine the wreck of the car and the blood on the pavement.

Matthew went over to the telephone kiosk that he used for his calls to suppliers. The man who had been driving the coach was inside sending his sad story back to headquarters. It must have been an empty coach. There were no passengers waiting for a new one.

The coach driver came out. '*El iba demasiado rapido*,' he said.

'*Si*,' said Matthew. 'Too fast.'

He put the pesetas into the tray at the top of the phone and dialled Leanda. He told her what had happened.

'Where is he?' she asked.

'He'll be at the medical centre now and later at the police station, I should think. Can you come down? I've got to get back to the bar. I can't leave Kim any longer in her condition.'

'I'm leaving now.'

'Drop in afterwards for a free drink.'

Kim was coping with a crowded bar.

'I think I need a new car,' she said.

'You saw it?'

'We heard the bump and saw you running down the road. How is he?'

'I don't know. I think he's concussed. He didn't seem to know that I was there.'

'Drunk?'

'Just a little. He was clutching his ribs. I wouldn't be surprised if he has broken a few.'

Manolo, the silent Spaniard who was thought to be in the pay of the authorities, was drinking at the bar.

'Your brother did you a favour,' he said. 'You are not allowed to own a car with foreign number plates if you have a business in Spain. Any day now they would have confiscated it and dumped it in the pound at Malaga. It would cost a fortune to retrieve. At least this way you will get insurance.'

'Thank you, Manolo,' Matthew said. 'I knew there had to be a bright side somewhere. What will happen to him?'

'A fine. Sixty thousand pesetas, I think. He didn't injure anybody.'

A £300 fine seemed laughably lenient to Matthew. In Britain it would have cost more and at least a year's loss of licence.

He bought Manolo a drink. Sometimes they played pool together. Despite his mysterious connections, he had occasionally proved to be a useful friend when Matthew lost himself in the labyrinthine alleys of Spanish regulations. Matthew suspected that he had been a Franco man in the old days when hopeful Socialists held covert meetings in wine cellars, and he had never got out of the habit of spying. Now that the Socialists were in government, and running into the problem that confronted their counterparts all over Europe – a better deal for the workers, or a stronger economy for the country – people like Manolo seemed to be waiting quietly for the emergence of a new Franco.

Leanda arrived later, pale with anger.

'I've seen him,' she said, pulling a stool to the counter. 'And a fine mess he's in.'

'What's the damage?'

'Two cracked ribs, a cut on the forehead from the windscreen and concussion. They're keeping him in overnight for observation.'

'A gin?' Kim asked.

'Please. What the hell was he *doing* careering round the country with two girls?'

'Not what you think,' Matthew said. 'They told me he was just giving them a lift from Benalmadena. He'd obviously been out on a bender.'

'I want a divorce,' said Leanda. 'The joke's gone on long enough.'

'Of course you don't,' said Matthew, shocked. 'Just relax, Leanda. It'll be O K.'

'What will be O K? I could be a housewife in Surbiton now, tripping up to the West End every now and again to see the shows. I could have a husband at the top of some respectable corporation. *I could have friends!*'

She started, quite unexpectedly, to cry at the elusiveness of this modest dream, and Kim went round the counter to put her arm round her.

'You've got friends,' said Kim. 'And you've got a house that most people would envy.'

'And I've got a drunken husband who is making a fool of himself on television when he's not in the *News of the World*,' she said, emerging from a pink handkerchief. 'I must be a laughing-stock among my old friends at home. Poor Leanda!'

The prospect of sympathy produced more tears.

'Nobody knows what a strain it is. Has been,' she said between sobs. 'Do you think my existence is *normal*?'

'Well,' said Matthew, but he didn't know what to say. Instead he pulled himself a glass of Cruzcampo and glanced round the bar to see if anyone was waiting to be served. Four Spaniards playing pool were more interested in the game than the beer.

'I'm a normal girl who wants a normal life. The semi-detached in the suburbs would do me fine. My God, it seems like a dream from here.'

Matthew was disinclined to believe this, but Leanda

was too upset for him to say so. She had always had extravagant tastes, even when Daniel was hauling himself up the computer ladder, and a semi-detached in the suburbs had never looked like being enough. A seven-bedroom house in two acres in the country, with five-barred gates, two dogs and a copse was more her style. In a desperate attempt once to reconcile himself to his brother's crime, he had even imagined that his wife's sybaritism was the real cause of his fall.

'Did he know that I was at the accident?' he asked.

'No, he didn't. I'm not even sure that he knew I was there. The doctor told me there were two girls in the car, in case they were relatives, but Danny didn't remember.'

'How are the girls?' Kim asked.

'They're all right. They've had stitches. They'll probably have my husband to thank for a few scars. The scars that he has inflicted on me are a bit deeper.'

The tears had left her eyes now, and had been replaced by a thoughtful anger. She picked up her gin for the first time and looked at Matthew.

'It's no good, you see?' she said, with an earnestness that almost hypnotized him. 'Life isn't meant to be this miserable.'

Matthew found himself toying with answers again: his brother wasn't easy to defend, particularly when you didn't have a list of the offences in front of you.

'You'll feel differently tomorrow,' he suggested. 'All we've got to do is cut down his drinking.'

'That's all,' she said. 'Why don't we do something easy, like reunite Ireland? He knocks back a bottle of whisky the way you'd eat an olive. He slides under the table, he sleeps in a ditch, he crashes a car. The millionaire from the public school is going to kill somebody one day, probably me.'

Her anger was unassuageable.

'I think,' said Kim, now established on the customer

side of the counter, 'that you've got to start feeling sorry for him.'

'Sorry? For him? What about me? He's made his bed. Why should I lie on it?'

'You married him, Leanda.'

'No, I didn't. I married an ambitious young computer executive who lived in London. A pretty abstemious computer executive, as it happens. Do you think my childhood dream was to marry a drunken bank robber? There was no mention of that on the day I changed my name.'

'I hesitate to say it,' said Matthew, 'but would you like another drink?'

She nodded and pushed her glass towards him. 'Do you know what he is?' she said. 'He's a bachelor. I don't know what I'm doing here.' She took her drink and put it down without trying it. 'Would you mind if I slept here tonight? I couldn't stay in that house on my own.'

The following morning when his brothers arrived to see him, Daniel was sitting up in bed doing a crossword. He had been given the free English edition of the Spanish newspaper *Sur*, and the clues were a lot easier than those in his normal puzzle. Resolve to put off what belongs to me, he read. Nine letters. He wrote in 'determine' and thought that if he could do a crossword there couldn't be a lot wrong with his head.

He had been through the paper half expecting to find a report of his own accident. Bjorn Borg was on the coast to discuss an expansion of his business interests; the world chess championship was about to start in Seville; a ship had slipped out of Malaga harbour, leaving passengers and debts; and time-sharing as a means of owning a piece of local property was now a dirty word and had been replaced by multi-ownership. But there was no mention of his crash.

It came as something of a surprise to be ignored by the press – perhaps he was about to be accorded the obscurity he had sought. He returned to the crossword. For a man with a hangover, two cracked ribs, a cut head and a police charge hanging over him, he didn't feel too bad.

His brothers came in grinning stupidly.

'Where's the bottle?' he asked.

Mark peered at the stitches in his forehead, and pulled a chair to the side of the bed. 'What bottle?' he asked. 'Medicine?'

'The bottle of encouraging fluid which it is customary to take when visiting the sick. Whisky, it's called.'

'We thought you may have had enough of that yesterday,' Matthew said.

'I didn't have any yesterday, so far as I can remember. I was drinking vodka Martinis, and pretending to be a Yuppie.'

'Well, you're not a Yuppie, you're a wally, kid,' said Mark. 'And if you don't ease up on the sherbet, you'll be a late wally.'

'Certainly a divorced wally, from what Leanda was saying last night,' said Matthew. 'A change in your life-style appears to be a bit urgent.'

Daniel looked at them in disgust. 'I've tumbled to your little ruse,' he said. 'You're trying to bore me to death.'

'It won't need boredom, Danny,' Mark told him. 'If the liver don't get you, the highway will. I thought last night might make you think.'

'I wasn't used to vodka, that's all. It's pretty tasteless and you hardly realize you're drinking at all. The last thing I remember was talking to two teachers from Edinburgh in Benalmadena.'

'Girls, were they?'

'They looked like girls, although I admit that's not conclusive round here. Have you seen the transvestites in Torremolinos? I tried to chat one up once and later saw her having a pee in the men's loo. What did Leanda say? She hasn't been in.'

'She saw you last night and she's coming in this morning. She said she wants a divorce,' Matthew told him. 'She looked like a person who has finally run out of patience to me, but I may have misread it. I think she's had enough of your playful little ways.'

'A divorce? That's a bit drastic, isn't it?'

'She's put up with an awful lot. She never even wanted to live here, let alone with a man who is three sheets to the wind most of the time.'

This news stopped Daniel for a moment. He stared down the bed at his feet.

'I don't believe she'd divorce me,' he said. 'She'd never go back to her mother.'

'There are other options,' Mark said. 'You need her, Danny. She's the only restraint you've got.'

'Who needs restraints?'

'You do, or you'll end up as a drunken stumble-bum, wandering round the bars in Mijas with your knuckles brushing the pavement. What's the food like in here?'

'Difficult to tell you what it's *like*. Wombat droppings probably comes closest.'

'The penalty of your lifestyle, kid. When are they going to let you out? If you lie in bed too long all your bile settles in your gall bladder and you get gallstones.'

'I can see that you two have come here to cheer me up. Divorce, gallstones, the wagon. What's the car like?'

'It doesn't really look like a car any more. It resembles a piece of modern sculpture that some bearded nut-case is exhibiting at the Tate.'

'Tell Kim she can choose what car she wants. If the insurance won't run to it, I'll buy it myself. What was the question? I've had a knock on the head, you know.'

A nurse came in with a glass of milk. She handed it to Daniel with a smile and went out without speaking.

'When are you coming out?' Mark asked.

Daniel looked at the glass. 'What is this drink?'

'It's called milk.'

'I remember milk. We used to have it at school. I shall pretend it's Pernod.' He thought for a moment and touched his ribs. 'They're going to let me out this afternoon, so long as I've paid. As I don't work, I'm not in their wonderful insurance scheme. The plan is that my chauffeur will be a policeman, and I'll be taken straight to court. Getting the driver into court after a road accident is about the only thing that Spain does quickly.' He drank the milk and made a wry face. 'Apparently if I hadn't been injured I would have spent last night in jail. I must admit that rather appealed to me, as an out-of-the-way experience.'

'If it's prison that you hanker after, I should think Scotland Yard would try to be helpful,' Matthew said. 'They're quite good at organizing that sort of thing.'

Daniel was glad to see his brothers go. The nuances of their conversation unsettled him. He returned to his newspaper and awaited the arrival of Leanda.

Leanda had endured a sleepless night on Matthew's hard Spanish sofa, but there were advantages in sleepless nights. She had been given time to think. She thought about the clear-eyed ambitious young man she had met in Harrods when she was still Leanda Plumridge, and about her wedding and the house they had bought in Holland Park. It had seemed then to be a life that was full of hope. She wondered, as she had wondered many times before, why exactly it had changed, why she now lived in a different country with, to all intents and purposes, a different man – why, in other words, Daniel, in a moment of madness, had stolen a million pounds. The conclusion that she usually arrived at, when her mind took this well-worn path, was that it was a problem, a challenge that puzzle-crazy Daniel could not resist. It was a brain-teaser, a riddle, a conundrum, and the financial jackpot that lay at the end of it was almost incidental. It was a conclusion that had certainly made it easier for her to accept the situation; she would not be here now if the money had been collected at the point of a gun. And then, as Daniel was fond of saying, nobody had lost anything from his little coup. The bank's customers had not been deprived of a penny, and the banks themselves mislaid millions in the under-developed world every month without batting an eyelid. But now she was not so sure. More recent events suggested that her husband had weakness built into him, and that the bank theft, so far from being a rather amusing aberration, was actually wholly in character with a man who found the world hard to bend to his will. Above everything else, she knew that the drinking was here to stay, and wasn't just a small part of his life. It was his life. He had the time, the money and the opportunity and nothing was going to stop him. She lay on the sofa and contemplated a future that filled her with horror.

Matthew, rising early to take the dog out, brought her tea. She pulled herself up on the sofa to drink it, and then went to the tiny bathroom.

Kim came in looking tired. 'I hope you had a better night than me,' she said.

Leanda thought that she looked as if she would give birth at any moment. 'It depends what sort of night you had,' she replied.

'They're all bad now and when the baby's born they'll be worse, by all accounts. What I'd give for a good night's sleep.'

Leanda nodded sympathetically, but actually felt envy. What were a few sleepless nights alongside the priceless gift of a baby?

When Matthew returned from his seafront walk, they ate boiled eggs in the kitchen. It was a subdued snack.

'I rang Mark at Jay's last night,' he said. 'We're going to see Danny this morning.'

'You go first. I've got some things to do,' Leanda said. 'It was kind of you to put me up.'

She did the washing up and then slipped away. She drove the Golf into the town and spent some time trying to find a parking space. Then she walked to the Banco Atlantico and withdrew 2 million pesetas. She did the same at the Banco de Jerez and the Banco de Bilbao, and then returned to her car and drove up to Mijas where she withdrew a similar amount from the Banco de Granada.

Back at the villa she parked the car and rang for a taxi, and then she started to pack. Forty thousand pounds, if she could get it out of the country, should keep her going for some time. She took a last look round the house without a tremor of remorse, and wrote the briefest of notes. It was stiflingly hot outside and the idea of rain, of seasonal fluctuations, seemed wonderfully attractive.

When the taxi arrived she asked the driver to carry two large suitcases to the car.

'*Aeropuerto*,' she told him.

She wouldn't get a cheap ticket at this short notice but there had to be a flight somewhere with an empty seat, even if it meant landing in Manchester or Glasgow. But she was lucky. Two hours later she was sitting on the Iberia flight to Heathrow. It was only when the engines started and she was belted into her window seat that the tears began to run down her cheeks.

The plane flew out over the Mediterranean, negotiated a shaky U-turn, and headed north.

Stooped by pain but adjudged fit to leave, Daniel was led from his lonely room to a shaded office where several people were waiting to see him. Leanda was not among them.

The medical centre itself seemed to have prior claim on his attention, requiring either evidence that his social security payments were up to date or, alternatively, hard cash. Once it was established, with the help of two languages, that he had made no social security payments, a small dark man with thick horn-rimmed spectacles pulled a carefully typed bill from a sheaf of papers on his desk and handed it to Daniel. It was for 40,000 pesetas, which he worked out to be about £200. It was time that Spain reorganized the currency, he thought. In the world of the peseta everybody was a millionaire.

'I've been waiting for my wife,' he said, 'to bring me money.'

Translated to a fairly crowded room, this piece of news drew expressions of consternation. The system did not run smoothly with penniless patients.

'No wife here,' said the man with the glasses.

'I must go to *el banco*,' he told them. He had always liked the bilingual approach, retaining the integrity of the guest while making some small concession to the host.

Two policemen, whom Daniel hadn't noticed, stood up at this news. They had been watching events from armchairs in the corner of the office. A conversation now ensued of which Daniel understood very little. It expanded and attracted other participants, some of them contributing simultaneously to the seminar. The debate reached such heights of passion and urgency that the bespectacled man's summary of its conclusions was a bit of an anti-climax.

'The police go with you to bank,' he said.

This, it emerged, was not a proposal, but a statement about the way that things were going to be, and Daniel was soon sitting in the back of another police car as it weaved its way through the crowded streets of Fuengirola.

In anticipation of further expenditure in court, he withdrew £600, and was driven back to the medical centre where the appearance of money created a relaxed and cheerful atmosphere that had been lacking before. They shook his hand and wished him well and gave him the date of an appointment he must keep with his doctor before the stitches were removed.

Ten minutes later he was back in the police car again, heading towards a less cordial reception.

The court, *el tribunal* – a tree-boo-nal, he reminded himself, in case he had to speak – sat in an old white building at the back of the town. A solitary magistrate in a brown suit sat at a high desk dispensing swift retribution on a succession of bag-snatchers, car thieves, dope sales-men, rowdies and, this afternoon, drunk drivers. Arriving without the company of a lawyer, Daniel found himself promoted in the running order and was soon listening to an account of his experiences the previous evening. He didn't understand a word, but the story was evidently a sad one judging by the wooden expressions that it induced. The magistrate asked the policeman who had related the tale a question about *el autocar*. Picking at the Spanish words that he knew, Daniel guessed that he was asking whether anybody on the coach had been injured. Reas-sured on this point, the magistrate announced a fine of 60,000 pesetas.

Despite the money that he had in four bank accounts, Daniel had never been extravagant. To have been separ-ated from £500 already today filled him with disgust, particularly as it was so unnecessary. He walked out into the sun to look for a taxi, and wondered what had hap-pened to Leanda.

He felt angry that he could be hauled before the courts without either his wife or his brothers turning up to offer him support. Supposing a mad judge had sent him to prison? There would have been no one there to hear of his fate or to know where he was. His anger could only be cooled by a drink.

He sat in a bar in the main street and drank a beer. It was as if his relatives had consigned him to a sort of family scrap-heap. He ordered a whisky. He didn't have to worry – a taxi driver was taking him home.

A second whisky brought his thoughts back to Leanda It became clear to him suddenly that something was wrong. There was a high point of great mental clarity in the early part of his drinking sessions which wasn't there earlier and certainly wasn't there later. And during this brief potent spell of insight and perception he saw that he should get home in a hurry. Leanda was ill, injured, dead or had left him. Nothing else could have kept her away.

He paid for the drinks and went out and found a taxi. It was an old vehicle that found the uphill journey to Mijas a struggle, and he drummed his fingers impatiently in the back.

He unlocked the gates with his special key and went in. Leanda's Golf was still in the garage, so she hadn't gone far if she was out. But if she was out she would have come to see him, not taken a leisurely stroll into Mijas. He was frightened now of finding a body on the floor, the victim of a robber's attack, which was common enough on this coast.

But there were no broken windows and nothing had been disturbed inside the house. He called her name and ran upstairs and called again. The silence alarmed him.

He found the note, appropriately, in the bar. Leanda didn't want him to miss it. It was scribbled in pencil on the notepaper she used to write home: 'Danny, I can't take any more. I've withdrawn 8 million pesetas to keep me going and am returning to England. L.'

The brusqueness of the note upset him almost as much as the contents. He stood motionless and read it again. He read it a third time and then, without moving his feet, reached for a bottle of whisky and poured himself a large drink.

She couldn't take any more, but the capacity to take had evidently not atrophied entirely: she could still take £40,000.

He poured the glass down his throat and refilled it.

When 'Cottage by the Sea' soared into the Top Ten in early September, one of the tabloid papers dispatched an alert feature writer to the Costa del Sol to 'write up' the unknown Englishman who spent his life singing in Spanish piano bars and had yet produced this beautiful, quintessentially English piece of popular music. The writer's name was Steve, and he was a surprisingly shy young man for such a strident calling. Mark was so pleased to see a journalist whose intention was not to probe, to expose and to humiliate his family, but merely to give his song-writing career a helpful push, that he insisted on buying the drinks that Steve would nevertheless claim back on his generous expenses.

Between Mark's stints at the piano, they sat on banquettes outside and discussed the recent history of pop music, lyrics and melodies, poetic inspiration, jazz, rock and soul, and which came first, the music or the words, while the yachts and the motor cruisers rolled in the water a few feet away. Mark chatted exuberantly, watching the cheap biro pen inscribe his authoritative words in a pad that looked as if it had been picked up in a street market. He was ecstatic. He realized that he had met his first fan.

Steve flew home, scribbling prolifically during the flight.

'It has taken an Englishman living in Spain and a Welshman living in America to revive the romantic tradition of the English ballad in its purest form,' he wrote. He wasn't quite sure what it meant, and nor was the sub-editor who put in some commas and then took them out again, but the sentence seemed to be saying something, which wasn't always the case with the sentences that arrived in shoals on the editorial floor, and eventually the Assistant Editor (Features) plucked it out, removed the last four words, and used it as one long headline in thirty-point type, laid in white over a dark picture of Mark that a local photographer was commissioned to take at the piano in Jay's.

His visitor the following evening was less welcome. Steve Finch came into Jay's wearing the uncertain look of a monk who has stumbled into a brothel. Alvin was playing and it was some time before he spotted Mark at the bar.

'I think we should talk,' he said, when he had found a path through the crowd.

Mark led him outside to the banquettes, which he was beginning to regard as his interview room.

'We have to discuss your *affaire d'amour*,' Steve Finch said, sitting down. He leaned forward, his hands together and his elbows on his knees, looking up at Mark's face in search of enlightenment.

Mark looked back at him, unsure how to react. He had nothing against Steve Finch, who had every reason to dislike him, but he was not going to allow him to assume the role of inquisitor.

'I don't see why we have to,' he said. 'Lots of other things to talk about.'

'The best thing to talk about is the future,' Steve Finch said. 'Nothing else matters much. I'm concerned about my future, and I need to know your intentions so far as Alison is concerned.'

'Are you planning to marry Emma?' Mark asked.

Steve Finch looked as if he was considering a truthful answer to this question, but his eyes told Mark that what he was really considering was what would be an appropriate reply in this situation.

'She wants to marry me,' he said, almost reluctantly.

'And you?'

'I'm concerned about Alison at the moment. She's my wife, in case you've forgotten.'

'I haven't forgotten, and nor has she.'

'I'm sure that we could work something out to the benefit of everybody. Cooperation is the *sine qua non*.' He looked at Mark now as if what was under discussion was a seat on the board.

'Do you think that divorce is a relevant concept in this day and age?' Mark asked him.

'No, I don't.'

'Nor do I.'

'But Emma does.'

'Well, Emma would.'

'Do I gather that you don't intend to marry Alison?'

'That's really something I'd prefer to discuss with her.'

Something snapped in Steve Finch then. 'Look, sunshine, you can do this the easy way or the hard way. I'm trying to save you money. I can sue for divorce on Alison's adultery. I can sue you for alienating my wife's affections. I can take you to the cleaners so that you can sing in there for the next ten years and you won't have a peseta. I'm in a better position. Nobody can touch me. Matthew has a pregnant girlfriend. He deserted his wife and skipped the country. Emma could get very nasty, and he can't hurt me.'

Mark nodded, more to himself than to Steve Finch. The deviousness of post-marital warfare was not a subject that he had learned. He had never had a wife, and he was dealing with a man who was about to acquire his third.

He said: 'What do you suggest?'

'I suggest you provide evidence of adultery so that I can get a quick, painless divorce. In return, no money will change hands. Emma's divorce will be a simple matter.'

A waiter called from the door to tell Mark that his return to the piano was overdue. He stood up and looked down at Steve Finch.

'All right,' he said.

*

237

The following day, emboldened by the ascent of 'Cottage by the Sea', he took Alison to look for homes. There were few places in the world where so many were being built so quickly or so well. People with no homes at all might be living in cardboard boxes south of the Limpopo, but round here those who already had several addresses in other countries needed new ones with four garages, a wine cellar and a swimming pool.

Awash with brochures, they drove around in Alison's Renault looking at luxurious developments that nestled between the mountains and the sea. Landscaped gardens, marble floors and satellite television were the sales pitch here, and the prices were high. They saw bijou houses, pastel-washed in pink, with hibiscus and bougainvillaea round the porch; seafront apartment blocks with shared swimming pools in secluded tropical gardens; and, down by the water's edge, town houses in one of the new beach-front villages with your boat tied up in the marina near your front door. Outwardly discreet, exceptional within, said the brochures. Nature and architecture working together.

'They look like the sort of places in which a girl could provide evidence of adultery,' said Alison. 'Do we have money?'

'We have great expectations,' Mark told her. 'In the meantime I can borrow.'

But he didn't want to buy a very expensive home. Unlike his brothers, he was not confined to this coast. Perhaps when the money rolled in he would want to buy a house in England, and use the Spanish home for only a part of the year.

In the afternoon they drove out on the Ronda road. Whole villages, with curving cobbled streets and fountains, were springing up in the wooded hills, designed to look as if they had been there for years. The traditional peace of the Spanish *pueblo* appealed to Mark, who was keen to put a few kilometres between himself and his drunken compatriots.

La Heredio was an Andalusian *pueblo* set on a hilltop 300 metres above the sea. No two houses were alike, but they each had wrought-iron grilles, mahogany doors and decorative tiles. The view was of the sea, Gibraltar and the mountains of Africa.

'The cheapest are 55,000,' said Mark.

'Pesetas?'

'Unfortunately not.'

'They'll be worth twice that in three years,' said Alison. 'They're lovely.'

'Is that a buy recommendation?'

'As your financial adviser, yes.'

'As my wife?'

'Get your chequebook out.'

They went into the sales office and Mark sat down to fill in forms.

FIFTEEN

KIM sat in the bar drinking Sprite lemonade and watching Matthew play pool with Manolo. She had pains in her abdomen that were new to her, and a backache which was quite different from others she had endured during what now seemed to have been an interminable pregnancy. Mild contractions had started that afternoon. She was hoping they would go away.

Matthew watched her from the pool table. That morning, having coffee in the El Toro bar in the square, where bright posters on the wall recalled long-forgotten *ferias* and bullfights, he had read his first booklet on the birth of babies and wondered if any couple had ever been so ill-prepared. There was no cot in the flat, no push-chair or baby clothes, no bedding or bottles or baby bath. Kim was superstitious. 'Let's wait until we have a baby,' she said. She had bought a few things that she would need in hospital and left it at that.

It was only when he was returning to the bar that Matthew remembered he no longer had a car. The plan all summer had been that he would drive Kim to the hospital in Malaga when the moment arrived, and now he didn't even have transport.

He sat in his bar when the pool game was over and made a list of some taxi numbers. Manolo had gone on to a bar in Las Rampas in the town centre, in search of information required in one office or another.

'You'd better close the bar,' Kim said. She had taken to going to bed earlier, but tonight she was staying up. She knew there would be no sleep.

'Are the contractions increasing?' he asked. He was suddenly learning new words.

'No, but we don't want the bar to be open when they really start, do we?'

The bar was empty at that moment so he locked the doors and pulled himself a Cruzcampo.

'Are you okay?' he asked.

She winced occasionally now, and he didn't know whether that was normal or not.

'I can't say I'm looking forward to the hospital. It would be bad enough at home . . .'

They waited. He found some dominoes under the counter and they had a game.

At midnight she said: 'Get a taxi.'

He rushed out of the bar and ran down the road to the telephone kiosk. The radio taxis were very efficient and he knew that one would arrive quickly.

Kim had collected her bag and was waiting by the door. 'They're every two or three minutes now,' she said. 'Is it coming?'

'It's on its way.'

But when the taxi arrived, the driver waved his hands.

'Hospital Materno-Infantil, Malaga,' Matthew said, ignoring the hand signals.

The driver said something which Kim picked up.

'They won't take pregnant women,' she said. 'Or not this pregnant.'

Matthew, starting to panic, would have dragged the man from the car and driven it himself, but the taxi had gone before he could argue.

'Manolo,' Kim said. 'Find Manolo.'

Matthew ran along the seafront in a real panic now. His mouth was dry, but his body was soaked with sweat. He hadn't run like this for years. It took him three minutes to reach Las Rampas, but it seemed like three hours. Why should his great talent for organization have deserted him on this of all nights?

He plunged into three bars in Las Rampas before he

saw Manolo, quietly drinking a gin at the bar. Manolo abandoned the gin and soon they were both running down the street to where he had left his little Seat 600. The one-way system held them up as they did a detour round the town to get back to Kim.

She was still standing outside, holding her back.

'I think we ought to hurry,' she said. She was the calmest person there. She climbed in the back because she said she would have more room, and Matthew sat in the front with her bag on his lap.

Once he was out on the main road Manolo drove at eighty miles an hour. He was sweating too. He hunched over the driving wheel, not speaking except to curse other vehicles which impeded his path. Kim, in the back, had started to groan.

Matthew couldn't remember being in a situation so fraught with disaster: if Kim didn't give birth on the back seat they would surely be killed on the road.

They reached the outskirts of Malaga in twenty-eight tense minutes. Posters supporting the ruling party, Partido Socialista Obrero Español, covered the brick walls, but the streets were strangely quiet for a city that stayed up late.

'I think my waters have broken,' Kim said.

'Where is the hospital?' Manolo asked.

'What? Don't you know?' Matthew shouted.

'I've never been there. It may be the Avenida de los Angeles. I don't know.'

'I was expecting to be in a taxi.'

Only Kim was thinking clearly now. 'Get one,' she said. 'We'll follow.'

A taxi appeared as she spoke and Manolo flashed his lights at it and pulled up. Matthew dumped Kim's bag on the front seat, jumped out and ran across the road to the taxi.

'Hospital Materno-Infantil,' he said. '*Rapido!*'

The two cars careered through empty, tree-lined streets, with Matthew urging the taxi driver to jump lights and Manolo struggling desperately to stay in touch.

'*Está muy cerca de aqui,*' the taxi driver said, and Matthew gathered they were getting close.

A minute later they pulled up outside an old building which turned out to be the hospital. They were greeted by a man with a gun. Manolo spoke to him and then rushed into the building, leaving Matthew to pay off the taxi. Manolo reappeared quite soon with a wheelchair and an official in a suit. He demanded to see their passports and their social security papers before Kim could be allowed in. She sat in the wheelchair, not speaking, while the man laboriously filled in forms. Matthew, impatient, wanted to get Kim into the hospital. The man with the gun moved closer to him.

Eventually the official waved them in, and Matthew pushed Kim into a long brown corridor with dozens of doors leading off into offices or wards on either side. They hadn't walked very far when the man with the gun stopped them. At first it wasn't clear why. Then a nurse appeared, a pretty, dark-haired girl who took the wheelchair from Matthew and started down the corridor. When Matthew went to follow, the man with the gun blocked his path.

'I'm attending the birth,' Matthew said in English.

The official who was standing near them suddenly revealed a knowledge of the language. 'It is not allowed in this hospital,' he said. 'Men, no.'

The evening had been taut enough with everything that could go wrong going wrong, and the bureaucracy was hard enough to cope with when he was relaxed. Matthew grabbed the man's gun arm, twisted it up his back and quickly had him helpless and face to the wall, with Matthew's knee in the small of his back, and his elbow in the back of his neck.

'I go in,' he said. He looked round to see the official

running down the corridor, and realized, with a slight feeling of dismay, that Manolo, his support and his interpreter, had gone – not wanting, perhaps, to be associated with Matthew's reckless behaviour.

Two doctors in white coats came running up the corridor. They stared, wide-eyed, at the scene which faced them.

'I want to attend the birth,' he said. 'My wife doesn't speak Spanish,' he added.

The doctors consulted. The man with the gun tried to adjust his face to a more comfortable position against the wall. One doctor left, and returned quickly with a white coat.

'Put this on,' he said. 'You can go in.'

Kim was in the delivery room with a doctor and two nurses. She was wired up to a machine that measured the size and frequency of her contractions. Studying the graph that the machine was compiling on a sheet of paper that was making its way to the floor, Matthew could see the size of her pain before she had felt it.

'Some people have epidurals, but apparently it's too late for that,' Kim said. Her head, to one side, was buried in the pillow.

Another machine was monitoring the baby's heart beats, for signs of distress.

'Do not push yet,' said the young nurse.

'She speaks English, thank God,' said Matthew.

'I was in London two years,' the girl said, smiling.

The doctor kept going out and coming in again. He never looked at Kim, only at the graph that was coming out of the machine and telling a story of rhythmic pain. It went on like that for two hours.

It was nearly half-past three when the nurses called the doctor in to examine Kim. He smiled at her for the first time.

'I think you're ready,' he said.

Matthew stood by the side of the bed, feeling that he

was, after all, in the way. The nurse told Kim to push when she had a contraction.

Suddenly a wet, greenish object shot from between her legs. It was shouting. The head must have been out before, but Matthew hadn't seen it.

The doctor had the baby in a towel. He severed the cord and held the baby up for Kim to see.

'It's a boy,' he said. 'He's good.' He checked the baby's hands, feet, mouth and nose and then gave him to Kim to hold. She smiled, but seemed too tired to speak.

'That's very clever of you,' said Matthew, kissing her. 'Be careful with him. He's going to look after you in your old age.'

The boy, unaware of the duties that were already being laid on him, seemed to be looking at them both. He didn't cry and his eyes stayed open.

A man came into the room now and with barely a grunt took the baby's fingerprints, then Kim's and then Matthew's.

'How extraordinary,' said Matthew. 'The baby isn't three minutes old and they want his fingerprints. He hasn't even given us a cloth to wipe our hands.'

But this strange episode, faintly disturbing through its associations, was nothing alongside the formalities which now engulfed him.

Once the baby had been weighed – 4 kilos and 400 grams – and placed in a cot by Kim's bed, Matthew was led out of the room, along the corridor and into an office by the official who had first met him at the hospital door. The Spanish way of doing things demanded that he provide the name of his father and mother – but no information about Kim's parents. He was then taken into another room where they not only photographed him but also took his footprints. Matthew had never had his footprints taken before, nor heard of anybody who had; he was beginning to feel like a character in a Kafka story.

But there was some light at the end of this strange tunnel. For the final demand of the hospital officials was that he visit a judge's all-night offices on the Calle Larios to sign a document which would enable the hospital to send Matthew a bill if his social security payments were found to be in arrears. He paid 14,000 pesetas a month in social security, and knew that he was not in arrears, but the baby would not be released from the hospital until they had the signed document, witnessed by a judge.

The Calle Larios was a fifteen-minute walk away. Tired, excited and confused, he walked it like a man in a dream. He was a father at last. There was a small person who was going to depend on him for a long time. It was a very odd feeling and he tried to picture the face in the cot. A teenager in the twenty-first century! What sort of life would he have? He would probably fly to Australia in half an hour, have television on his wristwatch, live to be a hundred, and go to his one-day-a-week job in his own small helicopter. Every generation seemed to have more fun than the last, although none appreciated the fact until it was too late. Perhaps he would become Prime Minister, perhaps he would be a mass murderer. Perhaps it would depend on how his parents treated him. Nature, nurture, environment, heredity. His head spun in the Spanish dawn.

The judge spoke perfect English. He sat in a large, gloomy office that smelt of Condal cigarettes, and he seemed to be glad to have a visitor. He examined Matthew's genuine passport, and then he watched him sign the document the hospital had given him. He signed it himself and hit it with a rubber stamp.

'The boy will be Spanish until he is sixteen – you understand that?' the judge asked, lighting a cigarette.

'I didn't realize,' Matthew said. He had never thought about it.

'At sixteen he can choose his own nationality, but until then he is Spanish.' The judge re-lit the cigarette which had gone out as soon as he had lit it. 'This gives you as the father the right of residence. You can't be extradited.' At this stage the judge allowed himself a small smile. 'Not even if the British police want you.'

Matthew smiled back at such a fanciful notion, but his heart jumped. He was free at last! The Inland Revenue could pound their tiny fists until the blood ran, but he was untouchable.

He walked back to the hospital with a stride that was noticeably springier than it had been on the outward journey.

It was six o'clock now and many people were going to work. When you took three hours for lunch you had to start early. To help them on their way some bars had already opened, dispensing coffees and the deep-fried churros which the Spanish liked for breakfast. It was their least important meal.

Matthew went into one and ordered a black coffee and a Veterano. It was an austere place, all white tiles and old furniture with one wall lined with vats. He sat at a table in the corner and thought about what had happened.

An exhausting, sleepless night, in which one disaster had seemed to follow another, had turned out to be wonderfully memorable. And now, free from the threat of extradition, he had a son. He drank his coffee and wondered what name he should be given. He had thought of a few when he remembered that the baby was, for the present, Spanish, and then the name was obvious.

He would call his son Juan, after a King who had taken this country from Fascist dictatorship to Socialist democracy in seven miraculous years, and then, in England, he could become John, after his grandfather.

He reached for the brandy and amused himself by imagining a notice in *The Times*: To Matthew Ward and Kimberley Jane Bradley (née Raynsford), a son, Juan.

*

There was no question of going to sleep. He was fizzing like a carbonated drink.

He left a message at the hospital where Kim and the baby now slept, and caught the commuter train out of Malaga. It rumbled over the cliffs through seventeen brief stops to deposit him fifty minutes later in the subterranean station at Fuengirola. He climbed into the brightest sunshine and looked for a taxi. Lady, impatiently entombed at Matt's Place, leapt willingly into the car, and Matthew told the driver to go to Mijas.

Sprawled on a sunbed on the terrace, Daniel was playing chess with himself on a board on the ground beside him. He had a bishop in one hand and a breakfast glass of champagne in the other. White was supposed to be winning, but black's game was full of concealed threats. He heard a taxi pull up and went indoors to consult the screen – even an unscrupulous hack from the gutter press would make welcome company now.

But it was Matthew and Lady, and he pressed the button which opened the gates and went out to meet them.

'You have a nephew,' Matthew shouted. 'He's sent me round to collect the present.'

'That's terrific, Matthew,' Daniel said. Unusually, they shook hands. 'You've reproduced yourself at last!'

'What a night that was! I fell off the bed twice. Where's Leanda?'

'I've gained a nephew and lost a wife. Drink?'

'Beer. I've got to go back to the hospital this afternoon. Biscuits and water for my dog.'

Daniel disappeared and returned with his order.

'What do you mean – you've lost a wife?'

'Leanda's flown home. Left me a note. Can't take any more. That sort of thing.' He looked at his brother. 'You did warn me.'

'What are you going to do?'

248

'There's not much I can do, is there? I can hardly chase after her, which I believe is the normal procedure. I hope that she and Mrs Plumridge will be very happy together, although I doubt it.' He sat on the sunbed and picked up his champagne. 'I don't like the idea of living on my own.'

'You'll drink too much,' Matthew said. He didn't like the look of his brother. The defection of Leanda had produced a wild look in his eyes. Psychosis loomed.

'When didn't I drink too much?' he said.

'It's always possible to drink more. Does Mark know?'

Daniel shook his head. 'I haven't seen him. I haven't seen anybody. I've been sitting here on my own for three days thinking about it.' He poured himself some more champagne. 'I want you to get Kim a car before she comes out of hospital. I'm going to give you a cheque. Twenty thousand pounds should cover it.'

'The insurance will pay.'

'Not that much it won't.'

He stared vacantly down at the tennis court and the pool. It seemed a big home for a small man.

'While we're talking about money, I want to take my loot out of your safe,' Matthew told him.

'You think it's safe to put it in the bank now?'

'It'll be in Kim's name. She deserves a little security. Have you attended a birth?'

'Fortunately, no.'

'I was thinking – there are two conspiracies of silence. One between men, and one between women. Married men never tell single men how bad marriage is, and women who have babies never tell women who haven't how awful childbirth is.'

'Bad as that, was it?'

'Bad.'

'But it doesn't sound as if you will be getting married.'

'Oh, I will. Kim isn't Emma, and I've got a son and

heir. He's Spanish until he's sixteen and as his father I can't be extradited. Emma's after a divorce to marry Steve Finch, so look for a couple of weddings in Marbella next year.'

Suddenly Daniel started to cry. Lady sniffed round him, confused by the unfamiliar noise. Matthew looked at the lawn sprinkler, turning in the sun, and wondered why the prospect of his own marriage should reduce his brother to tears.

'It's not that bad,' he said. 'I've heard that some marriages are actually quite happy.'

'Why am I always out of step?' Daniel asked. 'You and Mark will get married just as I lose my wife. Frankly, I don't like the look of the future. This villa might seem like the ultimate in living accommodation, but I've been bloody lonely here these last three days, and what does the future hold apart from loneliness? I was thinking in bed last night of changing my name and going back to England. Do you think I would get away with it?'

'For a while, but you couldn't spend the rest of your life looking over your shoulder.'

'The question is – what can I spend the rest of my life doing? Becoming a suntanned alcoholic isn't all that fulfilling when you're only twenty-five.'

'You never set about creating a satisfying life here. You were on holiday from the moment you arrived. I believe the suggestion was that you lay off the hooch and find yourself some useful work.'

'I did lay off the drink for a while. Leanda and I had the idea of having a baby to enrich our lives, but we couldn't even do that. The work idea ran into a language barrier.'

'Learning Spanish is the first thing you should have done when you got here, and there are plenty of jobs you could have done without it.'

Daniel refilled his glass and took a large drink. 'I developed an aversion to the classroom as a schoolboy. What jobs, anyway?'

'You could have compiled crosswords, seeing as you're obsessed with them. You could have written a book. *How I Made A Million*. I was in business here within a month of arriving and I didn't know twenty words of Spanish.'

'You were always a worker.'

'It's where the only true satisfaction lies, kid. As you're now finding out.' He finished his beer and stood up. 'How about a game of tennis, followed by a spot of lunch? After that, you can drive me and Lady to Malaga to see my son, seeing as how I don't seem to have a car.'

Daniel's enthusiastic response to this programme revealed the awful emptiness of his life, Matthew thought. The man needs something to do, but is too lazy to even think about what it could be.

He had slowed down on the tennis court, too, and missed shots that a few months earlier he would have returned effortlessly.

'I believe Lendl does without the pre-match champagne,' he said. At five-four down he threw up.

After a recuperative hour on the terrace and a light lunch, they drove into Malaga in the white Golf that Leanda had left behind.

'Have you been in touch with her?' Matthew asked.

'I don't know what to say to her.'

'Come back would do for a start.'

'I never lead with my chin.'

'Well, she can only hit it.'

'Yes, and I wouldn't like that. I'm going to end up like one of those British traitors in Russia who live alone in some chilly dacha. They're dead for a week before anybody finds the body.'

'You're a bit young to be contemplating your exit,' Matthew said. 'Turn left here – you can park in the street.'

Kim was sitting on the side of her bed, gazing into the cot and laughing.

'This child is a hoot,' she said. She had been moved into a ward where there were half a dozen other mothers with babies. It was surprisingly quiet.

'I've brought my crapulent sibling,' Matthew told her. He was feeling so bright on no sleep that he wondered why he had spent so much of his life in bed.

'How are you, Kim?' Daniel asked, kissing her.

'I've been doing my exercises. It's like being in the army in here. How are you?'

'Not firing on all cylinders, I'm afraid.' He looked down at the baby as if he had never seen one before. 'He looks like Matthew.'

'Well, that's a relief,' said Kim. 'I was afraid he might look like one of the others. He's had his first bath and thoroughly enjoyed it.'

Matthew bent over the cot. His son had black hair and waved his arms about a lot. He thought he had never seen such an intelligent baby.

He sat on the bed with Kim and told her about his experiences at the hands of Spain's bureaucracy that morning, and of the circumstances which had led him to choose Juan/John as the baby's name.

'I like it,' she said. 'Now he's here I have a shopping list.' She handed him a large sheet of hospital notepaper on which she had written: push-chair, crib, changing mat, vests, baby bath, bucket, towels and nappies. 'There are other things that I'll choose myself,' she said. 'Motherhood is all about spending money.'

'Terrific,' said Matthew, putting the list in his pocket. He bent down and lifted Juan from his cot. Segueing into the role of devoted father, he found, was no effort at all. The baby, happy to be raised from the boredom of his cot, turned in his hands to look at the view. Kim stood up and made a kissing noise to him.

This scene of domestic delight depressed Daniel, who sat on the bed saying nothing. It seemed to him that the less he had, the more everybody else received. It would be Mark next, no doubt brandishing twins.

'I don't feel too good,' he said, standing up. 'I'm going out for some fresh air.'

'Leanda has gone back to England,' said Matthew when he had gone. 'Juan's aunty has legged it. A trick she obviously picked up from her spouse.'

'Oh, no,' said Kim. 'What's he going to do?'

'That's what he wonders. He's tired of living and scared of dying is how it seems to me.'

He looked at his son who was now beaming up as if he had been given the best possible start to life's great adventure.

Matthew thought of the contrast between the smile of the baby and the scowl of the adult. A little experience of life was a sobering thing.

Mark and Alison drove up the coast in the early evening sun. They had spent the afternoon at their future home where Alison had taken a number of measurements that were crucial to her plans for furnishing and decorating. The plans were extravagant, but Mark found that he could face this unaccustomed expenditure without misgiving.

'Cottage by the Sea' had leapfrogged over more raucous offerings from new pop groups who had long names that sounded more like book titles and lodged itself at number four in the charts from where it looked challengingly at a song from the latest American teenage sensation, a girl in the throes of puberty; a new inferior version of a Nat King Cole classic, sung by a glassy-eyed Glaswegian with a crewcut; and a stirring rendition by a brass band that had surprisingly been elevated to pop prominence by exposure on a television series about Britain's imperial past.

A video of Tom Jones singing Mark's song (as shown on *Top of the Pops* and many other programmes) had now reached Marbella from Conrad Gambardella, and been played a few dozen times on the television and video recorder that Alison had provided in his flat.

The song jumped now from the car radio in Alison's Renault which was tuned permanently to BFBS, the British Forces Broadcasting Service that was transmitted for twenty-four hours a day from Gibraltar.

'What a clever man you are,' Alison said.

'You can't get away from me, can you?'

'That's the last thing I want.'

'I like the sound of this song.'

The man presenting the programme, who sounded exactly like every other programme presenter that Mark had ever heard, predicted that 'Cottage by the Sea' would reach number one before too long. Mark smiled to himself. He was sure that the man was right. Five versions of the song by singers whose names were known round the world were being produced in recording studios in America, and Conrad Gambardella's latest letter had suggested that it was always better to have two Rolls Royces, anyway, as the car attracted the destructive envy of vandals.

They left the main road at the Fuengirola turn-off and dropped into the little town. Tonight's mission, until work called, was to wet the baby's head.

'I must say,' said Alison as they pulled up outside Matt's Place, 'your brothers do seem to have action-packed lives. New babies, vanishing wives, dodgy money. Why aren't you like them?'

'I never had the education, miss, although I've done enough reading since to know that dodgy money is a bit of a euphemism.'

'Interesting is what they are,' she said, switching off the ignition and smiling at him. He smiled back, but he did wonder how she could consider becoming involved with a family whose scions had acquitted themselves so disgracefully, and whose shady behaviour was so far removed from the conventional moral standards of Steve Finch. Re-

254

bellion at thirty? A look beyond the kitchen sink before it was too late? A second attempt at life after a false start? He put his arm round her and went into the bar.

The champagne was out again. Three bottles stood in ice buckets on the counter, and Matthew was filling glasses from a fourth. Kim, in a loose yellow dress, was sitting on the customers' side, looking down into a wooden crib.

The previous day Matthew had collected her and the baby in an almost new Mercedes that was registered in her name. On the front seat were documents concerning her new bank account in which he had deposited £50,000, withdrawn nostalgically from the pillow in Daniel's safe. The rest of his money was now in his own safe in the bar, but his intention was to get Kim to take it to Gibraltar where it could hide and breed.

'This is your Spanish nephew,' Matthew said. 'He's having a rare nap.'

'I want to hold him,' Alison said. 'Isn't he beautiful?'

'It comes from the mother,' said Mark. 'Matthew's role was a small one.'

'I saw, I conquered, I came,' said Matthew, lifting Juan from the crib and giving him to Alison. 'He keeps going to the lavatory, which is a bit boring because he doesn't go to the lavatory.'

'How do you get to have one of these?' Alison asked.

'It's a bit complicated, actually,' Matthew told her. 'I'll lend you a book.'

'Give it to Mark,' she said. 'He's in charge of that sort of thing.'

Through the window they saw a white Golf park behind Alison's Renault. Daniel got out and came into the bar.

'I must have had eleven or eight pints by now,' he said. 'Where's the urinal?'

'I hate that word,' said Alison, putting Juan back in the crib. 'It sounds like one of those package holiday hotels. The Urinal Sol.'

255

Daniel came out. It was surprising how pale somebody could look after spending a summer in the sun. His pink shirt was flecked with dirt and his jeans seemed old enough to discard.

'Just a bottle of champagne then,' he said. 'This is one of my favourite bars, with the drink being so cheap.'

'Make the most of it,' said Kim. 'Matthew is selling it.'

'I'm losing my barmaid,' said Matthew. 'It's on the market for 22 million. Any offers?'

'What's that in proper money?' Mark asked.

'A hundred and ten thousand pounds. We're going to find a place in the hills like you. If we get near enough we might let you babysit.' He pulled a fresh bottle from the ice bucket and refilled their glasses. 'I'm not running this place on my own.'

'We're going to bring this child up in the fresh air,' said Kim. 'We're going to be honest rustics.'

'Well, semi-honest,' said Matthew. 'We're going to till the soil and feed the world. I used to be the richest of this trio and now I'm going to be the pauper of the clan.'

Mark raised a hand. 'You've reminded me,' he said. 'Talking about this clan, I have some news.' He pulled an envelope from a pocket in his shirt. 'I have a letter here from a relative. In case any of you had forgotten, our father, who art in England, is sixty next week and he's coming out here for the occasion.'

The news, arriving unexpectedly, seemed to deprive the others of the power of speech.

Matthew, his head full of other things, had completely forgotten this long-promised visit and the milestone of a birthday that it was to celebrate. Daniel, fearful of the confrontation, had pushed it from his mind several months ago and a memory damaged by alcohol was never likely to recall it. In fact he wasn't sure now that he had ever been told.

'Let's see the letter,' he said. The familiar brisk strokes

of his father's handwriting evoked a score of memories, many of them concerning his efforts at school, his successes or, more usually, his failures, as relayed home by the tyrant in the classroom.

Dear Mark, *it said*.

I'll be arriving at Malaga at 21.15 on the 29th, and would like to take you all out to dinner on my birthday the following day. Could you (a) meet me at the airport (b) book me into a hotel (c) book a nice restaurant for the 30th. Many congratulations on your record. I hear it everywhere. It has been the only consolation in a grim year.

Daniel gave the letter to Matthew.

'What does he mean, a grim year?' Matthew asked.

'Think about it,' said Mark.

'You and me,' said Daniel.

'I'm not looking forward to this visit,' Matthew said. 'I don't like the feel of it.'

Mark took the letter, returned it to the envelope and put it back in his shirt pocket. 'We're going to have to put on a show,' he said. 'It's his sixtieth birthday, for God's sake. I've booked him into the Dinamar, so he can walk across the beach to Banus, but what restaurant do we want?'

'Why can't he stay with one of us, anyway?' Daniel asked. 'We've got homes.'

'Perhaps he thinks it would be invidious,' Kim suggested. 'Which son would he choose?'

Matthew sat down. 'I hope to God he's going to be all right. I mean, he's going to be civil, isn't he?'

Alison laughed at his troubled face. 'Of course he's going to be civil, Matthew. He's going to find one son living with somebody else's flirty wife. He's going to find two other sons on the run from the police. One of them has just been deserted by his wife because he drinks too much, and the other has deserted his wife to father an illegitimate child by somebody else's. Why shouldn't he be civil? Just what a father always wanted for his sons, I should imagine. Sort of thing he dreamed about when they were in short pants.' She drank her champagne. Her stark résumé of their present situation produced a melancholy silence which almost echoed.

'Perhaps we should tell him not to come,' Daniel proposed eventually. The prospect filled him with dismay; he could see himself reduced again to the status of scolded schoolboy. 'Tell him the hotels are full. Tell him there's a lot of dysentery about. Tell him anything.'

'It's very touching to see these devoted sons longing to be reunited with their father,' Mark said. 'What did he ever do to you?'

'It's not what he's done, it's what he's going to do,' said Matthew.

'It's not what he's going to do, it's what you've done,' Mark corrected him. 'You have to face up to the consequences of your own actions in this world, kids. It's time to be brave.'

'Couldn't we bung him some money?' Daniel suggested. 'It's his birthday, after all. I could buy him a Bentley if we can find out how to switch the money to London.'

'Given the publicity you've managed to attract I should think that a Bentley would be a bit of an embarrassment at the golf club,' Mark told him. 'I thought you'd discovered already that money isn't the answer to everything.'

Customers were coming in now and Matthew left the anxious family conference to serve them. A lean Scandinavian demanded a blue lagoon, which Matthew had never heard of: it turned out to be a vodka, blue curaçao and lemonade. An Italian couple, bucking their national stereotype, wanted malt whisky. Two old ladies, newly widowed, newly rich, wanted nothing less than Harveys

Bristol Cream with ice. Life was much easier when people asked for beer.

The family conference, when he returned, had retreated with ice bucket to a table in the corner of the room, where the mood was, if anything, even more funereal. In fact nobody was speaking at all.

Matthew told Mark: 'If the source of our money is the cause of concern, you'll have to buy the birthday presents.'

'I imagine a gold watch would be acceptable from one of you. Something less ostentatious than a Bentley. You know what England's like. It's all gossip and envy most of the time.'

'I'll get the gold watch,' said Daniel. 'He can always give it away.'

'I'll buy him a camera,' said Matthew, 'so he can return with pictures of the sons that he is so proud of.'

Mark recoiled from the sarcasm attached to these promises. He wanted, above all, for his father to enjoy this holiday, and to forget for a while even if he couldn't forgive.

He said: 'I want you both to come to the airport with me. I want you to smile. I want to see a warm welcome. He may have complaints against you, but you have none against him.'

'I'll come and greet him,' Matthew said, 'but I can't imagine what is going to happen.'

'What's he like, anyway?' Kim asked. 'Matthew never talks about him.'

'The very memory makes him feel guilty, I should imagine. He's a fine man, isn't he, Matthew?'

'Don't go on about it, Mark. Yes, he is.'

'He brought the three of us up without a mother. He worked like hell to keep us together as a family, when relatives urged him to farm us out. His life is a story of grief and sacrifices, and I think that the golf club that he didn't join until he was fifty was his first genuine relaxation.'

'He's a good man,' said Daniel. 'That doesn't mean that I want to see him just at the moment. Is there any more champagne, or are we all going on the wagon until he's gone?'

Matthew went off and returned with two bottles.

'This was not intended to be a maudlin inquest into the Ward family's tribulations,' he said. 'You are supposed to be celebrating the arrival of Juan.'

A cry from the crib was a further reminder to them of why they were there. Kim bent over the baby and decided that he was hungry. 'I shall have to take him upstairs,' she said.

'But first,' said Matthew, 'a toast to my son and heir.'

'Who will welcome you with enthusiasm should you visit him when he's thirty,' said Mark.

They raised their glasses to the crib, but some of them were still preoccupied with dark thoughts about the baby's grandfather.

SIXTEEN

JOHN WARD exchanged his leather suitcase for a boarding card and went through passport control to the duty-free shop. He scanned the rows of cigarettes and drinks but, even at these prices, could find nothing that he wanted and he left the shop and went out to wait for his flight.

He had been dreading this day. Confronting his sons was a disagreeable duty that had hung over him all summer, and his destination was not the one that, in happier circumstances, he would have chosen. To him, Marbella was where men with criminal backgrounds ended up after the big house in Kent had begun to attract police attention. It was where you lived when you had graduated from armed robbery in Hatton Garden to the much more remunerative smuggling of cannabis from Morocco. It was a place renowned for its cupidity, its self-indulgence and its diseased beliefs; it affronted him.

He found a seat and sat down. His idea of a holiday was a four-star hotel in North Devon, with a five-mile beach for walks below his bedroom window and a choice of golf courses within a few miles. Perhaps when he returned he would book himself a holiday at Saunton Sands.

They called a gate number for his flight and he stood up and joined other passengers on the long trek to the plane. In this crowd of holidaymakers, informally dressed, noisily cheerful, he stood out, a tall, upright man in a grey suit with his grey hair carefully brushed back. All that was missing was a briefcase.

The passengers were allowed on the plane about ten minutes after they had been due to take off. He sat alone by a window and found the airline's magazine in the pocket in front of him. His midweek £116 ticket suggested that the flight would last more than three hours, but he knew that this wasn't true; Spain's clocks must be an hour ahead of Britain's. He opened the magazine and read that there were a thousand castles in Spain. He read that Africa was only fourteen miles from the Spanish coast. In the end he read the safety-procedure card to take his mind off the sons who were waiting for him. He had learned a long time ago that the world would break your heart if you let it.

He had never been to Spain. Flying down the west coast of France he began to wonder what it was like to live there. What interested him was the Catholicism which nagged at its mind and his. Why was it that countries that had endured a stringent Catholic regime with all birth control banned, countries like Ireland and Spain, had such absurdly small populations? If the Catholic fathers had had their way they would be the biggest countries in Europe by now. Something awful must have been going on in the homes – guilt, violence, perversions, kitchen abortions. And all caused by Catholicism.

But belief wasn't shed as easily as that. It pestered him still – he sometimes wondered, for instance, whether God was punishing him for not naming his third son Luke.

They flew over the Pyrenees and the light began to fade. He peered from his window at the strange country that lay beneath him: the lack of lights suggested that most of it was uninhabited.

When they began to drop over the mountains north of Malaga he saw that he would be arriving on time after all. He put his watch on an hour and wished that he had bought himself a drink during the flight.

They landed with a bump in the darkness. He waited to leave the plane, and then he queued to have his passport scrutinized by a man in a uniform. In London it would have been a chap in a suit. Finally, he waited longest for his suitcase. When other people's baggage began to appear, his didn't. The conveyor belt seemed to be full of golf clubs and push-chairs. He was beginning to wonder whether his suitcase was on its way to Hong Kong when it emerged through a rubber curtain and inched its way towards him. He snatched it up and marched out into the main hall of the airport building.

Three men in jeans and shirts stood against a wall about thirty yards away. One was a big, untidy man with black, curly hair. Next to him was a tall, thin chap with his hands in his pockets, and the third man, shorter and balding, had a hideous scar down the centre of his forehead. They were all very brown and they all needed haircuts.

He barely recognized his own sons.

'You all look thinner,' he said when they came over to him. 'Are you eating?'

He hugged them in turn. 'What happened to you?' he asked Daniel, who had seemed to be hanging back from his embrace.

'Car crash, Dad.'

Matthew took his case and led him outside to Kim's Mercedes.

'Whose car is this?' he asked, getting into the front seat.

'It's Kim's,' Matthew told him.

'I haven't met Kim.'

'You're about to. She wants to show you your grandson.'

'I didn't know I had a grandson.'

'He only arrived last week. We saved the news as a surprise.'

Matthew drove off towards Fuengirola, and John Ward stared out of the window at the Spain that he had never seen.

'It's great that you've come,' Matthew told him. 'It's taken long enough.'

John Ward looked at him. 'Don't confuse my presence with approval,' he said.

The reply was so formal that Matthew found himself edged into the same mode. 'I don't expect your approval, but I hope to enjoy your presence. Still,' he added, attempting to change the atmosphere with a light-hearted remark, 'we only did what you always recommended: show a profit.'

'A profit without honour.' Surprised to find himself making a joke, John Ward added: 'It's from St Matthew, Matthew. A prophet is not without honour, save in his own country.'

'It was a good joke, Dad.'

'What is my grandson called?'

'John. But at the moment he is Juan, because he has Spanish nationality until he is sixteen.'

'He's beautiful,' said Mark from the back of the car. 'You'll love him.'

John Ward didn't say anything. He was thinking that the only heir to be produced by three healthy sons was an illegitimate boy with a Spanish name.

They drove off the main road and into a pleasant little town and then through some backstreets until they found themselves on the seafront. It was a long seafront, with palm trees and a promenade, and John Ward, who was not disposed to enjoy this place, was pleasantly surprised. On the other side of the road from the sea was a row of shops, restaurants and bars. They pulled up outside one of the bars.

'It's closed,' said John Ward.

'But I'm going to open it,' said Matthew. 'Do you see what it says up there?' He pointed to the sign above the window: MATT'S PLACE.

'I see,' said John Ward. 'This is where the money is invested.'

Matthew showed them in, put on the lights and went upstairs to fetch Kim and the baby. John Ward looked round at the tiny bar. It was hard to imagine Matthew being satisfied with this after the media empire that he had created.

'What will you drink, Dad?' Mark asked, going behind the counter. 'I'll have to be going to work soon, and I'll show you to your hotel.'

'Whisky.' John Ward looked at his youngest son, now perched somewhat self-consciously on a bar stool.

'Where's Leanda?' he asked.

It was among several questions that Daniel was not looking forward to.

'She's gone back to England, I'm afraid,' he said. 'I'll have a whisky, too, Mark.'

'Do you mean for good?'

'So she says.'

'I'm sorry to hear that,' said John Ward. 'Why did she go?'

'She wasn't happy here.'

'Danny drank too much,' said Mark. 'She got fed up with it.'

'And Emma? What happened to her? She was flying out to see Matthew the last I heard.'

'She met a man here and now lives with him.'

John Ward took his whisky from Mark and drank a little. 'What extraordinary lives you people lead,' he said. 'So there will be no girls at my birthday party tomorrow?'

'Just your sons,' said Mark. 'Kim will be looking after the baby.' He thought his father had heard enough about the romantic lives of his sons for the time being, without introducing the subject of Alison who had decided anyway not to be the only female guest.

John Ward drank some more whisky and thought about the exhausting efforts he had made to keep his family together when his wife had died. Today they split up and formed new liaisons with the casualness of the zoo. Unfair, he thought. Animals were more dependable.

He stood up as Matthew appeared with a woman, and wondered whether standing up when a lady entered the room was now regarded as quaint and old-fashioned. The woman, a very pretty girl who looked to be in her late twenties, was carrying a baby.

'Kim, this is my father,' Matthew said very formally.

'Hallo, Kim,' said John Ward. 'May I hold him?'

'It's nice to have met you,' Kim said, passing him Juan. 'I was wondering whether I ever would.'

John Ward stared down at his first grandchild and found himself blinking back tears. The baby looked exactly like his own sons who had laid in his arms and carried his grandiose hopes all those years ago.

'Hallo, John,' he said.

'I have a surprise for you,' he told them the following evening over dinner. They were drinking birthday champagne at Don Leone's at Puerto Banus, sitting at the tables outside and looking at the yachts and the crowds. The canopies over the waterfront boutiques and restaurants gave the place the appearance of a film set, John Ward thought. The cars that cruised slowly between them and the harbour were all in the Lamborghini and Ferrari bracket, and some of the yachts would have cost several million pounds. He could see the appeal of the place and the champagne was helping him to enjoy it.

Daniel had presented him with a gold Rolex watch, and Matthew had produced a superb Pentax that zoomed in on its subject like a television camera. Mark had given him a present which had presumably cost him nothing – a copy of his record. It was the gift that he appreciated most.

The restaurant, with its al fresco setting and bright pink tablecloths, was the busiest in the port. 'Never eat in an empty restaurant is rule one down here,' Mark had said, and he had certainly booked them into the right one in the right place tonight. John Ward had researched it during a walk across the beach from his hotel that afternoon. The marina was a harbour that was called a port, built for the recreation of the rich by José Banús whose bronze statue at the end of a jetty now gazed approvingly across the crowded water at the slim, white buildings and the carmine bougainvillaea that covered them.

'What surprise?' Matthew asked.

'A golf-club friend of mine who is staying at Sotogrande has a boat down here and he has offered to take us out. A day trip into the wild blue yonder. Fancy it?'

'That would be fun,' said Mark. 'What sort of boat is it?'

'A motor cruiser, whatever that is. Are you two on?'

'Great idea,' said Matthew. 'I always hoped that Danny would buy a boat.'

'I'm a landlubber,' Daniel said. 'But I'll come for the ride.'

A waiter arrived with their Grand Marnier soufflé, which he promptly enveloped in flames. Three musicians, who would return later for the money, strolled among the tables making music. On the front a mime artist with a face concealed by white make-up was following different people in the crowd, imitating their walk and their gestures behind their backs. He produced ribald laughter among the diners and he, too, would be back shortly for the money.

'It's an extraordinary country,' said John Ward. 'The bank clerks are in shirt sleeves, yet the barmen wear bow ties. In Britain, the bank clerks must wear smart suits, and the barmen look like tramps.'

'A lot of things are the other way round,' Matthew told him. 'For instance, when you want a drink here, the bars are open.'

'I can see why you like it,' John Ward admitted. 'It has a lot of character.'

'A lot of shady characters, too,' Mark said. 'Present company excepted. There's a bar along there which is owned by a man who would get twenty years if he set foot in England. His name was on a list of wanted Britons sent to the interior ministry here when Spain joined the EEC.'

'What's he like?'

'Charming chap. Behaves impeccably. They all do. They have to. Spain doesn't mind if you've annoyed Britain, but if you annoy Spain it's a different matter.'

Matthew drank his champagne, relieved that his father's visit, after an awkward start, was proving so peaceful. He had been prepared for explosions and recriminations that might have split the family for ever, but his father had pursued a diplomatic course that had made the evening unexpectedly enjoyable. Occasionally, if you caught him off guard, he looked sad and even worried, but mostly he had tried to be agreeable company.

He looked a little sad now, and Matthew decided to jolly him along.

'What happened in the war, Dad?' he asked. It was a question they had annoyed him with as boys. John Ward, seventeen when the war ended, had never worn a uniform, a source of frustration ever since.

'The buses had wooden seats,' he replied as usual.

'Is that all you remember?' Daniel asked. 'What about the banana famine?'

'I remember Neville Chamberlain's message that morning,' said John Ward. 'Want to hear it? "I am speaking to you from the Cabinet Room at 10 Downing Street. This morning the British Ambassador in Berlin handed the German Government a final note stating that unless we heard from them by eleven o'clock that they were prepared at once to withdraw their troops from Poland, a state of war would exist between us. I have to tell you that no such undertaking has been received, and that consequently this country is at war with Germany. You can imagine what a bitter blow it is to me that all my long struggle to win peace has failed. Yet I cannot believe that there is anything more or anything different that I could have done that would have been more successful.'''

'He's learned it like most people learn Shakespeare,' Mark said.

'It made a big impression on me,' John Ward said. 'It was a very sombre morning. I was nearly twelve.'

'What I don't understand about this war that you were so sorry to miss,' said Matthew, 'is that we went into it to save Poland from the Germans and came out giving Poland to the Russians. Still, only 54 million people died.'

'That doesn't sound like a man who is brimming over with respect for politicians,' said Daniel. 'Not that I blame him.'

John Ward turned to his youngest son, who had been the most subdued of his guests, fidgeting, uneasy, refusing to meet his eyes.

'Talking about politicians,' he said, 'I noticed the other day that our great Chancellor of the Exchequer, Mr Lawson, was educated at your school.'

'A certain financial nous was obviously transmitted by osmosis,' Daniel said. 'Nigel and I just sort of picked it up.'

'I don't think a comparison between this particular pair of Old Boys will stand too much examination,' John Ward said, surprised at this stab at humour. He called for the bill. 'I would like to hear Mark sing in his piano bar now,' he told them.

'Well, it's your birthday,' Matthew said.

'I just can't believe that sixty years can pass so quickly.'

'So enjoy yourself, father. There's no other intelligent response to life – unless you're a Catholic.'

'I'm not a Catholic,' said John Ward, but even now he half expected to hear a cock crow three times.

They walked along the front to Jay's. The place was crowded as usual.

Mark found them a table, bought them drinks and went to the piano. Usually he started cold and felt nervous, but tonight he was helped by his father's champagne. He began with a trio of Neil Sedaka songs. John Ward watched, fascinated. Playing beautiful music while people talked seemed to him to be one of the hardest ways to earn a living. He had, he realized, always underestimated his eldest son's dedication.

He looked at his second son. Matthew was listening to the music and tapping a finger on the table. Whatever it was that had driven him to the wealth he had so briefly amassed, had gone – leaving behind a more peaceful person, freed from his demons and his tensions, and seemingly content with the world.

Mark's last Sedaka song was 'The Hungry Years'. He was thinking of Alison, whose favourite it was, but as he got into it he directed the words at his young brother, who looked quite alone as he sat with his family in the corner.

We spun so fast we couldn't tell
The gold ring from the carousel.
How could we know the ride would turn out bad?
Everything we wanted was everything we had.

John Ward was thinking about Daniel, too. He looked much older than the young man who had worked in London; his eyes were almost middle-aged and the lower half of his face had that plumpness that arrives unwanted with the years. The questions he had wanted to ask him had not been appropriate to a birthday party, but he knew already that he had never seen a man who took his pleasures so sadly.

*

The pale-blue motor cruiser was fifteen metres long and had two 500-horse-power engines. Its maximum speed was thirty-five knots.

The owner, a tall, slim man called Bob, who came down to Spain several times a year to relive his days in the Navy, warned them that if they saw white tops on the waves it might get a bit bumpy, but the wind stayed below force four and they careered down the coast bows up.

Bob had suggested a trip to the Straits of Gibraltar – or the Estrecho de Gibraltar, as he called it – so that they could look at the brown coast of Africa from half a mile out, and at first they stood up top watching San Pedro and Estepona drift past. Their eyes began to water and then dried out and were sore from the salt-laden air. It was another hot day, but they were soon cold.

Mark was keen to see some of the blue Mediterranean sharks that abounded in these waters, but Bob said that at this speed they would only see fish that came out of the water, like dolphins or porpoises. In the event they saw none of them and Bob, the only man in the right wind-proof clothes, suggested they go below and warm up with a whisky.

They sat on a comfortable U-shaped bench seat round a small table and opened a bottle of Johnny Walker which Daniel had thoughtfully brought along. It was surprisingly quiet – the engines were rubber-mounted and well insulated.

'Couldn't we land in Ceuta?' Mark asked. 'I've never been to Africa.'

'You'll need a passport,' Matthew said. 'Have you brought it?'

'No, but Ceuta is Spanish. We're not leaving Spain.'

'I'll ask Bob later,' said John Ward.

The sea flashed by outside but nobody felt warm enough to go up and look at it. Daniel poured them a second whisky. His father watched him put his own glass to his mouth rather too quickly.

'I have to ask you, Daniel,' he said. 'Why did you do it?'

It wasn't a question that he could raise during a birthday party, but it was a question he wanted answering now.

'Do what?' Daniel asked, wondering without much hope whether he could possibly be talking about anything else.

'Take the money.'

'I suppose, in the current cliché, it seemed like a good idea at the time.'

'I was rather hoping for more than a cliché,' John Ward said. 'I hoped you might talk about motives.'

Daniel put his whisky on the table but didn't look at his father. This was the part that he had been dreading since the arrival in Malaga.

'It began as a puzzle,' he said, not for the first time, 'and I solved it. It was a question of odds and chances. It's something I'm good at.'

'What are the odds against tossing a head five times running?' Matthew asked. He wanted to derail this intense conversation.

Daniel barely hesitated. 'It's two to the power of five. Thirty-two to one.'

'He's clever,' said Matthew.

'What a pity the cleverness is misguided,' said John Ward, but he was not to be diverted. 'Having solved the puzzle, why did you feel obliged to put it to the test?'

'You've answered your own question, Dad. You have to test a puzzle to see that it works. Otherwise it's just a series of scribbles on a piece of paper.'

'All right, but you could have returned the money.'

'If I'd ever had any money, I probably would have done. As it was, the temptation was too great. You've always had plenty of money. Matthew was a millionaire. Emma had things that Leanda could never afford.'

John Ward put down his empty glass. 'You don't seem to believe that you should pay for your little theft?'

Daniel stared at him for the first time. His expression suggested that there was injustice in the air. 'I'm paying now, aren't I? Leanda's left me. I miss England but can never return to it. That part of my life is over and I can never go home. In a way it's a worse punishment than any judge could give me.'

Watching his son drinking whisky on a motor cruiser in the Mediterranean, and imagining the men in the factory making the cars that he sold, John Ward found this hard to believe, but he knew what Daniel meant. His existence was miserable and could not be changed. John Ward had been anxious to visit his house, to try to imagine the life that he had been leading, but no invitation had been given – no doubt in fear of this unfriendly cross-examination.

He said: 'You see yourself spending the rest of your life in drunken exile, do you?'

Daniel poured himself another whisky. 'Probably.'

John Ward stood up. 'I'm going to see Bob,' he said.

The three of them stayed below to help Daniel with the bottle.

'It's warmer down here,' Matthew said, filling his glass. 'I've sold the bar, by the way. To a fellow from Portsmouth. I'm off to a *finca* in the hills. Pool tables, vegetables and T-shirts.'

'You lucky bastard,' said Daniel. 'You'll land on your feet again.'

'While you shoot yourself in yours, do you mean?'

But before Daniel could answer this, there was an abrupt change in the movement of the boat and they realized that the engines had stopped. The boat seemed to come to a halt very quickly and was now wallowing in the waves, and turning slightly in the water.

'What's up?' Mark called. 'Run out of petrol?' He

273

looked through the window. To their right, the Rock of Gibraltar towered above them.

John Ward appeared at the top of the steps.

'I think we've broken down,' he said. 'Bob's gone to look at the engines.'

The three of them left the table and climbed up to the deck. Now that the boat had stopped it was marvellously warm. There was no breeze at all. They stood there for a while looking at the Rock. It was an even more impressive sight from the sea than it was from the land, but it made Daniel and Matthew uneasy.

Bob appeared with oil on his hands.

'The engines died suddenly,' he said. 'I don't know what it is. We'll have to go in.'

There were a lot of boats about and he started to wave.

'Don't you have flares or something?' Mark asked.

'Yes, but I'm not wasting them here. Everyone can see us.'

They had drifted slowly into Algeciras Bay – or Bahía de Algeciras, as Bob called it – and from the pack of boats bobbing gently in the sun one was making precisely for their stricken cruiser. It was a motor launch and it chugged towards them trailing a path of foam as straight as a French road.

'It looks like a police launch,' said Mark, shielding his eyes from the sun.

Daniel looked at Matthew. 'I'm not sure I like the look of this,' he said quietly.

Matthew patted him on the shoulder. 'Relax. They don't know who we are. No passports. Make up a name for yourself, in case they ask.'

It was a police launch and there were four men in uniform on board.

'Do you want a tow?' one of them shouted.

'Please,' Bob bellowed.

The launch came alongside and one of the men threw a

rope. Bob caught it at the first attempt and went to the front of the boat to fix it.

Soon they were moving slowly towards the harbour at Gibraltar.

'What happens now?' Daniel asked.

'We find a mechanic,' Bob told him. 'It shouldn't take long.'

'Are we going ashore?'

'It would be silly not to,' said John Ward. 'I've never seen Gibraltar.'

The police launch found a path between dozens of small boats that floated aimlessly near the new marina. There was a smell of fuel oil, and the noise of sea birds.

The launch had turned off its engines now and was floating gently towards the jetty. Two of the policemen jumped ashore and tied it up. Then they came back to Bob's motor cruiser and slowly pulled that in. Bob climbed out to speak to them.

'There's not a lot in Gibraltar,' said Daniel. 'I'm quite happy to stay here.'

'I think I'll stay on the boat, too,' Matthew said. 'I like it on boats.'

'Since when?' asked John Ward.

'Since I saw all those policemen in the uniform of an English bobby.'

'Thus conscience doth make cowards of us all,' said his father.

'*Hamlet*,' said Daniel.

'You see?' said Mark. 'Those public-school fees weren't wasted.'

The banter ended suddenly. Two policemen who had been conferring with Bob on the jetty jumped into their boat, rocking it slightly with their landing. They knew exactly who they were looking for and placed themselves immediately on either side of Daniel.

'Daniel Ward, you're under arrest,' one of them said

quietly. 'You will be held in Gibraltar until a flight can be arranged to London.'

Daniel sat down. 'I don't believe it,' he said. The scene had been enacted so many times in his head that he felt hardly any shock. 'What is this all about?' He had imagined himself saying that line many times, too.

'I think we all know what it's about, sir,' the other policeman said. 'If you will just come with us now it will avoid a lot of embarrassment.'

Matthew watched in horror, believing he was next. Mark watched open-mouthed, not believing what he was seeing.

But Daniel, immediately resigned to what he had often lived through in his mind, stood up and shook hands with his father and his brothers without saying a word. He left the boat between the two policemen and then shook hands with Bob on the jetty.

The three of them walked off without looking back.

'I don't believe this,' said Matthew. 'I must be dreaming.'

'Jesus!' said Mark. It had all happened so quickly that it didn't seem real to him either. 'They've got him. I never thought they would. They must have recognized him from pictures in the police station. They've probably got a wall covered with Costa del Sol fugitives.'

'He took it very well,' said John Ward. 'It was almost as if it was a relief.'

Matthew couldn't take his eyes off the three figures that were now climbing into a police car on the front. 'Poor bastard!' he said 'What must he be thinking?'

They all watched in silence as the car drove off, with Daniel beside a policeman in the back. It was too far away for them to see the expression on his face.

Bob jumped back into the boat.

'Well,' he said.

Mark shook his head by way of reply.

'What an absolute disaster the boat breaking down just there,' he said finally.

John Ward looked at him. 'What makes you think,' he asked, 'that the boat broke down?'

Jay's was jumping. Alvin was taking the crowded bar on a rollicking tour through the rock-and-roll years – Little Richard, Elvis, Chuck Berry, Ricky Nelson and Jerry Lee Lewis. The music caught the crowd, stopped the conversation, and produced an accompaniment of claps and cheers which created just the sort of wild, vibrant atmosphere that Jay's customers appreciated.

Waiters hurried about with trays of expensive drinks, and the speakers outside relayed Alvin's strident piano and its forceful message to the evening strollers on the front: come on in, the music's lovely.

Mark arrived with his father at half-past ten. He bought them drinks and they sat at the corner table that John Ward had come to prefer. Matthew had left them to open his bar and demonstrate its limitless potential to the buyer from Portsmouth who was in need of instruction and encouragement.

After a long and dismal lunch in Gibraltar, the boat trip back had been like the journey home after a funeral. The Mediterranean, dazzling outside in a sun that thought it was still July and not the first day of October, had been ignored, and John Ward had sat below with his two sons not talking very much and not even drinking the whisky.

'I had to do it,' he had said when the silence became unbearable. Nobody answered him and he sensed a mood of reproach that he wanted to dispel. 'Daniel recognized the quotation from *Hamlet*. There is another from the play. "I must be cruel, only to be kind."'

'It's hard to imagine your little brother languishing in

one of Her Majesty's dungeons,' Matthew said. 'Even harder to imagine it as kind.'

John Ward was anxious to defend himself now, to explain, to justify. 'He was obviously very unhappy. At least this way he will be happy eventually.'

'How long,' Mark asked, 'is eventually?'

'I'm told he will only get two years. With good behaviour he could be out by the end of next year, and then he will be free to live in England and not have to spend the rest of his life in exile. That's what he wants, isn't it?'

Matthew opened the whisky. He needed a drink even if nobody else did. The episode had been more traumatic for him because for several awful moments he had expected to be arrested too.

'What do you mean – you were told?' he said. 'Who told you?'

'I took some advice in London.'

'You came out here to do it.'

'As a matter of fact, I didn't. I had arranged with Bob that I had the option to do it. It depended on what I found when I got here.'

'What did you find?'

'A son who was drinking himself to death. A son who had driven his wife away, and was miserable and desperately homesick. A son whose life had lost all purpose. A son who seemed to do nothing positive except crash cars. One way or the other he would have been dead in five years, Matthew. You look at me accusingly, but that is the one salient fact you should hang on to. He would have been dead in five years. Now he'll be able to start his life again. I've given him a second chance. He might even get Leanda back.'

'I doubt she'll want a jailbird for a husband,' Matthew said. 'Mrs Plumridge won't be all that enthusiastic, either.'

The boat spun through the water but, for all that they

were noticing, they could have been sitting on a bus. The African coast was passing them on their right, silent, sun-baked and mysterious, but their thoughts were of other places: Pentonville, Wormwood Scrubs. The contrast which Daniel was about to experience was almost biblical in its severity: from a luxurious villa to a crowded cell, from champagne to slops, from sunshine to the darkest shade. It was a prospect so terrible that Matthew wondered whether it would have been more merciful if Daniel had quietly died one night after drinking two whiskies too many.

'I suppose it will be like being back at public school,' he said after a while.

Mark was a thousand miles to the north in a hushed but crowded room where men with strange wigs and de-nunciatory tones set about the quiet destruction of his misguided brother.

'What will?' he asked.

'Being in prison. Regimented from dawn till dusk, punishments if you step out of line.'

'The reluctant company of other restricted males,' said Mark.

'When they told me that public school was a unique and comprehensive preparation for life I didn't realize what they meant,' said John Ward. 'I'm going up to get some air.'

He opened the door and they heard a plane climbing after take-off from Gibraltar.

'I wonder if he's on it,' Matthew said.

Mark shrugged. 'What I'm wondering is, what happens to the money? Supposing he says he's spent it? Can they get the house? Will Leanda fly back and scoop the pool?'

'He'll probably come out of prison and still have the loot. A prison sentence is expiation for the crime, isn't it?'

Mark pondered this and began to smile. 'I must say it

would be a bit odd if he was a free man next year and still a millionaire.'

They both liked this idea and Matthew began to smile too. He poured himself another whisky and watched the Sierra Bermeja, which stretched from Estepona to San Pedro, protecting the coast from unpleasant weather from the north. It would be different now without Danny, but it would be different, anyway, without the bar. A quiet life in the country with a wife and child was something he had never imagined for himself, but he was looking forward to it. He had never hankered after England as his brother had. If, after a couple of years, he grew bored with Spain, he would change his name and go to America. The future had always seemed interesting to him and he had never been afraid of it.

They went up top to watch Bob steer the boat into Puerto Banus. It was a complicated business, but Bob finally managed it. They all stood on the jetty and shook his hand.

'I'll square up with you at home,' John Ward said.

Matthew was anxious to be off to see his buyer. He would never again get within ten miles of Gibraltar. The place was pleasant enough, but he always seemed to be a gibbering wreck when he left.

Now Mark and his father were sitting in Jay's listening to Alvin's rock and roll. John Ward looked shaken by the events of the day. He twisted his beer glass round and round in his hand. He wanted to talk. He wanted his eldest son to approve of what he had done.

'What do you think, Mark?' he asked.

Mark thought his father looked worried, less sure of himself, older – as if the day had aged him. 'I was wondering – why Danny and not Matthew?' he asked.

John Ward nodded. 'I must admit that at first I had thought it would be both of them, but when I saw my grandson I knew that it couldn't be. Matthew has a son to bring up, the boy needs a father. Anyway, I make a distinction between what they did. I was never too fond of the tax man myself. On top of that, Matthew has been working this summer, not drinking. He's tried to create a life here and I admire him for that.'

'I'm not sure you ever forgave Danny for mother's death,' Mark said.

John Ward looked distressed at this suggestion. 'That is grossly unfair, Mark. I gave him everything. When you were a boy I had no time. When Matthew came along it wasn't much better. But I lavished time, love and money on Daniel because by the time he arrived I had time and money and I didn't want him to suffer through having no mother. When I think of the money I spent on his education, the sense of waste is almost unbearable.' The reference to his wife had stirred his anger. He clenched his fist and leaned across the table. 'And how did he repay me? Through the *News of the World*. Through the television news. You can't imagine what torture I went through at the golf club.'

'Yes, I can. Golf clubs are very primitive places.'

'I've been through hell, Mark. Did the boy owe me that?'

'No, he didn't.'

Mark looked across the room to get a signal from Alvin that he had only two more songs to do. The glass in front of him that collected tips was already full of notes. The theory at Jay's was that the Americans tipped the best because they wanted to be liked, the British hardly tipped at all because they were too mean, the Italians didn't tip because they were too poor and the French didn't tip because they didn't understand it.

He said: 'I'll have to play in a minute. Are you OK?'

His father, staring into the distance, hardly heard him. 'The funny thing is,' he said, 'that the son to whom I gave the least, has repaid me the most. I'm very proud of you, Mark. You should be very proud of yourself.'

'I think the gratification of ego becomes more transparent to you when you get to my age, unless you're a complete prat.'

'What on earth does that mean?'

'I'm too old to get big-headed.'

Alvin was rounding off his stint with a rousing version of 'Shake, Rattle and Roll'. A lot of the customers were joining him, singing, clapping and banging the tables.

Mark finished his beer and tried to make the adjustments that were necessary to face this baying crowd. Alvin was a difficult act to follow tonight. Perhaps something quiet and tender would provide an acceptable contrast.

A waiter came through the crowd and told him that there was a telephone call. He made sure his father was comfortable in his corner, and worked his way through the packed customers to the phone on the wall in the back room. Alvin finished his performance to tremendous applause, and a silence fell on the bar as no pianist replaced him.

Two minutes went by before Mark appeared. When he walked across to the piano he seemed to be a foot taller.

He sat on the stool and pulled the microphone a little nearer.

'Hallo, and thank you, Alvin,' he said. 'I was going to start with a Hoagy Carmichael selection tonight, but I've just had some amazing news on the phone. Sorry about the delay. A song I have written, called "Cottage by the Sea", has today reached number one in the charts in both Britain and America. So I think I had better sing it.'

The applause which greeted this announcement was louder than anything that had ever been heard in Jay's. It rang round the room, deafening conversation.

When it died down, Mark began to sing. He sang gently

and romantically and, as he sang, he looked across at his father in the corner of the bar. To his surprise he saw that tears were running down his cheeks.

But Mark did not know why.

FOR THE BEST IN PAPERBACKS, LOOK FOR THE

In every corner of the world, on every subject under the sun, Penguin represents quality and variety – the very best in publishing today.

For complete information about books available from Penguin – including Pelicans, Puffins, Peregrines and Penguin Classics – and how to order them, write to us at the appropriate address below. Please note that for copyright reasons the selection of books varies from country to country.

In the United Kingdom: Please write to *Dept E.P., Penguin Books Ltd, Harmondsworth, Middlesex, UB7 0DA*

If you have any difficulty in obtaining a title, please send your order with the correct money, plus ten per cent for postage and packaging, to *PO Box No 11, West Drayton, Middlesex*

In the United States: Please write to *Dept BA, Penguin, 299 Murray Hill Parkway, East Rutherford, New Jersey 07073*

In Canada: Please write to *Penguin Books Canada Ltd, 2801 John Street, Markham, Ontario L3R 1B4*

In Australia: Please write to the *Marketing Department, Penguin Books Australia Ltd, P.O. Box 257, Ringwood, Victoria 3134*

In New Zealand: Please write to the *Marketing Department, Penguin Books (NZ) Ltd, Private Bag, Takapuna, Auckland 9*

In India: Please write to *Penguin Overseas Ltd, 706 Eros Apartments, 56 Nehru Place, New Delhi, 110019*

In Holland: Please write to *Penguin Books Nederland B.V., Postbus 195, NL–1380AD Weesp, Netherlands*

In Germany: Please write to *Penguin Books Ltd, Friedrichstrasse 10–12, D–6000 Frankfurt Main 1, Federal Republic of Germany*

In Spain: Please write to *Longman Penguin España, Calle San Nicolas 15, E–28013 Madrid, Spain*

In France: Please write to *Penguin Books Ltd, 39 Rue de Montmorency, F-75003, Paris, France*

In Japan: Please write to *Longman Penguin Japan Co Ltd, Yamaguchi Building, 2–12–9 Kanda Jimbocho, Chiyoda-Ku, Tokyo 101, Japan*

The Nudists

Simon Venables, honeymooning under the scorching Mediterranean sun, has just seen the woman he should have married. She is a pneumatic blonde called Pym whose two page three assets leave Simon sick with lust. But Pym is married to dynamic Ben Brock, brash adman, brimming with cash from the lucrative pharmaceuticals market. Meanwhile, back in Thatcherite Britain, penniless Nick Bannerman is bashing out *Battered Husbands*, the misogynist mega-seller that will hoist him into the world of designer sex and driven success that Ben Brock already enjoys. Soon, these three parties will find themselves in a tangle of crossed destinies on a holiday to remember.

'Comic, happy and readable all at once' – *Daily Telegraph*

'Infested with the Porsche-driving class who holiday round swimming pools and return to stone-clad homes in Wimbledon' – *The Times*

The Secret Lemonade Drinker

Before Bobby met and married Caroline he believed in sex, drink and a good time. He still does. In his infinite wisdom Dr Grimshaw has proclaimed Bobby as sterile as a surgeon's knife and, since his wife's raison d'être is to become the mother of four, a little marital disharmony ensues. When Bobby's best friend and boss, Roland (candidate for the Nobel Prize in celibacy), hears of Caroline's plight, he feels sure he can help her out. (He's all heart, Roland.) Meanwhile, Josie walks into Bobby's life and undresses . . .

'I laughed and I laughed, reading it in the state of tremulous excitement which must be the nearest we novel reviewers come to an understanding of heavenly bliss. Thank you, Mr Bellamy' – Auberon Waugh, *Evening Standard*

'A very funny first novel. Bawdy, witty, sometimes touching, the book more than lives up to its zany title' – *Sun*

FOR THE BEST IN PAPERBACKS, LOOK FOR THE

PENGUIN BESTSELLERS

Illusions Charlotte Vale Allen

Leigh and Daniel have been drawn together by their urgent needs, finding a brief respite from their pain in each other's arms. Then romantic love turns to savage obsession. 'She is a truly important writer' – Bette Davis

Snakes and Ladders Dirk Bogarde

The second volume of Dirk Bogarde's outstanding biography, *Snakes and Ladders* is rich in detail, incident and character by an actor whose many talents include a rare gift for writing. 'Vivid, acute, sensitive, intelligent and amusing' – *Sunday Express*

Wideacre Philippa Gregory

Beatrice Lacey is one of the most passionate and compelling heroines ever created. There burns in Beatrice one overwhelming obsession – to possess Wideacre, her family's ancestral home, and to achieve her aim she will risk everything: reputation, incest, even murder.

A Dark and Distant Shore Reay Tannahill

'An absorbing saga spanning a century of love affairs, hatred and high points of Victorian history' – *Daily Express* 'Enthralling . . . a marvellous blend of *Gone with the Wind* and *The Thorn Birds*. You will enjoy every page' – *Daily Mirror*

Runaway Lucy Irvine

Not a sequel, but the story of Lucy Irvine's life *before* she became a castaway. Witty, courageous and sensational, it is a story you won't forget. 'A searing account . . . raw and unflinching honesty' – *Daily Express* 'A genuine and courageous work of autobiography' – *Today*

Goodbye Soldier   Spike Milligan

The final volume of his war memoirs in which we find Spike in Italy, in civvies and in love with a beautiful ballerina. 'Desperately funny, vivid, vulgar' – *Sunday Times*

A Dark-Adapted Eye   Barbara Vine

Writing as Barbara Vine, Ruth Rendell has created a labyrinthine journey into the heart of the Hillyard family, living in the respectable middle-class countryside after the Second World War. 'Barbara Vine has the kind of near-Victorian narrative drive that compels a reader to go on turning the pages' – Julian Symons in the *Sunday Times*

Rainbow Drive   Roderick Thorp

If Mike Gallagher (acting head of the Homicide Squad, Los Angeles Police Department) hadn't been enjoying himself in the bed of a married German movie producer, he wouldn't have heard the footsteps and seen the Police Department helicopter . . . 'Quite exceptional . . . powerful, gripping and impressive' – *Time Out*

Memoirs of an Invisible Man   H. F. Saint

'Part thriller, part comedy, part science fiction . . . a compelling, often frightening novel. H. F. Saint makes the bizarre condition of his hero believable' – *Listener*

Pale Kings and Princes   Robert B. Parker

Eric Valdez, a reporter on the *Central Argus* has been killed in Wheaton. His chief, Kingsley, suspects he was involved in the local pastime – cocaine smuggling. But, knowing Valdez's penchant for the ladies, it could be sexual jealousy. Spenser is about to find out. 'The thinking man's private eye' – *The Times*

Pearls   Celia Brayfield

The Bourton sisters were beautiful. They were rich. They were famous. They were powerful. Then one morning they wake up to find a priceless pearl hidden under their pillows. Why? . . . 'Readers will devour it' – *Independent*